SUDDEN

CONFLICTS

SUDDEN CONFLICTS

GARY BECK

Lillicat Publishers
USA

Copyright © 2017 by Gary Beck

www.lillicatpublishers.com

First Print Edition: April 2017

Print ISBN: 978-1-945646-13-3
EPUB ISBN: *978-1-945646-14-0*
MOBI ISBN: *978-1-945646-15-7*

Printed in the United States of America

To Nancy

Whose unwavering support sustains me every day,
without whom I would never accomplish my work.

Contents

Chapter One

The email was terse. "Peter Larkspur. Please come to room 1426 at 1:00 p.m. A.F. Rogers."

Who the eff was A.F. Rogers? I quickly reviewed our production schedule to be sure we weren't behind, then checked our last project report to Lou Perkins, our supervisor. Software simulations were optimum and we were ahead of the projected timetable. So what was this summons about? I couldn't think of any reason, so I dismissed it and went to lunch with my two project teammates, my closest friends, Clara Rodriguez and Thomas Jefferson Washington.

* * *

Clar and TJ had been my best friends since I attended Branville University School of Computer Sciences, just outside of Rochester, New York, in the small college town of Branville. In what later turned out to be a benevolent coincidence, we were assigned to the same dorm suite in a techno-geek environment. Suddenly I had freshmen roommates.

I walked into my assigned suite, apprehensive about who I'd meet. My worst fears were instantly realized. My future roommates were already there, standing in the shared living room. A huge, mean-looking black guy and a tiny, fierce-looking Hispanic girl stared at me silently. I didn't know which of them scared me more. I put down the plastic bag containing my limited wardrobe, but held on to my laptop and the new iPad I had won in a contest at high school. I looked back at them, waiting for them to tell me what to do, but they just stood there staring at me. After what seemed like painful minutes, I said nervously, "I don't think we'll be sharing each other's clothes."

We were frozen in a tableau for a few seconds, then they began laughing and the atmosphere suddenly thawed. Fierce girl stepped forward, put out her hand. "I'm Clar," and squeezed my hand firmly. Mean guy said softly, "I'm TJ," and swallowed my hand in the largest hand I'd ever seen, held it gently for a moment then let go, giving me what I could have sworn was a sweet smile.

We looked each other over for a few moments, politely appraising our new roommates. Then Clar said briskly, "We have to pick our rooms."

I said I didn't care which one I got and TJ nodded agreement, but Clar wouldn't accept our avoiding a decision.

"We're going to be living together for the next year, unless you annoy me and I poison you."

TJ and I looked at each other, but before we could respond, she said, "Just kidding, fellas."

I know I hoped she was.

"We need a system to organize our lives so we get along and don't get in each other's way. How about we pick rooms by seniority? I was seventeen in August."

"I'll be seventeen in October," I said.

"I'll be seventeen in November," TJ said.

"Well I guess the old lady picks first," she said, and the nickname stuck. TJ became Baby and I was Little Brother but we only used them when we were alone.

Clar was five feet tall, petite with a runner's body, long, dark hair, a heart-shaped face, and a tungsten disposition. Clar told us she grew up in the projects in the South Bronx, gladly left it behind in search of a new life, and wasn't afraid of anything. TJ was her diametric opposite. He was 6'5", 250 pounds, black as darkest night, with a shaved head, and fierce looking features that belied his gentle-as-a dove nature. He said he grew up in Albany and successfully survived the constant demands to participate in contact sports because of his size. His peers couldn't conceive that he had zero interest in basketball. All he wanted to do was study math and create things on his computer.

I was 5'11", 175 pounds, with short, blonde hair, blue eyes, a plain face that would have been nondescript except for my ears, which stood out noticeably from my head. I had been teased mercilessly in grade school, the kindest taunt was "Dumbo." I told them I grew up in Binghamton, without going into any detail. By nature, I was shy and only survived my classmates' nastiness due to my skills as a soccer player. I actually turned down two sports scholarships to attend Branville. I may have played soccer well, but my love was reserved for computers.

The next few weeks went by quickly as we adapted to classes and living together. We got along pleasantly, but distantly, yet that seemed to change when TJ discovered an overwhelming desire to cook. Our suite had a full kitchen and TJ raided the library for cookbooks, with a preference for gourmet fare. We thought he was nuts, until he made something French I couldn't pronounce that was delicious. He only came close to poisoning us once and when I looked at Clar accusingly, we almost fell down laughing at the look on her face.

TJ surprised me on my birthday with a magnificent cake with multicolored icing and red and yellow decorative flowers that looked so good it was almost a work of art. We sat there admiring it, reluctant to mar it, when one of the rowdies from down the hall poked his nose in the door.

"Hey. That's quite a cake. Can I have a piece?"

"No," Clar snapped. "Get out of our room."

"I was just being friendly . . ."

"Do it somewhere else," she ordered.

"Who the fuck do you think you're talking to, you big-mouthed bitch."

Clar was across the room in a flash, grabbed his arm in some kind of grip that made him yelp in pain, then hustled him out the door and slammed it shut behind him. She ignored his yell through the door, "I'll get you for this," and said casually, "We should start keeping our door closed."

"How did you do that?" I blurted, still shocked at how fast she subdued him.

"I have a green belt in Tae Kwon Do. I'll teach you, if you like."

"I like," I replied eagerly.

"Me too," TJ added.

"Good. We'll start tomorrow."

Before we could get back to admiring my cake, there was loud pounding on the door and angry voices demanding to come in.

Clar said, "We can let them come in and push us around. We can ignore them and have to face them later. We can call the campus police, who may or may not get here. Or we can face them now and probably have to fight."

"Let's fight," I declared, eager to prove myself to my tough roommates.

"If we have to," TJ said.

"I'll open the door," Clar said, "and we'll step into the hall. If we have to fight, let's do it there."

We went to the door and she threw it open. We stepped out and found ourselves facing four of the rowdy boys, who were a little surprised.

"What can we do for you boys?" Clar asked quietly.

"You insulted our friend," one of the boys accused.

"Then why did he have to bring you three with him?" she demanded.

Apparently he didn't tell his buddies how she tossed him out physically, so he let his friend do the talking.

"We wanted to make sure you apologize."

She laughed. "For what?"

"Whatever you said to him," the boy persisted

"He came into our room without knocking," she explained, "demanded a piece of cake and cursed at me when I said no. Then I threw him out."

"What do you mean?"

"Ask your friend."

His buddies looked at him and he said weakly, "She shoved me when I wasn't looking."

"You should apologize to Clar," I said.

"Fuck that."

Clar smiled. "We can let it go, or settle it right now. Your choice, guys."

They looked us over carefully, lingering for a moment on TJ, looked at their buddy who had lied to them, then the spokesman said, "Forget it," and they walked away.

Later that evening I brought half the cake to the rowdies' room and we established a polite truce.

The three of us became closer after that and spent more time together, though still not getting too personal. Unlike many roommates who went their own way in freshman year, we started to go everywhere together. After Clar taught us Tae Kwan Do in the gym, the only exception was the ladies' locker room. We were regarded as weirdos by our classmates, who themselves would be classic weirdos anywhere else, but they left us alone. Our professors quickly recognized our talents, abilities, and the dedication we brought to the learning process. We actually socialized more with our professors than with our fellow students.

Chapter Two

I think our friendship really started to develop when we surprised TJ on his birthday with gifts. Clar gave him the Gourmet Cookbook and I gave him an apron with the words Le Chef in black on the chest of the white garment. We watched in amazement as TJ cried.

"While I was growing up the only presents I got were at Christmas, underwear and socks . . . I'm sorry I'm acting like a baby."

"You're our Baby," Clar said gently. "Remember?"

He wiped his eyes, smiled, and said, "I didn't think I'd prove it so soon," and we laughed quietly.

"That makes you more special for us," Clar added, and I nodded agreement.

We all noticed the change in our relationship in the next few weeks. We were more comfortable with each other as we spent more time together. We were still too reserved about that part of our lives that shamed or embarrassed us to reveal it to someone else.

That barrier shattered suddenly on a bleak November morning, just after we got to class. We had just settled in and were powering up our laptops, when there were loud bangs and screaming in the hall.

"Those are gunshots," Clar declared. "Barricade the door!"

Everyone looked at her strangely, but TJ and I quickly pulled the professor's work table to the door and jammed it at an angle under the doorknob. Someone yelled, "I'm getting out of here," and several students started for the door.

Clar yelled, "Shut up and get down on the floor."

TJ stood next to her like a menacing mountain and the panicked rush subsided. The professor, an old guy in his thirties, devoted to Java, started to object. "What makes you think—" But pounding on the door, followed by gunshots through the glass silenced him.

"We've got to keep him out," I said. "Throw chairs at him if he reaches through the broken glass. Just make sure to stay out of his line of sight."

The attacker fired several shots into the room, which started a lot of the students screaming, then he tried to reach the lock, but we threw chairs at him, hitting his arm until he pulled back. Clar and another girl kept passing chairs to me and TJ, which we threw whenever his arm appeared. He fired more shots, cursed loudly, then moved on, followed by screams and shots from down the hall.

"What do we do now?" The professor asked Clar.

"We wait until the police come and tell us it's safe to come out."

"Thank you, Ms. Rodriguez. You saved our lives."

The students slowly got up and echoed him.

Clar walked to us and put an arm around each of us.

"The boys kept him out, and," she turned to the girl who helped her. "What's your name?"

"Maude."

"Maude helped too. Why don't we wait quietly and hope he doesn't come back?"

Now that it seemed to be over, some jerk in the back said, "How do you know it's a guy? Isn't that sexist?"

Clar looked at him. "Did you ever hear of a woman doing anything that sick?"

TJ and I stared at him until he sat down, and I decided to have a chat with him if he hassled Clar. About twenty minutes later, the police came to the door and told us they had the shooter but were maintaining lockdown until they were certain he was alone. Another hour later, we were told we could go and classes were suspended for the day.

That evening we opened a bottle of wine, sat in the living room, and talked about the terrifying rampage that afternoon. Three students were killed and fourteen wounded. We mourned them silently for a while, feeling the loss of the young people and the violation of our lives.

Finally, Clar said, "You guys were incredible. Have you ever been shot at before?"

TJ shook his head and I mumbled, "No."

"Gunfire went on all the time in the projects," Clar said softly. "One of my girlfriends was killed in the playground in a gang shoot out. I saw other people shot . . . I thought it would be peaceful here. That's why I came to Branville, to get away from the filth and violence. You're my family now, so I want to tell you about me . . . I was gang raped when I was thirteen."

We stared at her in shock, but before we could say anything, she held up her hand.

"I know you think I'm tough, but underneath I'm full of fear, anger, and hate."

I looked at her. "You're the bravest person I know. You *are* tough. You showed it today and many other times. We're here for you," and I looked at TJ, who nodded agreement.

"You show us every day that you're coping and facing your problems. You can handle it," TJ said.

"You have no idea how what happened eats at me."

"True," TJ replied. "But we have to deal with things, no matter how difficult."

"It's easy for you to say."

He took a deep breath. "I grew up in foster care. By the time I was eight I had lived in five foster homes, each one worse than the one before it. Then I lived in a group home until I came here. This is the first time I had a room of my own and roommates I liked."

"I had no idea," Clar said gently. "At least one of us isn't disturbed," she remarked, looking at me.

I laughed bitterly. "Yeah, well. I grew up on the wrong side of the tracks in Binghamton. My father was a drunk and my mother left when I was six. Five years later, the Susquehanna River flooded the city and wiped out my neighborhood. We lived in a FEMA trailer until I came here. No matter what, I'll never go back."

Clar started to laugh.

"What's so funny?" I demanded.

"I thought you guys had it so easy. A lot I knew."

TJ and I laughed, then I said solemnly, "We should make a pact to support each other. We did pretty well today. It'll only get better."

Clar stood up and beckoned us to her and we hugged.

"Take your hand off my ass, Pete."

"What makes you think it was me?"

"TJ's too polite."

We bonded together closely after the terrifying incident of the rampaging gunman. Maude, who was the only one in the class besides us who took action, started hanging around with us. It began gradually after she asked TJ for some help on an assignment. She came to our room one evening when TJ made a gourmet dinner and he asked her to join us. She quickly accepted, then he looked at us as if he did something wrong.

Clar reassured him. "Maude helped save our lives. She's welcome here."

After that, Maude was with us often. She was a little taller than Clar, perhaps 5'2", but heavier, about 120 pounds, with long, red hair, fair skin, a pretty face with freckles and an exuberant personality. She attached herself to TJ, and even though she was willing to have sex with him, he was too shy to do anything about it. They became good friends and were an amusing contrast on campus, the giant black man and the small redhead.

Other students came to us for help and we started a tutoring service, $100 for five hours. A lot of students had money and soon most of our spare time was taken and the money poured in. The only one we didn't charge was Maude. She had paid her way by defending us. Some students asked us to write term papers for them, at the going rate of $500. It was tempting, but Clar reminded us, "We have enough money for now. We may want to be professors someday, so we don't want any questions about our academic conduct."

We agreed because she was right. We each tutored two students a week, so we made $200 each. That was enough for now.

The year went by quickly and we zipped through our required class work effortlessly. Our professors got together with the department chairman and they proposed we take accelerated courses and finish our B.S. degrees early. This was very exciting and we began to plan a schedule for the fall semester.

We took summer jobs at a computer camp as teachers, not counselors. We were housed in an air-conditioned cabin and the first week was fun. Then the camp director told us we had to be counselors and live in the cabins with the kids. When we declined, reminding him that wasn't our agreement, he said we had to do it or get fired, so we quit. We spent the rest of the summer in the comfort of our suite at Branville U. developing an idea for a program to trace cyber intruders.

Maude didn't return for the fall semester and we missed her for a while, TJ longer than Clar or me. We fell into a satisfying routine and after a while even TJ forgot her. We were busy with class work, tutoring, Tae Kwan Do, socializing with our professors, and exploring cyber tracking. We were very busy and happy.

The environment at Branville U was so right for us that, after we got our B.S. degrees in two and a half years, we stayed on and got our M.S. degrees in a year, working as teaching assistants at the same time. It was a no brainer to continue to flourish in a fulfilling environment and we got our PhDs in a year and a half, while also teaching as adjunct instructors. Branville U wanted to retain us as faculty and offered an alluring academic package that would start us as assistant professors on a tenure track, with generous benefits. Our mentors were severely disappointed when we opted to leave the University for a start-up venture we had been planning since our second year together. Faculty and administrators bid us a fond farewell when we set out for what they considered the dangerous wilds of New York City. They told us we were always welcome to accept their offer and come back. It was a nice way to end our university life, which had been so good for us.

Our last unofficial act at Branville U. was to make a solemn pact not to celebrate our favorite rituals, our birthdays, until we got financing for our start up project, Cybersnarer, a tracking program to identify cyber-attacks, which would make us instant millionaires.

Chapter Three

New York City was a culture shock, even for Clar, who may have been familiar with the mean streets of the South Bronx, but Manhattan was another world. She admitted that her one class trip to a museum was a barely noticed visit to a foreign country. We quickly realized that we may have had a great idea for a software project, but we were completely unprepared for the realities of the city. We had blandly assumed we'd get a nice apartment in a nice neighborhood, then get used to the area before starting our search for start-up funds. That immediate failure should have been a wake-up call.

By the end of the first week's apartment search it became clear that a three-bedroom apartment was impossible on our budget. We spent the next few nights at a shabby, noisy, student hostel on the Upper West Side, near Columbia University. Each day our apartment expectations grew lower, as the size of what we could afford grew smaller. Our choice was simple, sub-let a small studio apartment in a nondescript building for $2,400 a month, or trek to the outer boroughs, probably the terra incognito of Brooklyn, an unknown land. Clar promptly vetoed that. So we signed a one-year lease for a living space a third the size of our college suite.

The building in the East twenties, between 2nd and 3rd Avenues was constructed in the

1970's, as cheaply as possible. The landlord tried to claim the apartment was a one bedroom, but there were no separate rooms, just an open space. The kitchen was tiny, with cheap appliances, but at least it was functional. A half partition separated the 8' by 10' bedroom from the living room/dining area that would have to be divided to create tiny sleeping areas for TJ and me. By unanimous consent, Clar got the bedroom. She also got one of the two windows that looked out on the building next door. The bathroom was so small that TJ could barely turn around in it. At least we had hot water and the toilet worked, though the bathroom door was so thin we could hear every sound the occupant made.

We were determined to make the best of it, and Clar buoyed our spirits by announcing, "As soon as we get our start-up money, we'll move into a good hotel until we can find a nice apartment. We might want to buy a co-op." We discussed the merits of co-op versus condo—about which we knew nothing—without reaching a conclusion.

We drew up a list of what we'd need now to furnish the apartment. We had lots of kitchen stuff from our dorm suite, as well as towels and linens. We wouldn't have a living room, so all we needed were beds, a large table for our computers and meals, comfortable chairs for each of us, and curtains and privacy screens for partitioning the bedrooms. We looked up some inexpensive stores online, ordered, then got ready for our next step in the great adventure . . . raising capital to finance our tracking project, Cybersnarer.

We had prepared a prospectus for potential funders and TJ had developed a list of possible investors. I got on the phone and started calling for appointments, but the only response I got was a suggestion to send a letter outlining our project. It was too early to be discouraged, but that was our first inkling that it wasn't going to be as easy as we had imagined while behind the serene walls of Branville U.

TJ started working on a secondary investors list, as we reduced our expectations from requiring 20 million dollars to five million. It was almost embarrassing to come down so quickly, but we consoled ourselves that we were being realists. Clar made up a budget for us and we decided we had enough money to last for six months, barring emergencies. We agreed to review our situation in three months, without really believing it would be necessary. We were confident that our prospectus, prepared by Doctors Larkspur, Washington, and Rodriguez, would surely be accepted by sensible investors.

By the end of our second week in the big city, we hadn't received one response from the 50 letters we submitted. With growing resignation that no one was stampeding to make an appointment to hear our presentation, we had to revise what was obviously an overly optimistic plan. TJ revised the letter, Clar fine-tuned the prospectus, and I went to the internet and drew up a list of corporations with a history of using competing software that we knew our system would do a better job of protecting against intruders—whether hackers or cyber spies— tracking the origins of the invasion, and then providing defense against future penetration.

After one month of 50 more letters and futile follow-up calls, our only response was from Parsec Systems, a medium-sized software development company that specialized in cyber security. However, instead of being interested in our project, they offered us jobs as software developers. We were of mixed minds about the employment opportunity. TJ was flattered and I was insulted. Clar was very practical.

"Pete, there's no point in getting angry at them. TJ's right. They obviously recognize our value."

"Then why aren't they interested in our project?" I demanded.

"I don't know," TJ replied. "At least they're interested in us. That's more than anyone else so far."

"Do both of you have to be so damn reasonable?" I asked pleasantly, which made them laugh and cleared the air of tension.

"I think we should send them a polite email," Clar suggested, "and continue our search for investors."

TJ and I quickly agreed, Clar sent the email, and I went back to my internet search for prospective funders.

Another month went by without responses and we found ourselves approaching the three-month deadline we had established to review our situation. The unproductive month had enhanced our frustrations and depleted our savings, without any indications of progress. So far, our stay in the exciting city had been limited to mediocre restaurants and a constant diet of take-out. We had certainly indulged in the almost endless variety of take-out, that in Branville had been limited to tasteless pizza from a national chain and some semi-toxic Chinese. Perhaps we ate more Thai and Japanese than we could afford, but it was a luxurious change.

When we finally sat down together, hopes a bit deflated, to consider our circumstances, Clar summed things up with her usual efficiency. "We have enough money for two to three months with our current expenditures. After that we have insufficient income to maintain us. We only have two options. We can go back to Branville with our degrees between our legs and become assistant professors, or we stay in New York City and get jobs."

It didn't take long to conclude there were no other options and TJ and I said we'd prefer to get jobs. Clar agreed, so our next concern was where we would work. With our qualifications, there was no doubt that any company would snap us up. The one requirement we had was that the lucky company would hire all of us. Three weeks later, we had each received several low-pay, not overly interesting job offers, but not together. This led to our second formal conference.

Clar took charge and presented the choices bluntly. "Either we take separate, unappealing jobs, or we inquire if Parsec Systems would still be interested in us."

TJ and I quickly stated our preference for Parsec and Clar sent them an email requesting an interview.

Chapter Four

On the first Monday of February, a dank, chilly day that turned the City of Dreams a dreary grey, we went to our interview at Parsec. They were located in an angular metal and glass building in Tribeca, surrounded by old, commercial loft buildings that made the new construction stand out like a science experiment on a football field.

Just before we went in, TJ said, "Let's go to the World Trade Center site when we're through."

Like all Americans, I had seen the horrific disaster over and over on TV. Like all Americans at the time, I couldn't imagine ever forgetting the sight of burning bodies leaping from windows, or the heroic first responders rushing into danger to save lives, perishing when the buildings imploded. Like some Americans, I got on with my life and the tragedy started to fade, until it became an historical memory, like Pearl Harbor, or the Alamo. I had mixed feelings about going there, but it was hard to resist visiting what was already a hallowed shrine.

Our visit to Parsec was a little different than we had anticipated. When we sent them our proposal we were confident, brash, even cocky. We had a great software project that they were privileged to have the opportunity to bid on. Now we were humble suppliants. We weren't quite begging, but we were wagging our tails respectfully.

Phil Hapgood, the C.F.O., who had earlier rejected our proposal as too speculative, smiled benevolently as his sleek, well-constructed blond secretary ushered us into his office. Phil was short, about 5'6", slightly plump, with a bland expression on his face. He had slicked-back, well-trimmed, dark hair, bushy eyebrows, pale brown eyes, a tiny nose, and a pouty mouth that seemed to have more teeth then the usual allotment. His grey, pin-striped suit cost more than our monthly rent.

Phil pyramided his hands, then said smoothly, "Welcome to Parsec. It's good to see you. I'm glad that you gave up your wild ideas and decided to use your talents practically."

I immediately bristled and Clar put a hand on my arm before I could say something confrontational.

Phil was oblivious to his effect on us, enchanted with the sound of his own voice and the temporary power he held over us.

"We can certainly find a niche for you at Parsec as software developers. You come highly recommended by professors and administrators at Branville University."

"You talked to them already?" TJ blurted.

"Of course. We always check thoroughly on prospective employees."

Clar brought us back to practical matters.

"If you don't mind, Mr. Hapgood, please tell us what we'll be doing and the salary."

"Certainly, Ms. Rodriguez. And please call me Phil."

"Thank you, Phil. And it's Doctor Rodriguez. Please call me Clara."

He gave her a cold glance, then said blandly, "You'll be working in Dick Pellicano's department, our C.T.O, to develop various user applications of our current software project, Trilateralization."

"What's that?" I asked.

Phil looked at me a bit disdainfully, as if I should know it, which instantly riled me, but Clar just looked at me and I settled down.

"Trilateralization allows tracking of an individual's location, moment by moment. The data, obtained from cell phone towers, can track the altitude of a person, down to the specific floor in a building. We're working on software that uses the cell phone data to predict a person's most likely route."

"That sounds like Big Brother watching," TJ said.

Phil glared. "It's a vital counterterrorism tool. I'm sure you'll see how valuable it will be in the war on terror." He paused and when we didn't respond, continued. "Lou Perkins will be your immediate supervisor. The starting salary is $60,000 a year, plus benefits, as well as an annual bonus and salary review," and he looked at us expectantly.

"We expected a higher starting salary," I said.

"Those are the slots we have open," Phil replied, with a take it or leave it attitude.

TJ and I looked at Clar, who just shrugged. It was obvious, like it or not, we didn't have a better option.

"Thanks for the opportunity, Phil," I said, doing my best to sound sincere. "We're excited about working here."

He looked less than enthusiastic. "My secretary, Mona, will give you your employment packages. You can start tomorrow. Welcome to Parsec." And he shook our hands, one at a time, lingering a moment with Clar.

We left with a combination of feelings: Relief that we had paying jobs and wouldn't have to return to Branville in shame and defeat;

resentment that they didn't value us very highly. Before negatives could take hold and spoil what should have been satisfaction that we solved our economic problems, TJ said, "I thought we'd start between $75,000 and $100,000. But there's no sense worrying about it right now. Once we establish ourselves, we'll get more from them, or look elsewhere."

"Let's not forget," Clar said cheerfully, "we'll have $180,000. We can manage with that for a while."

I felt my anger dissipate. $180,000 was a lot of money.

When we left Parsec, we forgot to visit the World Trade Center and instead walked to the Bowery then uptown. We stopped for pizza near St. Marks Place. It was much more expensive than the cardboard pies back at Branville, but it tasted much better. TJ saw a cheese shop across the avenue and herded us into an array of cheeses that we'd never heard of before. He selected half a dozen different kinds and mumbled something about making fondue. I almost said gezundheit. We made several more stops and bought steak, a variety of health and organic foods, wine normally beyond our budget, and pastries for desert.

"We can afford a special dinner tonight," TJ declared. "Now that we're employed."

Despite living with TJ for five years, I still couldn't figure out how a kid from foster care could blossom into a gourmet chef without any training. But I wasn't complaining. I had become used to fine dining.

After dinner we sat around the table, sipping wine, almost too stuffed to do more than burp and grunt for a while. Clar, who had eaten as much as TJ or me, never seemed to gain weight or require the same digestive respite we did.

"I've been calculating what our salaries come to after taxes," she said. "It should be about $40,000. Our benefits package covers medical and dental. If we don't live extravagantly, we can save about $40,000 for the year. That means we'll have a cushion when we leave Parsec."

"So you figure we'll work there for a year?" I asked.

"We should have a demo program developed by then," she replied.

"Do I stop cooking special meals?" TJ asked forlornly.

"No, silly. We love your cooking. Just no caviar sandwiches."

He chuckled, relieved.

"Just what is caviar?" I asked.

"Fish eggs," TJ explained.

"What's so special about fish eggs?"

"It's a great delicacy and very expensive."

"Why should anyone want to eat fish eggs?"

"You eat chicken eggs, don't you?"

"Sure. But that's different."

"An egg is an egg."

"Would you eat a skunk egg?" I challenged.

"Skunks don't lay eggs."

"You know what I mean."

Clar had been watching us, amused.

"Did you ever eat caviar, TJ?" she asked.

"No. But I'm looking forward to trying it when we can afford it. Right now an ounce of the good stuff is about $150."

"That's more than the dopers were getting for pot at Branville," Clar said.

"What do you mean by the good stuff? Are there fish laying cheap eggs like in a sweat shop?" I asked.

TJ laughed. "No. There are different kinds of caviar roe. Salmon, shad, weakfish. The finest comes from sturgeon, with different grades, like small eggs called sevruga. The best and most expensive is beluga."

"Can we talk about something besides fish eggs?" Clar requested.

"Sure," TJ said.

"Good. We need a plan to develop our project while working at Parsec. I suggest we work two or three hours a night during the week, we go out Saturday night to a movie, or something, sleep late Sunday, then work 5 or 6 hours."

"Sounds good to me," I said.

TJ nodded agreement.

"It doesn't have to be written in stone," Clar added. "We can do other things at other times, but we need structure to reach our goal."

TJ and I voiced approval.

"I'm going to wobble to bed and hope I digest before we go to work in the morning. Goodnight, Baby. Little Brother."

"Goodnight, Old Lady," we both murmured.

Chapter Five

Our first day at Parsec was a bit of a downer. We reported to Lou Perkins, who would be our project manager. Lou was short, chubby, nattily dressed, and definitely dweebish. He wasn't more than 30 years old, but his thinning hair, bland features, thick glasses, and pale skin made him seem like a slightly dehydrated nostalgia freak, yearning for his schoolboy past. He had a high-pitched, squeaky voice and was less than cordial in his welcoming address to the new troops.

"You may have impressed Phil, but this is the real world now, not the comfortable halls of academia. We have production schedules and our work product must be delivered on time to our clients, or they'll go to another company. We're always under pressure to produce results and there are no make-up exams. Your doctorates don't mean much around here. The environment is competitive, not protective."

He looked at us coldly and we probably had the same thought at the same time. *What a jerk.*

But TJ said pleasantly, "We appreciate your concern and we'll certainly do our best to fit in. Where will we be working and what will we be doing?"

Lou looked a little surprised at the large man's compliant attitude.

"Come with me," he said abruptly and went out the door. We followed him to a small room without a window, with three work stations that took up most of the space. It wasn't very appealing. He noticed our lack of enthusiasm for our new home away from home, but ignored our reactions.

"Make a list of what you need and I'll get it for you. I put your project on your laptops. It's a secure firewall system in early development. Look it over this morning and I'll be back before lunch."

We made ourselves as comfortable as we could and TJ suggested we request ergonomic chairs. We looked at each other resignedly for a moment, then turned on our screens. We quickly got absorbed in studying the program and scanned through it in less than an hour. We made separate notes, then discussed what we reviewed. Clar summed it up.

"They're on the right track, as far as it goes, but they're just creating another layer of protection, not solving the problem of how to keep out intruders."

"Do you think they know that?" I asked.

"We'll find out when we talk to Lou," TJ contributed. "That's if it's not too much trouble to talk to us civilly."

"What's with that guy?" I said. "He doesn't know us well enough yet to dislike us. Unless it's hate at first sight."

"He may feel threatened by us," Clar remarked. "After all, we have doctorates."

"That may not mean much outside of academia," TJ said. "These software development companies usually hire young kids right out of college, pay them as little as possible, then fire them when they've gotten their best out of them."

"How do you know that?" I challenged.

"Some of us weren't always busy hiding behind ivy-covered walls," he replied smugly.

Before I could respond, Clar said, "It's obvious that Lou doesn't like us, whatever the reason. We should discuss what our attitude will be and how hard we'll work on their project."

One of the many reasons I adored Clar was that she reduced problems to their basics, which allowed simple decisions. We agreed to treat Lou politely and let him determine, at least for the time being, how much they expected of us. We discussed our own project until Lou came back. Lou wasn't any more pleasant than earlier. He droned on for almost an hour about the urgent need for cybersecurity and how Parsec was in the forefront of cutting edge data protection. We listened and didn't ask questions, but we knew that what we had seen so far was hardly cutting edge. Lou finally wound down without really telling us any particulars about what we'd be working on.

When TJ asked if we had specific tasks, Lou responded impatiently, "You'll be given work assignments once you're familiar with our current program. Anything else?"

There didn't seem much point to further questions, so Clar requested ergonomic chairs, one extra-large. Lou just stared at her, then walked out. Clar started to go after him, then just shrugged.

"This hasn't been what we expected so far, has it?"

TJ and I nodded agreement, then TJ said, "Their system isn't very sophisticated. Do you think they're not showing us everything?"

"I don't know," I replied, "but something strange is going on here. They're either testing us, or they don't know what they're doing and expect us to bail them out. In any event, I think we should develop expertise in cybersecurity. Clar, how about you review all the current programs available for analysis. TJ, you analyze their program and draft improvements. I'll start reading all the literature on cyber tracking. We can review progress once a week."

This plan was so similar to our usual approach to problem solving at the University that we felt a little better about our situation.

We looked at the Lenovo laptops dubiously, each of us preferring other machines, but this was the company format. I started to make a smart-ass comment, but Clar held up her hand warningly. She picked up a yellow pad and wrote a note, then showed it to me and TJ. *It's possible they're monitoring us. We'll discuss it at lunch. Let's be discreet for now.*

We stared at her, wondering what prompted this reaction, but we trusted her, so we nodded acceptance. She smiled dazzlingly, revealing her inner self to the friends she loved. She crumpled the note and put it in her pocket.

"So what do you think of their program?" she asked cheerfully.

We discussed it for a while in careful, technical terms and concluded tentatively they were on the right track.

"Why don't we go to lunch," I suggested, "and we'll continue the discussion when we meet with Lou."

Most of the nearby restaurants were too pricy for us and we settled for the cheapest, with eight-dollar tuna sandwiches. But we had to eat. TJ consoled us by saying we could start bringing our own lunches. Once we were eating, TJ turned to Clar.

"What makes you think they might be monitoring us?"

"I just got this feeling that Lou was measuring us, and I wanted to talk to you privately before we relaxed there."

"Anything else?" TJ asked.

"Nothing I can put my finger on. But there's something about both Phil and Lou that doesn't feel right to me. Maybe I'm being paranoid, but I wonder if they monitor their employees by audio and maybe even video. Does that sound crazy to you?"

I winked at TJ. "You haven't been crazy before, Old Lady. I'll go along with you until we find out one way or the other."

"Me too," TJ said.

"Thanks, guys. I hope I'm wrong."

"Don't worry about it," I teased. "It'll give TJ a chance to practice silence."

This gave us a laugh, since TJ was generally closed-mouthed, unless we were alone in our apartment.

We met with Lou after lunch and each of us offered our comments on the work in progress. Lou didn't seem very impressed, and told us work assignments would be placed on our laptops in the morning. He left us with an admonition not to talk to anyone about the project and never to take our laptops out of the office. We told him we understood the need for security, but he didn't look reassured and left us with a barely polite, "I'll see you in the morning."

Done for the day, we went home, wondering what we had gotten ourselves into. TJ cooked a special dinner to celebrate our first day at work, something French, unpronounceable, and delicious. I waited until we finished to talk about the day.

"Tell us about what happened today, Clar. It was a bit strange."

She looked pensive for a moment, then said slowly, "It was strange. I had the same mixed feelings you and TJ had. Glad to have a job, regret that we couldn't fund our project, maybe

29

some resentment that our work product was far superior to theirs . . ." We nodded agreement and she went on.

"I just got this sense that something was wrong. I didn't know what, but the thought kept flashing through my head that something else was going on."

"What made you think they monitor the place?"

"I don't know."

"Do you still think that?" I asked.

"I don't know."

"Why would they bug their employees?" TJ said.

"Either they want to know what we think of them and their product," I replied. "Or other reasons."

"Like what?" TJ insisted.

"Finding out more about what their employees are doing during working hours."

"Then you don't think I'm nuts?" Clar asked.

"I know you're nuts, or you wouldn't be with us," I replied, and after the laughter died down, I added, "Let's assume you got some kind of . . . I don't know . . . premonition. We'll behave like good little employees, until we find out more, one way or another."

"Should we start looking for other jobs?" TJ asked.

I looked at Clar, who shrugged.

"I don't like Phil. And I dislike Lou even more. But we need the money. Let's give it three months, then discuss it again."

TJ and I nodded agreement and I said, "How about dessert?" which turned out to be French, pronounceable, and the best custard I ever ate.

During the next few weeks we formed a routine of a run before breakfast, prepared lunch brought from home, and dinner at one of the many restaurants on 3rd Avenue. The restaurants on Park Avenue South were much more expensive, so we avoided them, and tried Italian, Thai, German, Indian, Turkish and Japanese, thoroughly enjoying the diversity.

Work was less relaxed but manageable. Lou never expressed anything positive and he was completely impersonal, treating us as if we were androids, rather than humans with feelings. This was functional for us; we didn't have to be friendly, just efficient. We slowly got to where we said hello to some of the other developers, but they were involved in other projects and we didn't have much interaction. They were particularly closed-mouthed about what they were doing and expressed no interest in what we were working on.

I didn't have Clar's feeling of something wrong, but I began to notice some peculiarities. The place was too orderly, almost regimented. No one sang, made jokes, or did silly things to blow off steam. No one wanted to get to know us and they didn't go to lunch together. Some of them stayed late, but we always left at 5:00 p.m. I never heard of software development without people working long hours, with lots of pressure. I didn't want to worry my friends who were already wary, so I decided to wait a little longer and see how things developed. I smiled at that thought.

Chapter Six

During the next month we settled into our apartment, explored the neighborhood and joined a Tae Kwon Do Dōjō. Sensei Omura put us in a class for a week, then rated us. He scheduled Clar to test for brown belt at the next testing, scheduled me to test for green belt and TJ for yellow belt. The only reason TJ wasn't ready for his green belt test was his reluctance to hit anybody, except for self-defense. His size intimidated almost everyone, so he didn't feel the same pressure I did to be able to resist bullies. We had made real progress with Clar leading us, but now we were ready for more structure and discipline. Omura insisted on physical training that included rigorous exercise and running. So each morning we got up early and ran two miles at the East River walkway. We didn't see many boats, but the run was exhilarating.

We almost always went to 3rd Avenue for shopping and dining, but one day, on an impulse, we went east to 2nd Avenue. We found some great places that quickly became favorites. There was a pleasant Italian restaurant between 28th and 29th Streets, the Ale House on 30th Street, with dozens of different beers that we were tempted to try, and a specialty food store across the street, with really nice prepared food. We started buying most of our staples at a supermarket on 30th Street, so we frequented those few blocks regularly. TJ cooked for us two or three times a week, as the spirit moved him and we either ate out the rest of the time, or got prepared food.

One evening we went to a movie and on the way home Clar started talking about how we should take advantage of the cultural opportunities of the city. I confessed that I didn't know anything about culture and TJ said he didn't either. Clar, looking a bit self-conscious, admitted she didn't really know much, except for a school trip once to the Metropolitan Museum of Art. All she remembered, she said, were big pictures of naked ladies, which made us laugh.

"But we're living here. We should at least try new things," she urged.

I didn't want to admit that culture scared me, so I asked, "What do we do?"

Now Clar was on the spot and TJ and I looked at her expectantly.

"There are concerts, dance, opera, theater, and all kinds of museums. We could go to the modern art museum and see how we like it."

"Sounds like a good place to start," I said.

The next Saturday afternoon we went to the Museum of Modern Art, known as MOMA, which TJ called Mommy, until Clar gave him that behave yourself look. It was so crowded that people kept bumping into us when we stopped to look at a picture. Except for a few realistic type pictures that didn't quite look right, we didn't like anything, especially the abstract paintings that didn't make any sense to us. There was a big painting by Monet of water lilies that was nice to look at, but people kept walking in front of us and taking pictures of it, until we gave up in disgust. We agreed that if we had a fine arts education we might understand what we saw, but at the moment big pictures of naked ladies made more sense than a big red painting with a thin, white stripe.

Saturday night we went to a concert at a small hall in Lincoln Center. The audience was well dressed and babbled non-stop about tonality, dissonance, and percussive transitions. We had no idea what they were talking about. There were about twenty musicians in the orchestra and we didn't recognize some of the instruments they were tuning up. The lights dimmed, but the audience kept talking until the music finally drowned them out. If you could call it music. We couldn't. It sounded more like a work gang at a construction site, making deafening noise with pneumatic drills and sledge hammers. We left early with pounding headaches, as well as evil looks from our neighbors for our premature departure. On the suffering scale, it was much worse than the museum.

Sunday morning, we slept late, brunched on bagels and smoked salmon which we enjoyed, and read the New York Times. We decided not to work on our project for a change and went to a dance recital at a theater in Chelsea. The program informed us we were going to see a troupe dedicated to bridging the gap between the natural movements of animals and the artificial motion of man. The six dancers were large, muscular women, three white, three black. They hopped, leaped, scurried up and down to recorded animal sounds that didn't relate much to what they were doing. I guess I expected beautiful ballerinas in tutus moving elegantly. I found it hard not to laugh. TJ and Clar were as bored as I was and we left at intermission. It wasn't as annoying as the concert, but not to be repeated. I began to get the feeling that culture may not be for us.

The next week of work seemed to follow the routine that had become typical. We got to Parsec at nine, worked until noon, ate a prepared lunch in a nearby park when the weather was nice, then met with Lou in the afternoon, which was always tense and unpleasant. We went home with a feeling of release that didn't bode well for our future at Parsec. But we were together, earning our livelihood, and following our dream of developing a start-up that would satisfy us professionally and make us independently wealthy. It wasn't as secure as college, but we were managing, so there was no point complaining.

Saturday night we went to see a Broadway musical that was loud and colorful, but if there was a story, we couldn't follow it. The show felt so artificial and by the numbers that we walked out after the first act. The thought of opera, with fat ladies in tights squalling away, persuaded us to forget culture for the time being. We were busy enough with our Tae Kwon Do training as we prepared for testing and working on our software project, so we agreed we didn't need self-inflicted torment. For the time being an occasional movie would be entertainment enough. We half-heartedly discussed buying a TV, but decided to wait a while, then consider it further. Our one indulgence was eating at restaurants and we couldn't get over how many there were in the immediate neighborhood. As part of our plan, Clar opened a bank account in our names and made sure we deposited money each week.

We became comfortable with a weekday routine of a run in the morning, 9-5 at Parsec, dinner, then work on our cyber tracking program for three hours, three nights a week. Two nights we went to the dōjō. On Saturday we ran, did our shopping, went to the dōjō, and worked on our program. Sundays we slept late and explored different parts of Manhattan, studiously avoiding cultural attractions. We discovered that Little

Italy was so small it was barely Italian. Other ethnic neighborhoods we read about in a guidebook were also disappearing. The German area around East 86th Street was gone, except for a restaurant and butcher shop. The Ukrainian section in the East Village was just about gone. Only Chinatown kept growing bigger and bigger.

For two weeks we ate lunch in different restaurants in Chinatown, which was probably big enough by now to be China City. Some of the restaurants had reasonably priced lunchtime specials, so our budget didn't collapse. We always ordered different dishes that we shared, until we finally grew tired of Chinese cooking. One restaurant, New York Noodle Town, was our favorite. The waiters were surly, the menu was in Chinese that we couldn't read, and we enjoyed every minute there, so unlike the staid Chinese restaurant in Branville. The food was good, so when the current fad passed, TJ suggested we just go there once a month, or so. We quickly agreed, no doubt remembering their roast duck dishes.

We were still trying to adjust to working at Parsec, which Lou, our stress producing supervisor, didn't make easier. For whatever reason, he no longer allowed us to see the program's code, despite our having signed non-disclosure agreements. He expected us to find flaws and identify problems without our being able to go to the source and evaluate the functionality. It was a superficial process in which we observed malfunctions, but couldn't diagnose why they occurred. Lou just wanted us to tell him what was wrong, rather than let us fix, test, and go to a field trial. It was frustrating because we really couldn't do anything challenging, just report glitches.

Things went on this way for a while, and one night, before we started work on our project, I said, "Do you think they don't trust us, or is there some other reason they won't let us see the source code?"

"They don't trust us," Clar replied quickly.

"Maybe not," TJ said reasonably. "But there may be other reasons they're not telling us."

"Like what?" Clar challenged.

TJ shrugged. "I can't think of one at the moment, but they could be compartmentalizing."

"We could ask Phil," I suggested.

"I don't know if we should do that," Clar murmured softly. "We're getting paid. We're working on our project. We're eating so well I'm starting to get fat. Soon I'll be a *mamasota* . . ."

We quickly reassured her and she continued, "I'll admit it's frustrating and I'm beginning to resent them, but I think we should wait a while. We're making great progress on our project. I'd hate to have to start job hunting after such exciting results."

TJ and I looked at each other.

"Do we go along with the Old Lady," I asked, and when he nodded yes, I suggested, "Let's try it for another three months and see how we feel then."

They agreed and we went to work on our project, reasonably content for the moment. When we finished for the evening, TJ said, "I wonder if we should consider temporarily changing our project plan."

"Why?" Clar asked.

"I've been following the cyberattacks going on lately and they've changed from a few years ago."

"How?" I said, intrigued.

"Now they're trying to destroy the systems they penetrate, rather than steal information. Remember that Saudi Aramco attack, where they used the Shamoon virus to replace company data with an image of a burning American flag? It failed because there was a separate operating system from the administrative system."

"What's your point?" I asked.

"The new attacks are trying to destroy data, or to manipulate industrial machinery and take over or shut down the networks that deliver energy or run industrial processes. Perhaps we should consider building a defense program while we're working on Cybertracking."

"I think TJ may be right," Clar said. "In the current climate, the only customer for source tracking would be the NSA. They're having so much trouble with that info leak that they'll probably bury our program so deep we'd never see it again."

"That makes sense," I added. "Besides, if we identify the source of the Chinese attacks we could start the first cyberwar." They were too engrossed to get the joke.

"Don't misunderstand," TJ cautioned. "We shouldn't stop working on our program, just consider starting another project, a firewall program."

Clar and I nodded agreement and I asked, "When do we start?"

"Before we make a final decision to go ahead," Clar interjected, "we should consider how that might affect Parsec. They're paying us to work on a defensive firewall."

"We don't know their code," I said. "As long as we don't use anything they've done and we work on our own time, I don't think there's a conflict. Maybe it's time to get a lawyer and have him review our non-disclosure agreements and advise us what rights of theirs are proprietary."

"Good idea, Pete. You get crème brulée tomorrow night," TJ offered.

"Mmmm," I crooned.

"Stop drooling," Clar remarked. "I'll look up all the companies that have been attacked recently. TJ, you look up all the viruses of the last ten years. Pete, start a lawyer search. We need someone who knows cyber security and cyber law. Let's start tomorrow."

"Agreed," TJ and I murmured, then I added, "We should find out how much corporations will pay for protection."

They both laughed and Clar said, "You sound like the mafia."

"It's just business, lady," I growled in a low voice, which really cracked them up.

Chapter Seven

After training strenuously for weeks, on a rainy Saturday afternoon we had our first test at the dōjō. TJ got his yellow belt, I did really well and got my green belt, but Clar had some problems. She did her forms perfectly, with power and grace, and broke two boards effortlessly. Then she had to spar with a macho dolt who kept taunting her. It was supposed to be light contact, but the dolt kept hitting her hard after they stopped. The first time he mumbled, "Sorry." The second time he said, "I slipped." The third time he landed a solid shot on her shoulder, aimed at her chest, and he grinned like a jackanapes. He started to say something, but before he got it out Clar delivered a snapping kick to his groin. He let out a howl of anguish, slumped to the floor holding himself and Clar said, "Sorry, I slipped." TJ went to him, helped him up, and whispered something that made him shy away, but TJ held him tightly and smiled sweetly.

Sensei Omura, who had observed the bout closely, tapped TJ lightly on the shoulder.

"Thank you for your assistance, TJ san. I don't think that Bernard san requires further help."

TJ immediately released him, bowed to Omura and returned to his seat. Omura turned to Clar.

"You have passed brown belt test as expected. You will begin black belt training at your next session. Congratulations."

Clar bowed, and said, "Thank you, sensei," as Omura walked away.

"What about me?" Bernard asked.

"If you remain with us, you may continue green belt training until you are ready for brown belt."

"That's not fair," he protested. "I did better than anyone else."

"You insulted your sparring partner, then bullied her. That is not our way. Change or depart."

Bernard stared at him, trying to decide how to respond, then just shrugged and walked away.

"I'll let you know, Omura san."

We watched him head for the locker room and Clar started to speak, but Omura held up his hand.

"No need to intervene for him, Clara san."

She grinned elfishly. "I was going to offer to teach him some manners."

Omura turned his head to hide his smile, bowed to her, then left.

TJ took us to a celebratory dinner at the Oyster Bar, a wonderful seafood restaurant deep in the caverns of Grand Central Terminal. It was surprisingly quiet considering all the trains coming and going. The décor was bland, but clean, with mosaic tiles in some of the arched ceiling areas. We sat at the counter, a novel experience for me, and looked at the menu board that listed about 25 different kinds of oysters. TJ got into a discussion with the counterman about the merits of the oysters. He finally ordered a selection of four kinds; a dozen for him, a dozen for me. Clar refused to even taste them, comparing them to various nasal fluids, and ordered a shrimp cocktail, that she raved about. The rest of the meal was acceptable, but a bit pricey, not to be indulged in regularly.

On the way home I asked TJ how he knew so much about oysters. He said with a smile, "I looked them up online and took a quick course."

"Well, you passed with flying colors. Did you like them?"

"Some of them were okay, but some were too slimy."

Before I could reply, Clar said, "I don't know how you can eat anything that looks like snot."

"You could taste them before being judgmental," TJ interjected.

"Blech! Never."

"Well, let's agree to disagree," he said gently.

"For being so reasonable, big fella, you have to carry me home." She leaped on his back, wrapped her arms around him, and urged, "Let's go."

We walked down Lexington Avenue and TJ didn't even notice the burden. At our building, he helped her down gently.

"You walk the rest of the way."

She smiled sweetly. "Of course, Baby."

We talked for a while, then went to bed early, satisfied after a very nice day and evening.

Sunday morning, we got a phone call from one of our favorite Branville U. professors, Charles de Croix. He quickly told Clar, "I expected to be here for a few days, but I have to go back this evening. I'd like to see you before I leave."

Clar gave him our address and urged him to come for brunch. TJ made French toast and after we greeted Charles we sat down to eat.

Clar, grinning mischievously, asked, "What are you doing here, Charlie?"

He laughed. "Is that how you talk to a full professor?"

"Then you've had enough to eat," I quipped.

"Not quite. This is a lot better than the faculty dining room."

"Which was better than the student cafeteria," TJ remarked.

"Enough about food," I said. "We know this isn't a social call."

He nodded, embarrassed. "I'm here as a recruiter for the department. We want you back. We have a special offer of fellowships that would let you work on your software project, teach two classes, and be on a tenure track."

He looked at us expectantly, and after looking at us, Clar said, "That's a generous offer. You know we love Branville and we were very happy there. Things haven't gone exactly as we planned, but we're determined to make a go of it. Once we've accomplished our goals, we'll talk about coming back."

Charles stayed for a few hours and brought us up to date on developments and gossip at Branville U. We were delighted that all our old friends were doing well. Just before he left he told us about a plan to encourage faculty to develop new software and market the products through start-ups, approved by the University. This was obviously aimed at us and it was flattering to be valued, but we declined, at least for the present. Charles promised to keep after us until we came to our senses and returned to Branville U.

After he left we talked about the offer for a while. Clar apologized for rejecting it without discussing it with us first. We quickly reassured her that we agreed with her and there was no need to talk about it. Then TJ asked wistfully, "What if we fail here?"

"Then we go back to Branville whipped curs," I replied, "pitied by everybody for not making it in the real world."

"We won't get whipped," Clar asserted.

It was obvious that we were still determined to succeed with our project.

Chapter Eight

Shortly after our third month at Parsec, we had an unusual experience. At our weekly meeting with Lou, he expressed dissatisfaction with our progress. This was a first for the three of us. No one had ever been unhappy with our efforts before. I hotly demanded specifics, ignoring TJ's signal to remain calm, but I was outraged. Who was this dweeb to criticize us? Lou mouthed some meaningless generalities about not solving problems and not living up to Phil's expectations, said in a sneering tone implying that he didn't think much of us in the first place.

Clar had been watching him intently, a taut raptor considering prey. "If you have a complaint about our work," she said, "you'll have to give us some specifics, so we can make adjustments and improve our functioning."

"We don't have to improve our functioning," I blurted. "We're working in the dark without source code. All we can do is chart problems, not fix them. If you want better results, give us the tools we need to produce them. Even you should understand that."

He was shocked at my vehemence and looked at TJ and Clar, assuming they'd rebuke me, but they just stared at him coldly, outraged as much as I was by his attitude. I guess he realized he went too far and mumbled vaguely about discussing the matter with Phil. He slunk out without another word, leaving us fuming.

We sat there quietly for a few minutes without any inclination to work. When Clar suggested an early lunch, we got up and left. It was a grey November day, without a hint of sunlight, but it wasn't too cold, somewhere in the 50's. We walked east until we came to West Broadway, passing all kinds of restaurants, but we didn't have any appetite. TJ finally brought up what was on our minds.

"Why do you think he did that?"

By this time my temper had cooled down and I replied softly, "I don't know why, but it was obviously meant to provoke us."

"Right," Clar said. "We have to figure out why he did it and find out if he did it with Phil's approval."

TJ and I nodded agreement, and TJ said, "Let's talk about it tonight. I don't feel hungry, so let's walk around for a while and give Pete some time to calm down."

"I'm calm," I protested. "I just don't want him to think we'll accept whatever shit he wants to dump on us."

"If Pete didn't confront him, I would have," Clar asserted. "He has a hell of a nerve insulting us like that. I was tempted to kick him in the . . . head."

TJ and I grinned and TJ murmured, "You're more violent then Pete, Old Lady."

Before I could respond, he continued, "Let's head back to the office."

Lou stopped by in the late afternoon to drop off some discs and didn't say a word about the incident. Neither did we. We left for home at five o'clock, wondering what was going on and determined to find out. We ate dinner out at a German restaurant not far from our apartment and while we ate we discussed what happened earlier. We didn't reach a conclusion, other than we didn't want to take Lou's abuse.

I didn't admit it, but I was still angry despite denying it to my friends. Clar was absorbed in an action game where a scantily clad woman kicked or shot the crude men who tried to prevent her from completing her mission, rescuing sex slaves in a third world brothel. TJ was busy chatting on line and I reminded myself to find out what he was up to. It didn't seem like he was discussing recipes. I played online poker, not for real money of course, and despite my reckless play was ahead over $5,000.00. I wasn't tempted to play for real money, since I didn't have the requisite skills. I just wasn't in the mood for my usual game, online chess.

By unspoken consent we didn't work on our project that evening and just before we said goodnight, Clar asked TJ, "What have you been up to online? I know it's not cooking info."

TJ actually blushed and I had no idea how he managed the pigmentation.

"I . . . I've . . ."

"Yes?" Clar encouraged.

"I've been going on an online dating service, talking to different girls," he said in a rush.

"How can you be sure they're girls?" I teased.

"The service screens them and I'll find out if I ever get up enough nerve to meet someone."

"Well, it'll be good for you to go on a date," I commented.

"I get nervous thinking about it. I don't know how to talk to a girl."

"You talked to Maud back at school," Clar reminded him.

"She was different, real nice, and gutsy too."

"We'll help you prepare. Right, Clar?"

"Of course. By the way, my family invited us to dinner this coming Saturday. Would you like to go?"

"Sure." TJ and I replied loyally.

"You don't have to if you'd rather not."

"We want to go, Clar," TJ reassured her. "How about I cook a Spanish dinner for them?"

"That would be great. They'd get a kick out of it. Let me ask Mama, just to be sure she doesn't mind."

Clar made a quick phone call and Mama thought it was very funny having a guest come and cook dinner for them. TJ was enthusiastic about a chance to try a new cuisine and asked Clar to tell us about the South Bronx.

"My grandfather was from Puerto Rico. He joined the army during the Korean War, then came to the Bronx when it was still a nice place. In the 1960's, when my father was a boy, thousands of rural Puerto Ricans came to the Bronx in search of a better life. They didn't know anything about city living and nobody helped them. They scared their neighbors with their rough ways and the white people moved out, leaving abandoned buildings behind that the landlords burned for the insurance money. The Bronx became the symbol of urban decay."

She paused to assess our interest and we urged her to go on.

"My father got married and moved into the projects, which were supposed to be a nice alternative to the tenements. But the gangs made life difficult and between drugs and violence it wasn't easy growing up there. My world shattered when I was raped, but somehow I kept going. I got a scholarship to My Lady of Hope parochial school, then Branville, where I met you."

"That's quite a story," I said. "We'll look out for you now."

TJ stood up and hugged her. I joined them and tears poured down her cheeks. After a minute she wiped her eyes, then whispered huskily, "Thanks, guys. That's the first time I've cried since the rape."

"You don't have to be tough all the time," TJ murmured.

"Maybe not now," she replied.

We said goodnight a few minutes later and went to bed with another level of closeness growing between us.

Chapter Nine

Lou was just as unpleasant Monday afternoon at our usual review, but he wasn't confrontational. In fact, for him, he could have fooled some people into thinking he was human. I wondered for a moment if Phil had told him to treat us more politely, then dismissed the idle thought. Just before we went back to the office after lunch, we agreed that if Lou didn't insult us again, we wouldn't bring it up. We weren't making much progress on our assigned tasks, but the reasons were evident and we had mentioned them to Lou several times. Without source code, we couldn't do very much and we decided to talk to Phil in two weeks, if there were no changes.

That night we went to the Bronx and the trip on the "6" train was an eye-opener for TJ and me. It was just after rush hour, but the car was still crowded with mostly overdressed-for-work black and Hispanic passengers sweltering in the overheated car. The train came out of the ground in the Bronx and became an elevated line, but it was dark outside and the windows were fogged with our exhalations, so we couldn't see very much. Clar pointed out Yankee Stadium, which didn't mean much to non-baseball-fans. Judging by the lighted buildings there were no skyscrapers, but it was reassuring that there were signs of life. TJ and I hadn't mentioned our apprehensions of going to the Bronx to Clar, so at least it wasn't a wasteland.

Gary Beck

On the walk from the subway we passed
several blocks of two story houses, neat and in
good repair. Only high chain link fences in the
small front yards hinted at the need for security.
Bronxvale Houses was a pleasant surprise. We
didn't see any bands of thugs hanging around, no
dope dealers, prostitutes, muggers. Just average
people hurrying home after work, staring at us
curiously, but politely. Unlike our imagined
decayed public housing, Clar's building was
clean, functional and well maintained.

Clar's family greeted her tumultuously. Papa
and Mama hugged her tightly. Older brothers
kissed her, younger sisters surrounded her. Our
greeting was more reserved, a handshake from
Mama, a nod from Papa, suspicious looks from
brothers and their wives, but the young sisters
couldn't take their eyes off the packages we
carried. TJ had brought enough food for a rifle
platoon and I had teased him about it. Now I saw
how right he was.

He instantly won everybody over when he
said, "*Mucho gusto, Señora Rodriguez. ¿Dónde
está la cocina?*"

She beamed, led him away and that was the
last I saw of him until dinner was served. TJ
made a huge pot of sea food *paella* that everyone
devoured until they could eat no more. Then he
served *flan* that was so light and creamy it was
even better than *crème bruleé*. He was adopted
into the Rogriguez clan and by power of
association so was I. When we said goodnight a
chorus of Rodriguez voices urged us to return.

After Clar kissed everyone, she said, "Next
time we visit we'll have start-up money and we'll
come in a limousine."

Mama assured her she always wanted to see
her, rich or poor, and we left with a warm feeling
that our friend was loved and supported by her

family. Her brothers insisted on walking with us to the train station, their pride in their bright sister shone from their adoring looks. The ride back to Manhattan was uneventful and we went to bed early for a change.

A few days later we talked about our progress on creating a firewall system. TJ was studying the major virus attacks of the last ten years, Clar was compiling a list of companies that had been attacked, and I had narrowed the lawyer search to one woman with good credentials, who offered a half hour consultation free. We decided to see her as soon as we had solid results of our search, which would take another week. So the next day I made an appointment for the following Thursday.

I guess my strong reaction to Lou made him back off, because he acted as if nothing had happened. We continued what we considered meaningless tasks at Parsec, but at least the atmosphere wasn't worse. The big treat for us came the night we decided we were far enough advanced with our tracker program to consider a test. Clar outlined a plan.

"We can rent time on two servers from two different providers. Once we set up a format, Pete will attack us using one server and TJ and I will track your attack using the other server."

"That might be too easy," TJ said. "We know where the attack is coming from."

Clar started to nod agreement, but I said, "The program doesn't know."

They looked at me wide-eyed for a moment, then grinned.

"Good point, Pete," Clar remarked. "TJ, you rent the servers. I'll prepare the application. Pete, you plan the attack. Let's do it as soon as we can."

"How about I rent a server you don't know? That'll make it more of a challenge"

"Keep in mind," TJ reminded us. "This is not a real trial."

"Don't be a programmer," I teased. "It's an adventure. Let's enjoy it." And we cheerfully went about our preparations.

All our energies went into organizing this test and we felt so good that the stifling atmosphere at Parsec didn't bother us for a while. TJ made a list of time rentals on servers and he and I selected our own server providers, without telling which ones we selected. I took a camera photo of Lou when he wasn't looking and used it as an attack image, with him dancing on hot coals while being prodded with a pitchfork by a red devil. I arranged to use Clar's brother's computer, without telling her, and Charles' computer at Branville. I sent the virus originating in the Bronx, then bouncing around various sites, until it hit Clar and TJ's machines.

I hadn't told them when I'd launch the attack and they found out when they saw Lou getting jabbed in the ass, which they thought was very funny. They activated Cybersnarer and within a few minutes traced the attack back to the original point, through several servers to my machine. We congratulated each other, did a victory dance, then babbled about the wonderful program, until TJ, cautious as usual, brought us back to earth.

"Let's not get too excited. It was a very simple test."

"But it worked," I insisted. "And it's the first trial. It did everything right. What more can you ask for the first time?"

"You're right, Pete," Clar said. "It worked. TJ's just trying to keep us from going overboard."

"I know that. I just want to enjoy the moment."

TJ grinned. "Me too. How about we go out for a beer?"

"Lead on," Clar said.

We went to the Ale House on 30th Street, which was packed with fans watching a baseball game. We got a table in the back and quietly discussed the test. When we finished the analysis there was no doubt that Cybersnarer performed its first operation with flying colors. The next step would be a more complex test that would reveal any problems, but we decided to talk about it tomorrow and just enjoy the feeling of accomplishment. We had a couple of beers, sticking to Brooklyn breweries for some reason, and happily walked home. TJ asked where I got the idea to virus Lou.

I smiled. "Just wishful thinking, I guess," which gave us a laugh.

Thursday we took a long lunch hour and went to see the lawyer, Bonnie Carrington. She had a high-power office in the Seagram Building on Park Avenue. Her receptionist, an android blonde with a pretentious British accent, looked us over disdainfully, until I said, "Doctors Larkspur, Rodriguez, and Washington to see Ms. Carrington."

"You're doctors?" she asked, startled.

"Yes," Clar snapped. "And you're a receptionist. So get to it."

The chastened android mumbled into her phone and a moment later Bonnie Carrington rushed out.

"I'm so glad to meet you," she gushed. "Sorry to keep you waiting."

Even Clar thawed after her enthusiastic greeting. She led us into her office, which had a great northern view of Park Avenue, asked what we would drink and sent for coffee, then asked cordially, "What can I do for you?"

I outlined our Cybersnarer program, so she'd know we were serious players, then told her what we were working on at Parsec and that we were considering doing our own firewall program, as long as it didn't create a conflict with Parsec.

Bonnie had been taking notes, looked them over, then asked, "Do you intend to use any of Parsec's technology or intellectual property?"

"No," I replied. "Anything we do will be our original work."

"Then unless you duplicate some part of their program, I don't see that you're liable."

She looked over the non-disclosure agreement we signed, and concluded there was no restriction on our doing our own project.

We thanked her, I said we'd retain her as soon as we were ready to form a company and we got up to leave.

"May I ask you a question?" Bonnie said.

Clar rolled her eyes, expecting the usual how young we were, but nodded yes.

"Why are you working at Parsec, if you have such a hot program?"

"We had a choice," TJ explained. "To become professors, or go for a start-up. When we couldn't raise funds, we took jobs so we could earn money to continue to develop our programs."

"I may know some possible backers. Send me your proposal and I'll see what I can do."

"Sure," I said. "And thanks."

Clar and TJ echoed me and we left, hopeful that Bonnie might actually find some serious start-up money.

Chapter Ten

We followed our usual routine on the weekend, running, the dōjō, and working on Cybersnarer. Sunday evening, we reviewed TJ and Clar's research. TJ presented a list of viruses. We all knew Stuxnet that attacked the Iranian nuclear project, Agent.btz that attacked the Pentagon's computers, Poison Ivy, a remote access trojan, that secretly controlled the infected computer, and the Zeus Trojan, which TJ explained was the malware of choice for cybercriminals to steal identities.

Clar smugly told us, "Cybersnarer will catch Zeus users."

The pride in her voice was obvious and we eagerly agreed. We discussed Conficker, a worm that crawled into millions of Windows-based PCs around the world.

TJ piqued our interest when he said, "No one knows what it was meant to do. The best guess was to steal financial data, but it was never used for a specific purpose, which still worries security experts."

"Maybe we should look into that sometime," I mused.

"Not until we finish our current projects," Clar reminded me.

"Of course," I said. "Tell us about your list of companies that were attacked."

"It's every big company you can think of: GE, IBM, Apple, banks, brokerage houses, every part of the government—especially the Pentagon—and the Treasury. The biggest vulnerabilities are the power grid, water supply, transportation, and communications. Unless they have better firewall systems than they describe, a cyber-attack could cripple the country without firing a shot."

"Then our firewall project will have real value," TJ said.

"We'll have to put a lot more time on it," I added.

"Right," Clar said. "We'll have to set a new schedule to allocate more time. Do you think we need someone with firewall experience?"

"Not yet," TJ replied. "Let's assess what we can do first, then we'll consider if we need help."

"Why don't we review a new work plan tomorrow night," I suggested. "After we finish our regular session on Cybersnarer."

We called it a night and went to bed a little giddy from the new info and work plan.

Monday morning at Parsec we got a real surprise. Lou was actually pleasant. Granted he had a forced, insincere smile, but it was better than his usual nasty, confrontational attitude. At lunchtime, Clar and I expressed our suspicions of the odd behavior, but TJ dismissed our concerns.

"What do you care what's going on in that malbot's head. It's better than his normal unpleasant self, which makes work easier for us."

Clar went on about it for a while, but TJ refused to speculate, cutting off any more discussion with, "What could he possibly gain? Let's talk about something more interesting."

Clar subsided, but it was clear that she wasn't satisfied.

I guess I should have been more suspicious of Lou. After all, the only people I trusted were TJ and Clar. But I was so absorbed in thinking about Cybersnarer and the new firewall project that I ignored Clar's concerns, accepting TJs assessment that it wasn't worth worrying about, and forgetting that Clar was generally right about people.

I was so happy about our progress with Cybersnarer that I decided to make the next test much more challenging. I hadn't done any hacking for years—well not real hacking. I may have poked around a site or two, just to keep tabs on research that interested me, but I didn't steal or do anything malicious.

I waited until TJ and Clar went to bed, then I outlined an attack plan on my iPad. I selected entry points on various gateway machines that led through a dozen random businesses, restaurant chains, bookstore chains, none of which were tightly firewalled and my penetration wouldn't disrupt anything. I picked one insurance company with reasonably good firewalls, but it was far from military encryption. I set up a network map and decided to organize the attack from the server used by TJ and Clar. In the morning I'd suggest we have the next test in a week or so. I went to bed and slowly drifted off to sleep, fantasizing that the final test of Cybersnarer would be to track a Chinese attack. I had a strange dream about being very tiny and riding electrons on the information superhighway, stopping at atom shipping centers, but I forgot most of it after I woke up.

Lou was still insincerely pleasant the rest of the week. I was at the point where I couldn't decide whether I detested him more when he was nasty, or when he gave us the greasy smile that looked like it pained him. But Clar didn't say anything about it, so I let it pass without comment. We were too busy to bother with anything that didn't require our immediate attention. TJ was busy checking the various attack mechanisms, while Clar was studying defensive firewalls. I was evaluating the successful attacks that we knew about in order to isolate the most dangerous, and prepare to defend against them.

Saturday night we went to see a movie, an action shoot-em-up, blow-em-up, with a bunch of old stars who should have been home in bed instead of kicking bad-guy-ass. It was silly, but gave us a laugh. On the way home I told them the name I came up with for our firewall program; Castle Keep. They loved it. Clar described a beautiful picture of medieval knights fighting off a band of ugly trolls trying to capture the castle. I mentioned crossbowmen and Clar added boiling oil. We were really getting off on siege craft, when TJ interjected, "Why don't you wait until I can do a domain name check?"

"There better not be another one," Clar growled, "or I'll . . ."

"And I'll join you," I added.

"Why are you two always so violent?" TJ asked teasingly.

"Let's show him," Clar urged.

We each grabbed one of his arms and pulled him back and forth, chanting to each other, over and over, "You're more violent."

"No. You are."

Until TJ held his arms at his side and we couldn't move him.

"Killjoy," Clar muttered.

"Spoilsport," I accused.

TJ suddenly wrapped an arm around each of us, pulled us close and hugged us.

"Don't worry. I still love you."

"Now whose being violent?" I accused, and we laughed the rest of the way home.

A notable event occurred a few days later. After weeks of cruising internet dating services, followed by chat room exchanges, TJ made a date to meet a girl for dinner.

The complications began when he turned to me and asked, "Will you come with me, Pete?"

Clar burst out laughing. "That's a hoot. The king of shyness taking the prince of inexperience."

We both looked at her indignantly and I blurted, "At least he's trying. Not like someone we know."

"What do you mean by that?" she demanded.

I hadn't meant to upset her, so I tried to reply tactfully, "We know why you don't date. We just worry that you're missing something important in your life."

"You know how much we care about you," TJ said.

She softened at our obvious concern.

"I know you care. I'm just not ready to get involved."

"How about we arrange a triple date?" I suggested. "This way TJ and I will make sure you don't get into an uncomfortable situation."

"Thanks, Pete. I'll think about it. Can you imagine what we'd look like?"

"We'd look fine," I asserted.

"I'll let you know. Are you going with TJ?"

Now I was on the spot.

"I don't think I'd be very helpful."

"I need you as my wingman." TJ looked at me expectantly.

What else could I say to my best friend.

"Sure."

"Is it alright if the girl is black?"

"Of course. Will she put out?"

"Pete. You're a low beast," Clar declared.

"Why? Because I want to get some experience?"

"That's not the way to say it," she replied.

"I wouldn't say it to her."

"I should hope not," she murmured. "You have to build a relationship carefully. I'll teach you some basics on how to get along with a girl."

"How do you know so much about it?" I asked.

"I may not be out there, but unlike you stoops, I know what's going on."

"We'll appreciate your help," TJ said, and gave me a warning look not to say anything else, so I just nodded enthusiastically.

Suddenly TJ and I had developed a social life, at least in preparations for the big event, a first date. Clar instructed us how to dress, how to eat, how to talk about casual things, and in general to be relaxed and try to have a good time. We didn't dare ask where she acquired this sophisticated knowledge. During the next week she outlined various questions the girls might ask and critiqued our answers. I suspected she was making things up as she went along, but I didn't know anything, so it was helpful. Each night we worked on Cybersnarer, Castle Keep, and dating techniques. Things were definitely looking up.

Work was routine, the same mindless tasks, except smiling Lou was beginning to look like the Joker in one of the Batman movies. But we managed to ignore him and deal with the tedium of repetitious chores. TJ arranged our date for the following Saturday, which was greeted with a combination of enthusiasm and trepidation. I proposed our second test of Cybersnarer for Friday night, which delighted TJ and Clar.

I got completely absorbed in preparing the second test and was careful to not let TJ and Clar discover what I was doing. I suspected that Clar was hacking into my computer, so I wrote some guard code that would trigger a 'Caught you. Ha, Ha, Ha', at her entry. I set up a shell account with a cloaking service to hide my identity. Then I created a network of anonymizers, using a series of 30 servers in disparate geographical locations. It wasn't very sophisticated compared to the real cyber-attacks launched by highly skilled hackers, but I thought it was a fair challenge for a second test.

TJ and Clar had been looking at me strangely for a few days. I finally said, "What?"

"You've been walking around mumbling and cackling to yourself," Clar accused. "We thought you were heading for a nervous breakdown before your big date."

She and TJ were laughing at me and I replied with as much dignity as I could muster, "I'm not the least bit nervous. I've been enjoying my preparations for the second test of Cybersnarer. I'll have a few surprises for you this time."

"I hope so," she snapped. "My momma could have made a better attack the first time."

I pretended to be hurt. "Then let her do it."

"Aw. Did I hurt Little Brother's feelings? What a sensitive little boy." But she caught my smile and whacked me on the arm. "Play with me? I'll teach you a lesson," and she dropped into a combat stance.

"Peace, violent one. I surrender."

"You better," she growled. "Do you really have a good attack?"

"You'll find out."

"That sounds exciting," she said.

TJ nodded and offered, "We're looking forward to it. How good is it?"

"We'll see," I replied. "It's nowhere near the real thing, but it'll be a real test."

"I can't wait," Clar enthused. "If we track the attack it'll prove Cybersnarer works."

"Maybe," TJ cautioned. "It's got to do a lot more than track a controlled attack."

"Don't be a wet blanket," Clar urged. "If this works, after we get our start-up money, the test will be to launch a real attack on a target, then set up a tracer route and track it back to its I.P."

"You got it, girl," I responded happily.

Chapter Eleven

Thursday night Clar gave us a date tutorial. She asked TJ to tell her everything he knew about the girls, starting with their names, ages, where they worked, everything.

"I can only tell you about Lakeisha. I only know her friend's name, Janet, nothing else about her."

"So you're going to let Little Brother meet an absolute stranger?"

She teased but before he could respond, said, "Tell us about Lakeisha."

"Sorry, Pete," TJ murmured. "I didn't think . . ."

"Don't worry about it. Tell us."

He opened a page on his laptop. "Here's her picture."

Lakeisha was a very pretty, dark-skinned girl, with short hair. Her most noticeable feature was large, intelligent looking brown eyes. Clar and I commented on how pretty she was and Clar glared at me when I whispered, "She's probably a man."

TJ ignored my remark. "She's 20 years old, a junior at N.Y.U., majoring in micro-biology. She likes Asian food, classical music, and ballet."

"Uh, oh." I groaned. "That means going to culture."

"It wouldn't kill you," Clar declared.

"You're only saying that because you won't have to go," I muttered. "Oh, well. What about Janet?"

"All I know is she's her roommate. I don't have a picture."

"She'll probably be a man," I grumbled.

"Then you'll say goodnight and leave," Clar snapped. "What's the plan?"

"We're going to meet at a Japanese restaurant on 3ʳᵈ Avenue and if we want to spend more time together we'll go to a nearby Starbucks."

"That sounds very sensible," Clar approved. "Let's discuss what you'll talk about. Later I'll pick out your clothes."

"I can dress myself," I protested.

"Don't worry," she cooed. "You can put them on by yourself. Now here are some basic guidelines. You can tell them where you were born and grew up, but nothing about the circumstances, that's personal business. You can tell them about school, developing software projects for cybersecurity, but no details. You can talk about running and Tae Kwan Do. TJ you can talk about your interest in gourmet cooking. Don't mention me."

"Why not?" TJ asked.

"Our relationship is none of their business, unless you get to know them really well. Any other questions?"

TJ looked at me and I shrugged, "You prepared us."

"One more thing. This is supposed to be fun. Try to relax and enjoy yourselves. You're very special guys and these girls are lucky to meet you."

"Thanks, Clar," TJ said huskily.

She smiled that dazzling smile that only we and her family saw, then turned to me.

"Don't be crude, Pete. These are college girls, not street tramps."

"What's the difference?" I asked immediately and they both grabbed me. TJ held me and Clar mussed my hair.

"It's a good thing I know you're not the pig you pretend to be."

I smiled sweetly. "What about the last lesson?"

"What?" she asked.

"How to have sex."

She flushed for a moment, then said, "When I'm ready, it'll have to be someone as special as you guys."

TJ and I hugged her and I said, "We won't let you go out with anyone who doesn't deserve you."

"Thanks," she whispered, then fled to her room.

Things were getting even stranger at Parsec. Friday morning, at our usual meeting, Lou was actually pleasant. Of course, we could see he wasn't sincere, but if it made life at work easier, so be it. We discussed it briefly at lunch and after several guesses our best conclusion was that Phil must have spoken to him, even though we hadn't complained. It got weirder. Lou stopped by just before we left for the day and wished us a good weekend. This was totally out of character for the troll, but I just mumbled, "Thanks." We got out of there with a peculiar feeling of unease, that we promptly forgot about as soon as we were outside.

TJ took us to dinner at a small French restaurant on East 33rd Street, off 3rd Avenue that was really nice. The atmosphere was what we imagined Paris would be like, the service was welcoming and efficient and the food was good. By the time we headed home, I was mumbling to myself, to the amusement of TJ and Clar, as I reviewed my preparations for the simulated attack.

When we got to the apartment I went to my room, checked that everything was set and immediately launched the attack. It took a few minutes for them to realize the attack was on, but they activated Cybersnarer and sent it on its way. It took less than two minutes for Cybersnarer to track the attack through the series of servers and penetrate the cloaking service I used to hide my identity.

I was a little disappointed that I couldn't conceal the attack, but delighted that Cybersnarer worked so well. We babbled and cackled to each other about our triumph and TJ opened a bottle of champagne, Dom Pérignon, that he bought for the occasion of a successful test. I said that I never tasted champagne before and we had a big laugh when TJ and Clar admitted they had never tasted it either. We proclaimed it a wonderful drink and vowed to make it a regular habit once we were rich. We were drunk with the wine and the test and talked for hours about what we'd do with all the money that would soon be rolling in. The most popular topic was a three bedroom, luxury apartment in a building with a swimming pool. We went to bed in a sweet haze.

Chapter Twelve

We slept a little later than usual Saturday morning and were definitely creaky on the run by the East River. When we got back, TJ insisted we eat a big breakfast, with lots of coffee and by the time we left for the dōjō, we were beginning to feel slightly human. Sensei Omura greeted us with his warm courtesy and informed us the next test period would be the first Saturday in December. He said we were all eligible for the next level, Clar, black belt, me, brown belt and TJ, green belt. We thanked Omura for his confidence in us and told him we were excited about reaching the next level.

"You have worked hard, and with proper attitude. I am pleased to have you here," and he bowed and walked away.

We bowed to him, then congratulated each other on our progress, and I couldn't help saying, "Things are really going well for us."

As we finished dressing for the big date night, closely supervised by Clar, TJ reminded me of two conditions for the night, everybody pays for themselves so there's no financial obligation or embarrassment, and anyone can leave at any time, without criticism or complaint.

"That's a relief," I sighed. "I thought I'd be stuck all night."

"It doesn't apply to you," TJ blurted, with a hint of panic in his voice.

"Don't be mean, Pete," Clar said.

"What if my girl adores me and TJ's girl takes off?"

TJ looked alarmed at the prospect of rejection and Clar said soothingly, "It's a get-acquainted date. TJ's girl will love him. It's you I'm worried about."

"What do you mean?" I asked.

"You get carried away sometimes and I'm afraid you'll scare your girl off."

"Don't worry. I'll be on my best behavior."

"Remember it, for TJ's sake."

"Yes, Old Lady."

She gave me an exasperated look, then saw I was teasing and managed a weak smile.

We met the girls at the Japanese restaurant on 3rd Avenue and 18th Street. They were nervously waiting outside when we got there five minutes early. We introduced ourselves and the oddest thing happened. It felt like we already knew each other and we were immediately comfortable together. I guess I stared too obviously when Janet took her coat off, because she said, "Do you like what you see?"

"Very much," I replied instantly.

"You look as if you never saw a girl before."

"Not one as pretty as you."

I must have said the right thing because she gave me a big smile. I didn't notice what I ate that TJ ordered for me. Janet and I babbled away through dinner and I wasn't aware of what we talked about. I had almost forgotten about TJ and when I looked at him he was so comfortable talking to Lakeisha that I didn't worry about him.

By popular consent after dinner we went to Starbucks, and on the way there I had to smile at our physical appearance. Lakeisha was about 5'2" and she looked like a child next to TJ. Janet was 5'10" and made me seem taller. We sat close together at the tiny table and I could feel the heat of her body racing through me. She was a dancer studying modern ballet and was very surprised when I told her about our running regimen, and preparing to test for a brown belt in Tae Kwon Do. She asked if she could run with us some time and when I asked if she ever ran she said no.

"You'd have to build up to it, otherwise you'd injure yourself. We run two miles every morning."

"What are you talking about? Feel this leg."

I did, and didn't stop until she said, "That's enough."

"You're in good shape. Very good shape," I added with a leer, which made her smile. "But you can't just run without preparation."

"Will you help me?"

"I'd be glad to take care of your body."

"I'm sure you would," she grinned, then smacked me playfully.

She was really enjoying herself and I began to realize for the first time how my life had changed for the better. I had a doctorate, I was an athlete, soon to be an entrepreneur, and I had the two best friends in the world. There was no reason that a smart, beautiful girl couldn't like me.

We walked the girls back to their dorm on East 23rd Street and made a date for next Friday night, Janet kissed me goodnight, with a taste of tongue. I couldn't tell if I was falling in love or in lust, but it felt good. TJ was walking on air and we didn't talk much on the short walk home. Just before we went in, I said, "Thanks, TJ. I hope you feel as good as I do."

"Definitely. And thanks for coming with me."

"Anytime," I said fervently.

We slept late Sunday morning, not our usual habit. I tried to ignore the commotion of Clar's cleaning and vacuuming frenzy as long as possible. So did TJ, but we finally gave in and joined her in the kitchen for breakfast.

She looked at us disdainfully.

"It's a good thing I know you don't drink or use drugs, so there must be another reason for your pathetic lack of energy." Before either of us could reply, she said, "You have ten minutes to get ready for our run," and she walked away, dismissing our feeble moan of protest.

But she was right to push us. Halfway through the run we snapped awake and picked up the pace, until Clar finally demanded, "Slow down, you show-offs."

"How about an extra mile this morning, TJ?"

"Sure, Pete. Maybe two."

She whacked us both, then sprinted ahead and she was still laughing when we caught up to her.

Later that day she made us tell her all the details of our date. When TJ described his evening with Lakeisha I realized I was so involved with Janet that I hadn't noticed how things were going for TJ. I started to apologize, but TJ cut me off.

"If I had a problem you would have been there for me."

"Of course. I just feel really badly because . . ."

"Forget it. I had a great time."

Clar's interrogation was thorough and she pronounced herself satisfied when she was positive we hadn't revealed any details of Cybersnarer or Castle Keep.

"I'm glad you both had such a good time. I must admit I'm a little jealous. I hope those girls realize how special you two are."

TJ and I looked at her in amazement. This was so unlike Clar that it took us a moment to respond.

"You're the most important woman in my life," I declared. "And you always will be."

"The same goes for me," TJ stated.

"Thanks, fellas. The Old Lady is watching the boys grow up."

"How about the boys take you out to dinner?" TJ said. "There's a nice Spanish restaurant on 2nd Avenue."

Chapter Thirteen

TJ and I were feeling so good Monday morning we almost danced to work. We were both obviously infatuated and Clar teased us about dating college girls.

"They're twenty years old," I protested. "College juniors, not teeny boppers."

"I don't know," she said sadly. "I hoped you boys were ready for women."

TJ picked her up and carried her in his arms.

"We're waiting for you. Right, Pete?"

"Right, TJ. Your refusal to date us forces us to look elsewhere."

"You boys are too young for me. You couldn't handle it."

"TJ seems to be doing alright and I'll carry you if he gets tired."

Clar suddenly shouted, "Help. I'm being kidnapped. This bad man is abducting me."

This being New York City, except for a few quick glances, no one paid any attention to her and we all laughed the rest of the way to work. On the elevator ride to our floor we put on the serious work faces that let us tolerate the tedious job.

We each had an email on our machines asking us to report to A.F. Rogers, in room 1462, at 1:00 p.m. We didn't know who that was and TJ quickly looked him/her up on the company website and he was the chief financial officer. We speculated for a few minutes why the summons, but couldn't come up with a good solution, so we worked until noon, then went to lunch.

* * *

We got to room 1426 promptly at 1:00 p.m. and a shapely blonde receptionist, virtually a clone of Phil's receptionist, greeted us crisply and asked us to be seated. After waiting almost ten minutes, I was getting impatient, but just before I stood up and complained, the clone said in a throaty voice, "You can go in now."

A.F. Rogers turned out to be a bland looking man in his early thirties, wearing an expensive suit and a garish tie with lemons and limes. His face was almost one dimensional, with a bored, supercilious expression.

"Please have a seat."

"What's this about?" I demanded.

He looked at us coolly, then said, "I'm sorry to inform you that the project you've been working on has been cancelled. We have no choice but to let you go. We will give you three months of separation pay and extend your health benefits for six months."

He looked at us as if he were giving a weather report.

"You mean I've been fired?" I asked, shocked.

"Not fired. Separated."

"What's the difference?" TJ asked.

"The project is terminated; therefore, your positions have been eliminated. My secretary will give you your separation packages. If you have any questions, feel free to call. My card is in each package. Thank you for your efforts at Parsec. Good day."

Part of me wanted to whack his indifferent face, but I controlled myself, looked at Clar and

TJ, who just shrugged. We left his office, stopped at his secretary's desk and got our packages, retrieved our personal things from our office, then left the building.

"What now?" Clar asked.

"Let's go home," I replied.

"Do you feel separated?" Clar joked.

"I feel fired," I replied.

"So do I," TJ added.

"They gave us a very generous separation package," Clar reasoned.

"I still feel fired," I muttered. "We've got to talk about this."

"Later," Clar said.

We didn't talk much on the way home. I was angry, TJ was brooding, and Clar was trying to put a good spin on our situation. Once the door shut behind us, temporarily locking out the traumatic world, we changed into comfortable clothes and by unspoken consent drifted into the kitchen. Without asking, TJ poured apple juice for us and we sat there looking at each other.

"I have to tell you that I do feel fired," Clar finally admitted.

"They may have sweetened it by severance . . . I mean *separation* pay," I said, "but we've been fired."

"They could be telling the truth that the project has been cancelled," TJ offered.

"Does it matter how they say it?" Clar said bluntly. "They let us go, dispensed with our services. Whether we like it or not, that's a fact."

"What are we going to do about it?" I demanded.

"What can we do?" TJ asked.

"Nothing," Clar replied. "They didn't break any laws or violate our rights. They simply let us go. I know it's humiliating, but there's nothing we can do about it. I suggest you curse them, Pete, if that'll make you feel better."

I shrugged. "Not really. In a way it's a relief. We never liked that place and they never appreciated us."

"So what's next?" TJ asked.

"I suggest we take a week off," Clar proposed. "Maybe go somewhere for a few days. We've never had a vacation and we've been working our asses off non-stop for years."

"That's a great idea," I said. "Where shall we go?"

"Well, we don't want to spend a lot of money." Clar pointed out. "We may need it. So we can't go very far. Any suggestions?"

"How about Disneyland?" TJ said.

Clar shook her head. "Too far. Too expensive."

"We can't go anywhere warm, because we'd have to fly," I said. "So if we can't get sun and sand, we want someplace interesting."

"Like what?" TJ asked.

I thought for a moment. "Atlantic City? Washington, DC?"

"I could write a program for blackjack and we could win a lot of money," TJ said.

"We can't afford to lose money," Clar stated. "Washington sounds good."

TJ looked slightly dejected at the rejection of his money making scheme, but nodded agreement.

"We can rent a car, stay at a cheap motel, see the sights and forget about Parsec," I explained.

"Let's do it," TJ said.

"When do we go?" Clar asked.

"Tomorrow. We leave early, stay two nights and come back Thursday. I'll reserve a car today."

"I don't have a driver's license," Clar said.

"Neither do I," TJ added.

"Then I'll do the driving. When we get back, both of you should get learners' permits, then get your licenses."

"I'll find a motel online," TJ said.

"I'll make a list of what we should see," Clar said.

I smiled at the two people I loved most in the world. "It sounds like fun."

It might have seemed crazy to someone else that we were celebrating getting fired, but it was a great feeling of release. We didn't like Parsec from the first day, using it as a means to an end. The second test of Cybersnarer proved that we had a valuable product and it would only be a matter of time before we got funding for it. I sent our lawyer, Bonnie, a summary of the test, then packed for the trip.

The drive to Washington was uneventful, and we easily found the motel that TJ selected, then we were off sightseeing. We saw all the monuments we had read about in school and we were as disturbed as everyone else at the defacement of the Lincoln Memorial. We breezed through the National Gallery, true tourists, spending less than 1.9 seconds per picture. I guess we are visual art challenged. We spent the entire second day in the Smithsonian.

We looked at the capitol building from a distance on Thursday morning, but had no desire to see it up close. We weren't very political, but we had followed the refusal of legislators to help people who lost jobs and homes, and wondered who they were working for. We did take a White House tour, hoping to get a glimpse of the President, even though we wouldn't admit it. We had a great time on a whirlwind trip, our only extravagance a meal at a famous restaurant where the elite gathered. TJ and Clar slept on the drive home, Clar occasionally snoring with grunts and snorts. I dropped them off at the house, returned the rental car, went home, and fell sound asleep as soon as my head hit the pillow.

Chapter Fourteen

We went for our run on Friday a little later than usual, then went to the dōjō for a workout. We relaxed the rest of the day, casually cruising the internet looking at recent virus attacks on government agencies, especially the Department of Defense. Again Clar reviewed our wardrobe selection for our date, and she pronounced sweaters and slacks appropriate for the evening.

Clar looked at us fondly, then turned to TJ, "I'm so glad you learned to dress middle-class, especially now that we're living in New York City. I could just imagine what might happen to you if you went around wearing a hoodie like that Treyvan Martin, who got shot in Florida."

"When I got to Branville I realized I had a chance to remake my life. I was a big, black kid out of foster care, statistically doomed to early death from drugs or violence. I was determined never to look street again. The school may have accepted me, but my roommates treated me like a person, not a racial representative, and helped me become a man. I loved you for that.

"We did it for each other," I said. "I was treated like white trash all my life, even when I had the highest grades in high school, until I got to Branville. You two are the best thing that ever happened to me. I just wish I could do more for you."

They both beamed at me and Clar said, "We were all potential victims of stereotypes who refused to let our past defeat us. I love you both and am so proud of us." She got up and pulled us to her in a hug.

"Pete. Take your hand off my ass," and she smacked my arm.

"How do you know it's me?" I asked, mock-innocently.

"TJ would have the courtesy to ask."

"You're just prejudiced against white trash," I said, rubbing my arm where she hit me, which gave us all a laugh.

Before we left for our date I turned to TJ, "Just so you know, I'm still angry at Parsec."

"Do you want me to give them an SQL injection?"

"What's that?" Clar asked.

"It's an attack that infects a computer system with malicious software that lets attackers steal or manipulate the contents of the system."

"Where did you learn that?" I asked admiringly.

But before TJ could reply, Clar shook her head. "I'm just as angry as you, but we're not going to waste our time on them. Besides, they're still paying us and giving us medical benefits. Let's forget them and go on to better things."

"I can't argue with that," I murmured, "but it would still be nice to punish them."

"Forget it. Now you boys get out of here and have a good time."

I was still brooding about my anger at Parsec on the way to meet the girls and TJ said, "I can infect them, if you like."

"Thanks, TJ. We shouldn't do it without Clar though."

"You're being pretty reasonable about it."

"I listen once in a while."

"I know. I was just teasing you."

We went to meet the girls at their dorm on 23rd Street and 3rd Avenue, a new building that looked more like an upscale condominium, rather than a college dormitory. While we were waiting in the lobby, TJ struck up a conversation with one of the security guards, who told us the building was intended to be a condo, but somehow N.Y.U. acquired it. He snickered when he told TJ that some of the students were living in the penthouses. By this time, I was listening intently and heard his cynical remark that all big universities were landlords, often slumlords, and constantly expanded at the expense of the surrounding community. I didn't comment, but had to wonder at the economic awareness of a low paid security guard.

I was about to question him, when the girls arrived. They arbitrarily canceled our plans to go out and took us to their room, which turned out to be a former one-bedroom apartment, now connected into three small bedrooms, with a kitchen and tiny living room. It was bigger than our apartment, and much nicer. Music was playing softly in the background.

Lakeisha led TJ into the well-equipped kitchen, placed a shopping bag on the counter, and announced, "There are the ingredients for a gourmet French dinner. Now we'll see if you can really cook."

"Can I see the recipes?" TJ asked.

"Why?"

"I generally cook for three. I just want to verify the amounts."

"Who's the third person?"

"Our roommate, Clara."

"You live with a woman?"

"Yes."

"Do you sleep with her?"

"No," he replied indignantly. "She's very special and Pete and I love her."

"I didn't mean to offend you."

"Alright. Let's get dinner started."

"Have you known her long?"

"Since freshman year in college. We've been through a lot together. We're life and business partners."

"I'd like to meet her."

"We can arrange something."

While TJ cooked and Lakeisha got in his way, Janet and I talked. She told me about her dancing, modern ballet, then mentioned that the music playing was Tchaikovsky's Swan Lake. She got up and twirled across the room on her toes and I asked, "How do you stay on your toes for a whole dance."

"Years of practice and you have to have good feet."

I decided to investigate her feet more closely at the first opportunity. We chatted away happily until TJ invited us to the table. Lakeisha declared when we finished eating that it was the best meal she ever ate. We hung out for a while, talking casually. Just before we left, the girls kissed us goodnight passionately and we made another date for Sunday night.

Clar's interrogation wasn't quite as intense as it was for the first date. She was reassured when TJ told her that Lakeisha surprised him with ingredients for a gourmet dinner to test him. She laughed when he described how they spent the evening talking, cooking, and eating.

"Was Lakeisha pleased with the meal?"

"She said it was the best she ever ate."

"Smart girl. I'd like to meet her."

"She wants to meet you."

"What did you tell her about me?" she asked suspiciously.

"Just that you're our life and business partner."

She glowed. "That's nice to hear. What about you, Pete? How was your girl."

"Janet's really exciting," I blurted. "She's a dancer, but real bright and interested in running with us."

"You boys seem to have lucked out. When do I meet them?"

"We're seeing them Sunday night," I replied. "We'll arrange a get-together then."

"Sounds good. We do have to set a work schedule for next week."

I nodded. "How about we keep it simple. We run in the morning. Go to the dōjō after lunch and work in the afternoons and evenings."

"We'll get a lot done that way," TJ said. "But the following week we have to start job hunting."

"It's doubtful we'll get jobs together," Clar murmured.

"You never know," I responded, trying to be upbeat. "I'll call Bonnie on Monday morning. Maybe she's made some progress finding investors for us."

"Don't count on it," Clar responded despondently.

"It's too soon to be discouraged," I countered. "We believe in ourselves and our project. It's just a matter of time before we succeed."

"You're optimistic. What happened to all your anger?"

"It's still there. But I have confidence in us."

"So do I," TJ added. "Pete's right. If we don't get anywhere in the next three months we can reassess what we're doing."

Clar smiled beatifically. "How can I resist two strong, determined men?"

Chapter Fifteen

We met at Starbucks Sunday night and talked for hours, completely absorbed in each other. We didn't notice the time until it was after eleven. Janet said throatily, "We had planned to take you to our dorm, but our roommate came back earlier than expected and I'm too embarrassed to take you to my room with her next door. What about your place?"

I couldn't imagine Clar listening to us making love.

"I don't think so. It would be awkward." Then I got a bright idea. "What about a hotel?"

She laughed. "Do you know how much hotels cost in New York City?"

"No."

"Well unless you're rich, forget it. Either two rooms, or a suite would cost at least five or six hundred dollars, and I'm not talking about a palace."

"We're not rich, but I bet TJ could find something on line."

"Let's not start our relationship in some cheap, tawdry dump."

I stoically tried to conceal my disappointment at not getting her body tonight.

"I guess you're right."

"Don't worry. We'll be together. Why don't we have dinner Friday night with our roommates and see where it goes."

"Sure."

We walked the girls to their building and ignored the nosey security guard, as we kissed for a while, then said goodnight. On the way home I told TJ about our hotel conversation and he said he'd do a search. I also told him about our dinner date for next Friday night that would include Clar.

"Why don't we have it at our place? I'll cook and everyone will get used to being together."

I picked him up as he gasped in surprise.

"You're getting strong."

"You're my main man, bright guy."

I couldn't tell if Clar was pleased or not at the prospect of dinner with the girls, but she didn't object. Then we talked about a plan for the week. She approved morning run, dōjō, afternoon and evening work on Cybersnarer and Castle Keep, which suited us.

The week passed quickly and between our physical exertions and work on our projects, the edge of anger at Parsec faded, but underneath I was still simmering with outrage. I had talked to Bonnie on Monday and she said she had two groups who had shown preliminary interest in Cybersnarer, and she would try to arrange meetings in the next week or so. I told her about Parsec letting us go and she thought it was a bit strange, but she felt the separation package was extremely generous, considering the short time we'd been there and not having a contract. She said she'd get back to me as soon as she had a meeting set up. When I disconnected I thought about her comment that the separation package was very generous and something questionable tugged at me, but I couldn't put my finger on it and dismissed it.

We'd enjoyed working out every day, and having afternoons and evenings for our projects. The only glitch on Friday night was Lakeisha and

Janet's roommate, Brinn, who turned out to be a lesbian. Clar assumed we knew. She didn't say anything, but underneath she was fuming, until I took her aside and assured her we'd never do that to her. She knew I wouldn't lie about that and relented, then gave me one of her dazzling smiles that could make me forget any other girl. She was very cordial to Brinn for the rest of the night. Brinn told her she grew up in Boston in a stuffy old house with control freak parents who expected her to go to Radcliffe and marry a lawyer or doctor, so she escaped to New York City.

The evening turned out to be pleasant for all of us. Later that night, after the girls had gone home, we teased Clar about her response to Brinn.

"Did you think she was hot?" TJ asked.

"She was very sweet and I enjoyed meeting her."

"Does she turn you on?" I asked.

"I'm not gay, Pete. You know that."

"Yeah. But it might be a good way to get over some of your hang-ups, without having to deal with a guy."

"Are you trying to fix me up?"

"We just want you to be happy," I explained. "If making it with a chick helps, we're all for it."

"That's very sweet of you, Pete. I'll let you boys know when I'm ready. Until then, please don't arrange things for me."

"Sure, Clar."

Monday morning, we started our job search. I guess we had been spoiled by the security at Branville, because this was the first time we had to look for work. We realized we had no idea how to go about it, which was humiliating and rekindled my smoldering anger at Parsec. TJ quickly did some research and selected twenty companies to approach, including Google, Facebook, Microsoft, and Apple. He got their application requirements and during the next few days we revised our resumes and prepared letters to go with them.

Saturday we tested at the dōjō and TJ easily got his green belt. I aced my forms and board breaking. My sparring opponent turned out to be Bernard, the jerk who abused Clar, until she paid him back with a well-placed kick. Despite sensei Omura's admonitions, Bernard's attitude hadn't changed. We touched gloves and he bopped me on the chest and started to poke me in the face, but I smacked him on the side of the head hard enough to sting, and smiled pleasantly. He rushed at me, enraged, and I moved aside, hit him in the kidney with a short punch and he doubled up and fell to his knees.

Sensei Omura had been observing us closely and announced, "Bout is over. Peter san pass brown belt. Bernard san can consider whether he wishes to continue to train here."

Bernard got up and started towards me, but Omura moved between us faster than I thought possible, took Bernard's arm in a pressure grip and walked him to the locker room. He gently told Bernard not to come back unless he apologized to everyone and promised to behave properly. No one felt sorry for him. Omura came back and observed the black belt tests. Clar went second, did her forms perfectly, broke three boards, then sparred with a woman who was obviously afraid of contact. Clar effortlessly and elegantly hit her lightly with hands and feet, easily deflecting her feeble attacks. Omura stopped them and awarded the black belt to Clar. TJ and I congratulated her, then we picked her up and carried her triumphantly around the dōjō.

Although it felt wonderful working on our projects, our lack of employment was a bit nerve wracking. We emailed letters and resumes to twenty companies on Thursday, slightly resentful that we were begging for jobs. TJ insisted it was applying, not begging, but I was resentful at first, being fired and, now, humbly job hunting. We were stars at Branville and I expected to be stars wherever we went.

"We feel this way because our egos are wounded," Clar explained. "It's not the worst thing to be reminded that we're in a different world now."

I had to laugh. "I didn't expect a fanfare of trumpets, or a key to the city, but this isn't what I pictured."

"We'll appreciate our success more because of this," TJ declared.

Clar and I stared at him, then I responded, "You're getting very philosophic."

"I bet Lakeisha's softening him up," Clar said.

"He was pretty soft to begin with, like a teddy bear," I added.

"I dare you to find anything soft," he challenged.

Clar suddenly jabbed him in the stomach with her knuckles and he whooshed and doubled over.

"Told you so," she smirked.

"I wasn't ready," he protested, breathing hard.

"Always be ready," she replied smugly.

Friday morning, we had a major mood swing. Bonnie phoned me early and said two groups were potentially interested in Cybersnarer and she could schedule presentations on next Wednesday and Thursday afternoons. I told her to go ahead and she said she'd confirm the time. TJ and Clar were delighted, but TJ cautioned us not to get our hopes up. He was becoming very reasonable, a good quality around here. Later in the day we got emails from a dozen companies asking us to contact their personnel departments to arrange interviews. Things were definitely looking up.

Chapter Sixteen

We spent a lot of time with the girls on the weekend and Clar was very comfortable with Brinn. Janet suggested that we work out a schedule so Clar and Brinn would be out at the same time, so TJ and I could be alone with her and Lakeisha, one couple in their dorm room, one at our apartment. The only thing that stopped me from jumping up and barking was I didn't want to offend Clar's sensibilities. I told Janet that TJ and I would work on it, but we'd have to be sure Clar didn't mind. I couldn't help gloating a little that Janet's delectable body might soon be mine.

After the workout at the dōjō Monday morning, we went home and checked our email. We each had more responses from companies asking us to contact them to set up an interview. Clar and I both got a response from AOL. This was encouraging news, since we had enough money, for the time being, to pick and choose and even decline an offer if we didn't like it. TJ was disappointed that we wouldn't work together, but felt a little better when I reminded him we didn't get the jobs yet.

We worked on Cybersnarer after lunch and I noticed Clar was acting strangely. She was muttering to herself, while her fingers were flying over her keyboard, increasingly urgent. She became aware that I was watching her, turned slowly and put her index finger to her lips, requesting silence. At first I thought she was kidding, as she scribbled away on a piece of paper, got up and handed it to me. Before I could say anything she pointed at the note and indicated I should read it, which I did.

I think I've been hacked. My machine is running slower. Give the note to TJ and signal him not to speak. Nod your head if you understand. Then check your machine. She seemed too serious for it to be a joke, so I handed the note to TJ and signaled him to be quiet. After he read it, he nodded that he understood. I turned to my computer and, now that I was alerted, immediately saw it was running slower. I looked at TJ who was getting upset, then turned to Clar, pointed at my machine and mouthed, *It's running slower.*

She stood up and said in a casual voice, "I need some espresso. How about we go to Starbucks and recharge our batteries?"

"Sure," TJ said.

"Let's go," I confirmed.

We didn't say anything until we were outside, then I turned to Clar. "What do you think happened?"

"I know what happened. We've been hacked."

"Any idea who?" TJ asked.

"My guess would be Parsec, but we'll have to find out."

"If it's them," I muttered angrily, "they'll be sorry they messed with us."

"Why didn't you want to talk about it inside?" TJ asked.

"Our dedicated machines are connected to the internet. They could also get into them physically, which means they may have broken into our apartment. I figured they might plant bugs to learn as much as they can."

"That makes sense," he said. "What do we do about it?"

"First thing," I answered, "is to get a bug detector and verify if anyone's listening. There's a spy shop on East 34th Street that should have one, or we can look it up on the internet."

"Then let's go to this spy shop and not use our machines until we find the problem and fix it," Clar said.

"We should get at least one new machine," TJ said, "so we can keep working."

"Good idea," I responded, "and we'll have to carry it with us at all times. It sounds like a job for Baby Brother."

A very helpful man at the spy store, who didn't look the least bit like a secret agent, sold us an inexpensive radio frequency detector. He cautioned us that professionals used spread spectrum bugs that an RF detector wouldn't pick up. Just before we left he advised us if we didn't find anything and still thought we were bugged, we'd need an experienced technician with a spectrum analyzer, and he could recommend someone.

We were discussing where to get a laptop, when I suddenly had a terrible thought. I turned to Clar and TJ.

"If they bugged us with listening devices, what if they put in cameras?"

"If they've been watching me undress," Clar growled, "I'll cut Phil's balls off, and Lou's."

I couldn't help but grin at my ferocious roommate.

"I'll help you."

"Me too," TJ chimed in. "What do we do now?"

It was very clear to me.

"If they're watching us, we can't use the RF detector. In fact, we can't do anything in the apartment that would let them know we're on to them. We either search for cameras and risk their seeing we discovered the surveillance, or continue our normal routine, until we figure out how to verify there are cameras."

"I don't know if I could live with the feeling that they're watching me," TJ said, "especially if I bring Lakeisha to my room."

"I couldn't stand the thought of their watching me," Clar declared.

"Then it's decided," I said. "Let's go home and search."

On the way to the apartment I told them some of the places we should look.

"Light fixtures, smoke detectors, anything high enough where a camera could observe us. One very important point. Don't make any noise. If there are no cameras, then they won't know we're on to them."

I suggested I search the living room, TJ the kitchen, and Clar the bathroom, then we do our own bedrooms. There was no disagreement and we didn't talk on the way back, each of us preoccupied with the disturbing developments. When we got home we started searching immediately, not bothering to conceal what we were doing, since they'd obviously see us.

I realized they would hear us poking around, so I said, "Clar. Why don't you put on some of that soppy music you like so much?"

"Some people have no taste," she announced. She put on a CD of romantic Spanish ballads, performed by a group I had nicknamed "The Singing Sombreros."

It took more than half an hour to carefully check every possible spot to conceal a camera, until I concluded we weren't under visual surveillance. I checked the apartment with the RF detector and we found bugs in our bedrooms and one in a lamp in our work area in the living room.

A flare of rage raced through me and I vowed to myself that we'd get even, then I said pleasantly, "I don't feel much like working. How about we go for a walk, then have an early dinner at the Japanese restaurant?"

"Sounds good to me," Clar replied.

"I could cook dinner," TJ offered.

"No," Clar stated. "Let's go out."

"Okay," TJ replied. "I'll get my jacket."

As soon as we were outside, I stopped and said, "It's confirmed. We're being bugged."

"What do we do?" TJ asked.

"We go to Parsec and cut some *cojones*, if they have any," Clar growled.

"I'm with you," I said.

"We can't do anything to them until we have evidence," TJ responded.

"Who else could it be?" Clar demanded, and she and TJ looked at me expectantly.

"I know it's them," I admitted. "But without any proof, we legally can't do anything. And I'm sure not going to let the people I love most in the world go to jail for assaulting those sleaze balls."

"So you do love us that much," Clar murmured.

"Of course I do, hot stuff."

"Don't call me that," she snarled.

"I was talking to TJ," I replied with aplomb, which made us crack up with laughter.

A minute later, still smiling, Clar asked, "So what do we do?"

I thought quickly. "I'll call Bonnie and tell her the situation and find out what she suggests. We should copyright Cybersnarer immediately, and Castle Keep. Then they may pirate us, but they won't do it legally."

"Sounds good to me," TJ said. "What about the bugs?"

"I think we have to live with them," I replied slowly, "at least until we have an action plan to deal with them. Agreed?"

They reluctantly said yes, which was exactly how I felt, but we were being realistic. We'd been getting some lessons lately in dealing with unpleasant reality. We didn't talk much at first during dinner, then Clar reminded us, "We need to behave the way we always do, so they don't realize we're on to them."

TJ and I nodded agreement and he asked, "What about the girls? I don't think we should bring them here until this is resolved. I'm not sure I could have a normal conversation with them, knowing someone was listening."

"It'll seem normal to them if we have the girls here," I said. "Besides, if they hear Brinn trying to seduce Clar, they'll never listen to anything else."

"Nobody's going to seduce me," Clar declared.

"I know that," I replied, "but they don't. It'll keep them busy. Now remember. When we get home let's just try to be ourselves."

Chapter Seventeen

It was definitely awkward living with the bugs, as we tried to behave as our usual selves. I spoke at length to Bonnie and she said she'd start the paperwork for copyrighting our two projects. She advised me to videotape the bugs with a description of where they were, as evidence if we ever verified who put them there. She also suggested we hire a professional to discover where the monitoring station was, without alerting them.

She did have a piece of good news. She had set up a meeting for Wednesday morning with a group of investors who backed startups. "They're young, savvy, and looking for hot prospects. I think they'll love you guys."

"What about Parsec hacking us? Do I tell them our project has been stolen?"

"There's no proof Parsec did it, so don't use their name. And don't tell anybody else, especially potential investors. I'll register your copyright today and have a copy of your proposal, backdated from your first visit, and notarized."

"Thanks, Bonnie. You're a great help."

"That's what you pay me for."

I told TJ and Clar about the meeting Wednesday, which delighted them, as well as what else Bonnie told me. Clar insisted we hire someone right away, so I called the Spy Shop and he gave me a name and a phone number. I called Jack, described the situation and he accepted the job. He asked why we were being bugged and I explained we had a potentially valuable software program that someone may have stolen. He said since we're computer people, he'd pretend to be a server salesman pushing his product and we could talk about it while he checked the apartment. He said he could come by tomorrow and we made an appointment for late afternoon.

We took a walk to discuss recent developments. Somehow, despite the good news, we were still angry about the violation of our privacy.

"We need a plan to destroy Parsec," Clar declared.

"Isn't that a little drastic?" TJ replied. "We don't know for sure it's them and maybe not everyone there is in on it."

Clar looked at me.

"I appreciate TJ's good sense. But we know they did it. Yet I don't think we should actually do anything to them until we have proof," and I smiled wickedly. "But there's no reason we can't prepare a plan to do them in. Besides, they didn't treat us well and we didn't make any friends. We don't owe anybody anything."

"TJ?" Clar asked.

"Pete's right. I want payback as much as you do. Let's make a plan."

"Then let's go to Starbucks after dinner," I said, "find a quiet table and outline some basics."

"What are you smiling at?" Clar asked me, as we huddled together over coffee later that evening.

"We look like conspirators," I whispered.

"We are," she whispered back, which made us smile.

"Where do we start?" TJ asked.

"We have two basic choices," I replied. "We destroy the company, or we just destroy Phil, Lou, and E.F. Rogers."

"A. F.," Clar corrected.

"Whatever the eff."

"We destroy the company," TJ stated.

"Explain your reasoning," Clar said mildly.

I looked at her in surprise that she didn't just want to bomb them, but she looked at me and I realized she was making sure we decided carefully.

"We know who probably directed the attack," TJ said. "Phil, Lou, and maybe Rogers. But there had to be others. That worm Lou didn't break into our apartment. Neither did Phil. We can spend time, maybe months, trying to find out who else is involved. I say we target the company, with special attention to Phil and Lou."

Clar and I nodded agreement and the three of us grinned at each other like gloating avengers.

"We bankrupt the company," I proposed, "Bankrupt Phil and Lou, destroy their credibility so they can't function again in the software world, and ruin their lives to the best of our ability."

Clar leaned over and kissed me, a real shocker.

"I love you for your gentle mind."

Then she pulled TJ close, kissed him, and we put our arms around each other.

"You're quite a kisser. How about another?" I asked.

She smiled sweetly. "After we finish them off."

"I'll go phishing, penetrate their system, and find their vulnerabilities without leaving any trace of entry. Pete, you find Parsecs financial info. Clar, you get their personal bank info, especially off-shore accounts."

"We better buy three new computers," I said, "so we can all work at the same time. It's a good thing we made backups on discs, because we shouldn't do any new work on our infected computers."

"We shouldn't search for malware and we should continue to do some work on our old computers, so they don't know we're on to them." Clar suggested

"I'll outline a work project that won't reveal anything new," TJ said, then added, "What about the girls?"

"Let's have them here and TJ will cook so it seems normal," Clar replied.

We bought top of the line computers, paid for by Parsec's separation pay. On the way home, I stopped TJ and Clar before we went in.

"The salesman told me something interesting. Lenovo computers have been banned for use to access classified government networks in the U.S., Australia, Great Britain, Canada, and New Zealand, because they're manufactured in China and they're afraid of a Trojan horse."

"Yet Parsec uses them," TJ muttered. "We should look into that."

"After we destroy them," Clar declared.

The next few days were difficult, knowing they were listening to us, even though it was a relief they weren't watching. We followed our usual routine, a morning run, the dōjō, then work on our projects. TJ had verified that they weren't downloading our computers, so the only way they could currently know what we were doing would be if we said anything aloud. Clar cleverly suggested we go on made up interviews, so we could have time to talk during the day. Whenever we went out I left a tell-tale on the door, a hair carefully placed, that I checked when we came back. I was really getting into this conspiracy and spy stuff. I browsed Wikipedia, reading about spy craft and surveillance techniques. Every time we went out I checked if we were being followed.

Wednesday morning, we got up early, went for a run, then discussed an imaginary interview at AOL. to mask our meeting with the investors. We met at Bonnie's office and she introduced us to two women and a man. Jessica Robbins was a tall, slim, fit-looking brunette with a strong handshake. Elaine Valmont was a short, plump blonde, with a sweet-looking face. Mort Flinders was tall, freckled, red-headed, with piercing blue laser eyes. After I shook Jessica's hand, I shook my fingers as if she hurt me.

"Oh. I'm so sorry. Sometimes I forget what a strong grip I have."

"I'm used to macho women," I said, which drew a glare from Clar, but a smile from everyone else.

I looked them over, curious what rich investors looked like. They didn't look that much older than us, were causally but expensively dressed and looked very sure of themselves.

"If Dr. Larkspur is finished joking," Bonnie said, "let's sit down and start the presentation. Dr. Larkspur."

"Please, call me Pete."

We had refined the presentation after each time we did it, and especially prepared for today. I went through our backgrounds, the genesis of the project, the development process, and the two recent successful tests of Cybersnarer. I concluded with a brief description of Castle Keep, which I asserted would be the "mother of all firewalls." We took questions for almost an hour, so they had a fairly comprehensive overview of the project, even though they weren't computer experts. We shook hands as we said goodbye, and Jessica squeezed my hand hard. I didn't react and remarked pleasantly, "You do have a strong grip."

"I have a feeling yours is much stronger," she replied. "Do you work out?"

"I run and do Tai Kwan Do."

"I'm impressed. I just workout at the gym."

"Some things are better done by hand," I whispered suggestively, which made her laugh.

Bonnie had been monitoring our exchange with concern and said, "I'm going to meet with our new friends for a while. I'll call you later."

Just as we were going out the door, Mort asked, "How much capitalization are you seeking, Dr. Rodriguez? It's not in your proposal."

"Twenty million. Please call me Clara."

When we got outside, TJ turned to Clar. "I thought we were going to ask for ten million."

"Bonnie said they were friends. What's another ten million between friends."

Chapter Eighteen

Bonnie phoned me late Wednesday afternoon. I went into the bathroom so the bugs wouldn't pick up our conversation. She told me the investors loved the proposal and were tremendously impressed with us. They were going to consider the project and would get back to her.

"I can't believe how well you handled them," she added.

"Did you like my wrestling match with Jessica?"

She laughed. "You were playing around with big money. How did you know you wouldn't offend her?"

"Dr. Larkspur knows macho women."

She laughed again. "Well we have the second group tomorrow at one o'clock. Try not to wrestle with them."

"Not until we get their money."

She laughed and disconnected.

We had gotten into the habit of playing music whenever we were home, not loudly, so it wouldn't be obvious we were trying to defeat the bugs, but enough so we could whisper to each other without being overheard.

I told TJ and Clar what Bonnie said about our meeting. The positive response of the investors delighted them.

"Just don't mess around with Jessica again," Clar admonished, "at least until we have the money in the bank."

"It's cool," I replied. "They loved us."

"Love don't pay the bills," she retorted.

TJ and I smiled and he said, "You're a tough Old Lady," which made us laugh.

I reminded them of our meeting tomorrow at one o'clock, then we talked for a few minutes about our biggest problem, how to verify that Parsec was behind the break-in, theft, and bugging. TJ, who was our best hacker, said he'd go into their system and see what he could find out. If that didn't work, the only way to find out if it was them would be to break into their office late at night.

TJ and Clar were looking a little despondent so I said seriously, "I guess I have to brush up on my breaking and entering technique."

"Did you ever do a break-in?" TJ asked, wide-eyed.

"No, silly." Clar stated, then looked at me suspiciously. "Did you?"

"I'll never tell."

We left the bathroom and I said for the benefit of our listeners, "Remember we have an interview tomorrow at Google. One o'clock. I'm going to bed. Goodnight."

Without another word I went to my room, booted up my new computer and started a search for breaking and entering techniques, as well as any related useful skills.

We went to our next investor's meeting with a lot more confidence, casually dressed, expecting another young group. We managed to conceal our surprise when Bonnie introduced us to three older men. They were wearing dark-blue, pin-striped suits, regimental ties with heavy gold tie-clips, cuff links, rings, and wrist watches. It was enough gold to make Midas envious. They looked remarkably similar, an inch or two of difference in height, a few pounds difference in their well-fed bodies, receding hair lines, bland faces that revealed nothing, and greedy eyes.

They didn't offer to shake hands, so we got right to the presentation. They stared at us coldly as we took turns describing the project. They asked no questions and I couldn't tell if they understood what we were talking about. The more I watched them, the more they resembled fat fish I saw in a nature documentary, that just sort of hulked there until a smaller fish swam by, then they would grab and swallow them.

When we finished, they didn't say anything, didn't offer to shake hands, so I stood up and said, "Thank you," and led TJ and Clar out.

We stopped at a pizza shop and talked about the meeting. We agreed it was a strange experience. TJ said they reminded him of state officials who came once a year to the foster home—just as inhuman, not as well dressed.

"Do we want their money?" Clar asked.

"Sure," I answered. "We'll just require them to join the morticians' union."

They both cracked up and we made jokes about the three undertakers on the way home.

When we got to the door, I checked the telltale hair I always left and it was gone. I said softly to TJ and Clar, "Someone has been inside. Either we call the police, or we go in carefully if they're still there, quietly if they're not and still listening."

"Do you think they'll have guns?" Clar asked.

"Not if they're techies," TJ said.

"What do you think, Pete?" she asked me.

"Let's go."

I opened the door and went in quickly, ready, almost eager for a physical confrontation, but wary in case they were armed. TJ and Clar were right behind me. When we saw no one, we checked our bedrooms, then the kitchen and bathroom. We made a quick search for cameras, but didn't find any.

I got the RF detector, checked for bugs, and after a quick scan of where they had been, I said, "They're gone."

We looked at each other, with mirroring expressions of relief.

"Now that we can talk freely," Clar said. "Let's find out who's behind this."

"I'll get right on it," TJ said. "Remember, don't use our old computers to do anything new on Cybersnarer or Castle Keep."

We nodded and went to our rooms. I phoned Bonnie and she told me the investors were very impressed and would give serious consideration to funding us.

"I don't know if I want to be obligated to morticians."

She laughed. "Don't kid yourself. The group yesterday is just as tough. They're newer, hedge fund money and they think they're cool."

"I'd prefer to work with them."

"Because Jessica's a good-looking woman? What if they decide no and the older men come through?"

"I guess I'll go to morticians' school."

When she stopped laughing, I told her about the latest break-in and the removal of the bugs.

"So you can forget about it now, Pete, and get on with your start-up venture."

"We're not forgetting. They violated our privacy, stole our work, and eavesdropped on us. They're not getting away with it."

"What if it was the CIA, or the NSA?"

"I can't imagine they'd be that clumsy. But if that's the case, there's not much we can do about it now. It's too complicated to try and be whistle blowers now."

"I'm glad you have some common sense. What if it is Parsec?"

"Then we'll destroy the company."

"I don't think I heard that."

"No problem, Bonnie. Why don't you get us a lot of money? Talk to you soon."

I told Clar and TJ the good news that the morticians were impressed with us and were considering investing.

"You can't call them morticians if they fund us," Clar ordered.

"How about terminal expeditors?" I quipped.

"How about final dispatchers?" TJ added.

Clar tried to keep a straight face, but finally laughed.

"Remind me in my next life to pick dumb men."

"Do you think there's a next life?" TJ asked.

I cut them off before it became too theological.

"That would make you pretty dumb. Now that no one is listening, let's talk about Parsec."

"Do you want to wait until I hack their system?" TJ asked.

"It doesn't matter, TJ. We know it's them. We'll get them whether you get in or not. If you do, it'll be a lot easier than B&E, just not as much fun."

"You'd actually enjoy that," Clar remarked.

"Absolutely. Revenge is sweet, hot or cold."

"How do we do it?" Clar asked.

"Our goals include appropriating all of Parsecs money . . ."

"Nicely put," she said, and I grinned.

". . . changing their records so it's obvious they've been cheating their clients, informing their clients, disabling their operating systems so they can no longer function . . . planting evidence of hiring discrimination . . ."

"That's diabolical," Clar gloated.

"That's just for starters. We'll come up with more targets."

"What about Phil and Lou?" TJ asked.

"We'll bankrupt them, default their mortgages, if they have any. If they're married, we'll plant evidence of homosexual affairs, plant evidence of looting the company, overbilling customers, alert the IRS to tax evasion . . . have I left anything out?"

"Great beginning," TJ said admiringly. "Why don't you and Clar start planning the break-in. I'll pop into Parsec."

We had only been chatting for a few minutes, when TJ came back with a big grin.

"You're not going to believe this. I went in through the backdoors I had set up while we worked there and found our program on Phil's desktop. They didn't even protect it."

We shook our heads at their stupidity and he continued, "I deleted some of our code, put in some garbage to replace it so it won't be obvious there are changes, and installed a tool kit."

"What's that?" Clar asked.

"It's a program that conceals the compromise of a computer's security system," TJ explained. "It can represent a set of programs to subvert control of an operating system. It replaces system binaries so the user won't detect intrusion. I also left a tracer so we'll know when they use our program."

"You're just as evil as Pete," Clar declared.

He smiled smugly. "I learned it from you, Old Lady."

"So, no B&E?" I asked.

"Only if we need the discs," TJ replied.

"Then there's no point in breaking in. They have a million discs. I'd never find ours. They could be anywhere."

"Well, boys, it's time for a council of war."

"Now you're talking, Clar," I enthused.

It was the first time in several weeks that we could talk freely. It felt good. We decided that the attacks on Parsec, Phil, and Lou should happen simultaneously, so the shock would be overwhelming and there wouldn't be time for them to deal with all the problems.

I realized something and said, "The attacks can't come from our computers. We don't want any possibility of their tracing it to us."

"We can use an internet café," TJ suggested.

"I think they require ID," Clar responded.

I felt a fiendish smile spread on my face. "Can we use Parsec's computers to attack them?" I asked softly.

They both gaped at me and Clar said, "You are an evil genius."

"Thank you, ma'am," I replied modestly and looked at TJ.

"Great idea. We can use them against each other. But we'd still have to go in from another source. It can't originate from our computers."

"I'll check if we need ID at an internet café," Clar said. "If we do, can we make them?"

"Sure," I replied. "I'll make driver's licenses for Clar and me."

"What about me?" TJ asked.

"You're too memorable, TJ," I replied. "Clar and I can make ourselves look inconspicuous, but if anyone checks, they might remember you."

"But I'm the best hacker . . . "

"We know," Clar said. "You'll just have to prepare us, unless we come up with another way to do it."

"What if we rented a month-to-month office," he offered, "and Pete could break into other offices and we'd use their computers."

He looked at Clar hopefully, figuring I'd go along for the chance at B&E. But she shook her head emphatically.

"No way, TJ. We'd be too easily identified."

"Oh, alright," he muttered sulkily.

"You're going to love this," I gloated. "Phil will destroy Lou, Lou will destroy Parsec, and Rogers will destroy Phil."

They applauded and Clar shouted gleefully, "We're going to get Parsec," and TJ echoed her.

I held up my hands for silence and they looked at me expectantly.

"This one is for you, TJ. If there's an internet café in Harlem, you can lead the attack."

His eyes lit up with joy.

"Thanks, Pete. I'll never forget this. I owe you big time." Then a strange look flitted across his face. "Is it safe to go there?"

Clar started to laugh at the thought of our big, strong, martial artist apprehensive about going to Harlem, but she quickly said reassuringly, "Don't worry. It's been gentrified. Besides, we'll go with you."

"What's gentrified?"

"That's when rich white folks move in and the landlords raise the rent and force out blacks and Hispanics," Clar explained. "That's why it's safe."

"How do you know that?" TJ asked.

"I'm not a hick like you two. I grew up in the big city."

"The Bronx?" I teased.

"Whatever."

His radiant smile warmed the room. "I love you guys."

Chapter Nineteen

TJ cooked an incredible French dinner for us; soup, salad, sea bass, asparagus, and my favorite dessert, *crème brulée*. The only word I could pronounce was salad. As usual, Clar teased TJ about dessert, calling it *flan*, which always provoked a haughty lecture about *haute cuisine*, not common Spanish pudding. We dissolved into laughter when she made funny faces at him. Afterwards, he served brandy and brought out three long cigars. We didn't smoke, so Clar pointed at them and asked, "What are those?"

"These are fine Cuban cigars. Don't ask how I got them, or how much they cost. It just seemed cool to have brandy and cigars after dinner."

He showed us how to light them properly and we puffed away for a few minutes, until the smoke detector went off. Then we went outside and smoked for a while longer.

Clar gave in first. "I don't like it," and she tossed it in the gutter.

"Neither do I," I chimed in, and tossed mine.

TJ looked at us for a moment, shrugged and tossed his. "I don't either."

"That was very thoughtful, TJ," Clar said sweetly. "It'll be nice to try a lot of new things when we're rich."

We went back inside and the smoke had mostly cleared. Except for a lingering odor, the air was breathable, so we sat down to discuss our plans.

"We have three particular problems to deal with," I announced. "The girls, our investors, and the attack on Parsec."

"The girls are easiest," TJ said. "Lakeisha phoned me earlier and said they were going home for the Christmas vacation and wanted to see us before they left. She added that Janet was insistent we spend time alone."

Before I could reply, Clar said, "Let me know what night and I'll go visit my family."

"Only if you take a car service there and back," I insisted.

"I can take care of myself," she said belligerently, then gave me one of her dazzling smiles. "Thank you for caring, Pete. I will, just so you won't worry."

"That settles the girls," I said. "I'll call Bonnie in the morning and find out what's happening with our investors. That leaves Parsec."

"Once we have their financial data," TJ explained, "I'll write a few access and retrieval programs to get the money. We should find out where to send it, probably an offshore account in the Islands."

"I'll do that," I offered.

"Good. Then we design the attack format, get all the data we need to do everything we planned, verify it's all there, then set an attack date."

"How about Christmas Eve?" I suggested.

Clar giggled. "I get it. You always wanted to play Santa Claus."

We laughed at the thought and I replied in a deep voice, "We know who's been naughty," which cracked us up.

"Christmas Eve it is," TJ affirmed. "One they'll never forget."

"I just wish we could let them know that we sent them the presents," I murmured wistfully.

"Santa will be anonymous this year," Clar declared, then added, "We must never tell anyone, or we could end up in jail, or if we were lucky, just never work again in our field."

"It'll be our secret," I said.

Clar looked hard at TJ, "Tell no one."

"What if I get married. Can I tell my wife?"

"No one."

"Don't worry. I get the message."

I phoned Bonnie in the morning and she brought me up to date on what was happening with our investors. She told me our copyright was approved and we'd get an official notice in a few days. We chatted for a few minutes, and planned to talk again in a few days.

I told TJ and Clar the news. "The cool yuppies want to meet again after the holidays. Bonnie'll let us know when. The morticians want a six-month operating budget and a projected completion date."

"Oh," Clar moaned. "I know who you're going to ask to do it."

"It's not my fault you're better with figures," I said innocently, which earned a glare.

"Alright. I'll prepare a draft."

Janet phoned me just after we came back from our run and she sounded peeved. "I thought you liked me."

"I do. Very much."

"Then why haven't you phoned me?"

"I know this sounds lame, but we've been really busy working on our project, trying to get it done before we have to get jobs. But I think about you a lot."

"Too busy to call?"

"We've been going day and night. I want you to know I miss you and want to see you."

She sounded a bit mollified when she said, "My last final is tomorrow, Friday the 13th, and I'm going home to Rochester on Saturday. I won't be back until January 6th."

"I've got to see you before you go. How about tomorrow night."

"Your place or mine, big boy," she joked and I knew it was alright between us.

"Your place. How about I take you to dinner first. There's a nice Thai restaurant on 3rd and 28th."

"Meet you there at six," and she disconnected.

I told TJ and Clar about my date. TJ arranged to meet Lakeisha at our place for dinner. Clar phoned her mother and told her she was coming for dinner tomorrow night. We could hear her cry of joy that her daughter was coming home.

We went to the dōjō and, for different reasons, each had a vigorous workout. Sensei Omura complimented us on our efforts and said we should start to train soon for our next level testing. We showered and changed into street clothes.

On the way home we decided to start our preparations for the attack on Parsec. Before we started, Clar suggested that TJ do the personal bank information search and look for off-shore accounts, so she could concentrate on the operating budget and a completion date. He agreed cheerfully.

"I'll check out the internet cafés, before I start the drudge work," she said mock pathetically.

"What a martyr," TJ quipped.

"Didn't you study accounting in high school?" I asked reasonably.

"I'm going, before I display my temper."

"Did you know she had a temper, TJ?"

She grinned and went to her room and we went to ours. About ten minutes later, she yelled, "Fellas. Come here."

We went to her room and she said, "I talked to three cafés and checked a few online. They don't require ID All you do is pay by the hour. Some of them only have Wi-Fi, so we'll have to bring our own computers."

"That's perfect," I enthused. "We'll buy cheap Lenovo computers for each attack and toss them afterwards. That way we won't leave any tracks. Each of us will buy one at separate stores. When we're through with them we'll wipe all fingerprints, break them down, and discard the parts in different places."

"This is becoming a piece of cake," TJ said.

We worked the rest of the day and ordered pizza for dinner. We updated each other as we ate. Clar had started work on the budget, using samples from the internet as a guideline. TJ had easily gotten into the personnel bank accounts, both checking and savings, and found that only Phil had a substantial amount. He was going to search for CDs, brokerage accounts, and any other investments after dinner and then start the search for offshore accounts in the morning. I had been listening intently and nodding happily, and they looked at me quizzically.

"Parsec has a regular business checking account, Rogers and Phil are the signers, with $217,469.26." I paused for effect. "There is a special business account with Phil the only signer, with $1,634,300.48. What do you think of that?"

"I bet Phil is a naughty boy," Clar murmured.

"He's going to be one unhappy boy on Christmas morning," TJ said.

"I've got more. I had an email chat with a bank in the Cayman Islands. We can transfer money, freeze it, disappear it, as long as we're willing to pay substantial fees."

"What do we do with the money once we've got it?" TJ asked. "I don't want to be a thief."

"We'll donate it to charity," I replied. "Anonymously. Breast cancer or wounded veterans"

"You two are my favorite masterminds," Clar said. "I'm going to work for a while, then go to bed early."

We said goodnight, went to our rooms and instead of doing anything, I lay on my bed and fantasized about what Phil would do once he had been stripped of everything he owned.

Chapter Twenty

After we came back from the dōjō on Friday, Clar decided to leave early to visit her family in The Bronx, and then stay overnight. When she teased me by asking if I thought it was safe to travel by subway in the daytime, I reassured her that it was, but it would be a nice treat to take a car service.

"You sit back like a princess, relax, and watch the city that you'll become rich in."

"You're so sweet sometimes, Pete," and she kissed me.

"You're a great kisser. How did you learn?"

"It's in my blood, Little Brother."

"How about me?" TJ demanded. "Don't I get a kiss?"

"Has your mouth been anywhere it shouldn't lately?"

"How could you say that? You know me."

"You're a dog, just like your buddy, Pete. I should warn those girls about you two."

We objected vigorously and she teased us as she gathered what she needed for an overnight stay. Just before she left she turned suddenly, grabbed TJ's arms, climbed up him, and kissed him.

"Little Brother's right. You are a great kisser."

"Bye, boys. Remember to use protection. And don't use my bed," and she dashed out the door.

TJ made it impossible for me to work for the rest of the afternoon. First he cleaned the entire apartment, making more noise than a demolition gang leveling a condemned structure. Then he sanitized himself, singing horrible raps at the top of his lungs, while he washed, curried, plucked, powdered, and perfumed himself in preparation for his guest. The final straw was when he started his dinner preparations, an exotic French meal, and he chanted the recipes louder and louder. I didn't mind the French part, which almost sounded romantic, but a pinch of this and a dash of that, bellowed in painful decibels, was unendurable.

I grabbed my laptop, mumbled a surly goodbye, and went to Starbucks, where I could at least dislike strangers if they were too noisy. I finished my search for Parsec's accounts without finding anything new. Then I found a site that explained how to open an offshore account, how to set it up so it couldn't be accessed by anyone else, and how to transfer funds without being discovered. By the time I finished I was confident that TJ could penetrate Phil's offshore account and transfer the money to an account we'd set up.

I had gotten so absorbed in exploring how we'd pillage Phil's money that I had lost track of the time. When I checked the display for the time, I saw it was after six. I quickly shut down, stood up to put on my jacket and found myself face to face with Janet, glaring at me and punching her hand with her fist.

"I don't know whether to laugh, hit you, or go home," she muttered.

I didn't say a word, reached out, pulled her to me and kissed her passionately, the boldest thing I ever did with a girl. She resisted for a moment, then melted against me. It was a delicious, exciting feeling. I let her go and started to put on my coat to the applause of the nearby patrons, which I ignored.

"If you're not starving, how about we go to your dorm and order takeout later," I said daringly.

"I felt your thing poking me, so I guess dinner can wait."

"You better believe it."

She grinned. "Let's go."

It was only a few streets to her building and we seemed to float there. Tingles of anticipation shot through my body and I lost track of anything but the wonder of this beautiful girl with her arm around me. Everything happened effortlessly. We got to her room, our clothes vanished, we joined together, wild one moment, tender the next, until we came with a rush that left us panting, sweaty, with every nerve end tuned to each other's body.

"Wow," she whispered.

I didn't smoke and I wasn't cool, so I just whispered back, "Yes."

We lay glued together and she was as reluctant as I was to separate. We made love two more times, each one wilder and sweeter. Then we fell asleep in each other's arms. It was after 2:00 a.m. when I awoke and Janet stirred a minute later, kissed me tenderly, and said, "It's a little late for Thai food."

"I'm still hungry for you."

We made love again, then fell asleep, and I didn't stir until 8:00 a.m. I got dressed, kissed her on the forehead and she mumbled sleepily, "I'll call you when I get back."

When I got to the lobby, Lakeisha was just coming in. We hugged like old friends, said goodbye, and I walked home in a trance. TJ was snoring loudly, so I let him sleep a little longer. I felt completely invigorated and wanted to run, so I decided if TJ wasn't awake at 9:00 a.m., and if Clar wasn't home by then, I'd leave her a note with my route. Next time I checked, TJ was still playing a sinal sonata, so I left.

I may have been running a little faster than usual because I was so exhilarated, but when I noticed the trees zipping by, I slowed to my regular pace. When I got to the tennis courts I stopped for a moment to consider whether to go on or turn back. Just as I decided to go, a woman runner stopped next to me.

"I've seen you before. You run with that little girl and that big black guy."

I didn't particularly care for her tone, but she was a good looking, older woman, probably in her thirties, with a dynamite body. She was wearing top of the line running shoes, a designer warm-up suit, and lots of expensive looking jewelry. So I could at least be polite.

"That's right."

"Do you want some company?"

"Sure."

I continued at my regular pace and she kept up, but was obviously near her limit, so I slowed a bit and asked her name.

She was puffing a little, but managed to say, "Karen. Karen Haskell."

"I'm Peter Larkspur."

"That's a funny name."

"No. It's not."

"Touchy?"

"Not at all. It's a very poetic name, often unappreciated."

"Are you a writer?"

"No. I'm a software developer."

"One of those boy geniuses?"

"I'm not a boy anymore."

"How old are you?"

"Twenty-three."

"I guess I'm too old for you."

"Not if you can still get it up."

She flushed with anger for a moment, then burst out laughing.

"You're pretty fresh."

"If you mean I'm crisp, tasty, and firm, I have to agree with you."

"Would you like to go out with me?"

"That depends."

"On what?"

"Are you a rich, old lady?"

"That's crude."

"Perhaps. But I'm not rich yet, so I can't afford the places I want to take you."

"Do you expect to be rich?"

"Within six months to a year."

"You sound like all the other undergraduates, who have a great idea, if they can only find backers."

"I'm not an undergraduate and my partners and I are about to get investors."

"That's impressive. Are you going back to school?"

"What for?"

"An advanced degree."

"I have an M.S. and a PhD."

"Oh."

"I just want you to know I don't have much free time."

"You're awfully sure of yourself."

"Does that threaten you?"

"Not at all. I like a confident man."

"Give me your number and I'll call you."

She took out a card, wrote on the back and handed it to me.

"My private phone number is on the back."

I quickly glanced at it.

"You're a psychiatrist."

"Does that threaten you?"

"Not at all. They're generally not as crazy as psychoanalysts."

She laughed and her body sort of flexed and seemed to say *grab a spoon and dig in.*

"I've got to go. I'll call," and I headed home at an accelerated pace.

Chapter Twenty-One

We didn't do much on the weekend, an unusual occurrence for us. Clar worked sporadically on the investor's budget. TJ went food shopping, intending to cook all our meals. The biggest treat was a truffle omelet for breakfast Sunday morning. I was forced to admit it sounded better in French, *omelet au truffe*, which TJ appreciated. I idly looked at offshore banking account procedures, but didn't really make much of an effort. Since our only immediate objective was the destruction of Parsec, now that we made our initial preparations a kind of lull set in. The only reason I didn't worry was anticipation of the storm to come.

I kept thinking about the Parsec plan, even if it wasn't in a very orderly way. Ideas kept flashing through my mind in an erratic stream, touching on a particular, then moving on. It was clear that we knew what we wanted to do, had the skills to do it, so the next step was to organize each part of the plan in the appropriate order, divide who would do what, then make sure we covered everything. I was confident about everything, except where we'd do it. Somehow the internet café seemed too obvious. Then I remembered something I read a while back about Wi-Fi areas the city was establishing, with one in Lower Manhattan. I asked TJ and Clar to join me in the living room.

"Instead of using internet cafés, where we might be remembered, we can use a Wi-Fi area."

"Explain," Clar said.

"The city set up a Wi-Fi area along Water Street, between Whitehall and Fulton Streets. I'll do a test run in a taxi, to be sure it's working. I'll tell the driver I'm waiting for a friend, give him an extra twenty dollars and verify I can connect to the internet without any problems. If it works, our attack is easy. We'll rent a car, park somewhere on the street, do our business, then drive away."

"Whatever happened to that shy, innocent kid I met at Branville U.?" Clar asked.

I hung my head and shrugged woefully.

"I just fell into bad company," which gave us a laugh.

"We should take tomorrow off," Clar said, "resume our normal routine on Monday, not bother with any job interviews until after the holidays, and we should each think through the plan separately. We can finalize the plan over the weekend, with an extra day for last minute thoughts."

"Sounds good," TJ said. "It'll be a nice change to concentrate on one thing at a time."

TJ was right. It was a nice change to only think about one thing for a short while. Obviously it couldn't last, but it was a luxurious feeling. We ran and went to the dōjō, but otherwise we didn't talk much, only grinned occasionally as we recognized how much we were enjoying ourselves. I briefly considered phoning the psychiatrist for a date, then decided it would be crazy at a time like this. I didn't need any distractions right now and didn't want any complications when Janet returned, so the older woman would have to find a young stud elsewhere. But I remembered how hot she was and didn't throw her card away.

We bought cheap Lenovo computers on Tuesday at separate stores, then TJ reinstalled the operating systems we'd need for our Christmas present to Parsec. On Wednesday I took a taxi to Water Street and had him wait. I logged on to the internet and it only took a few minutes to make sure we could function in the Wi-Fi area. Everything worked as intended, so I didn't bother telling the driver I was waiting for someone. He was wearing a turban and I assumed he was an Arab.

"What part of the Middle East are you from?"

He glanced at me. "I'm a Sikh, from India," then he looked away.

The meter read $14.00, so I put two twenties in the slot, got out and walked away. I didn't know what a Sikh was, but I didn't want any trouble and kept my head averted as he drove off. I took a taxi home and told TJ and Clar the good news that the Wi-Fi area was functional. Then I reserved a rental car, a black Ford SUV, with tinted windows, for December 24, 25, and 26, at a place on East 31st Street.

Clar was surprised at how expensive it was, but was reassured when I reminded her we were using Parsec money. I was concerned that I had to give the rental agency a credit card number, but Clar insisted there was no possible connection that could tie us to Parsec, and TJ agreed.

As a special treat, I told them to get learner's permits on Thursday and I'd give them driving lessons as part of our holiday celebration. This excited them at the moment almost as much as the imminent attack on Parsec and they thanked me profusely.

We sat down together Friday afternoon and began to divide the objectives between us, with TJ doing the record changes and attack on Phil, Lou, and Rogers. Clar would add incriminating items to their computers, and notify the IRS and mortgage companies. I would handle all the money transfers. The plan was definitely shaping up.

We were feeling very relaxed that night, confident that we were ready. We idly chatted once again about whether or not to get a TV. Suddenly, Clar got a very strange look on her face, and sat up.

"Boys. I regret to tell you we've been thinking with our balls, not our brains."

"What do you mean?' TJ asked.

She shook her head sadly.

"We've been enjoying the torments we were going to do to Parsec."

We nodded enthusiastically.

"Unfortunately, we can't do them."

"Why not?" I demanded.

"Because it just occurred to me that all those things happening at the same time would indicate an outsider attack. Lou wouldn't tip off the IRS about Phil. Rogers wouldn't cause a default on their mortgages. Phil wouldn't give Rogers away if he was having a homosexual affair. Anybody with half a brain would investigate, and we'd be the prime suspects. Discontented former employees with the skills to do those things will be the obvious first one's looked at. No matter how well we cover our tracks we still might be vulnerable. I don't think we should risk our future to get even with those *pendejos*."

I thought about what she said and, however reluctantly, was forced to agree.

TJ said, "You're right. The only thing we might get away with is taking the money, because that'll seem as if they did it to each other."

"I was really looking forward to outing Phil," I joked. "How about Rogers steals Phil's offshore account, Phil takes the Parsec account and Lou steals ten or fifteen thousand covering his trail with a phony bill for a new server?"

"Sounds pretty easy to me," TJ replied. "Let's do it."

"Let's," Clar echoed.

"That makes it real simple," I observed. "TJ and I can do it in five or ten minutes. We won't need the car. We'll just go to Water Street, pull out the computers, push a few buttons and be on our way. TJ, can you place a fake server bill in their files?"

"Sure. No problem."

"Then correct me if I'm wrong, but we're ready." They nodded agreement, so I added, "I met this woman the other day. If we don't have to rehearse tomorrow, I'll phone her and see if she's free tomorrow night."

"What about Janet?" TJ asked, shocked.

"I'll see her when she gets back."

"I told you he was a dog," Clar said.

They stared at me and I said flippantly, "Every dog must have his . . . look guys, I never had much luck with girls, so this is a good thing for me. It doesn't change my feeling for you."

"It better not," Clar warned. "Or she . . ."

"Don't worry. I love you both."

This reassured them, but they still looked at me a bit oddly, discovering another side of me. That night I thought about Karen and her hot body. I phoned her in the morning and got a recording that informed me Dr. Haskell was not available until January 2ⁿᵈ, and gave me a number in case of emergency. I dialed her cell phone, got her voice mail and left my name and number. She phoned a few minutes later and told me she was in Hawaii and would return January 2ⁿᵈ. She wanted to chat, but I said goodbye abruptly, a little frustrated that her flesh was unavailable.

We went to a movie Saturday night at the complex on 2ⁿᵈ Avenue and 31ˢᵗ Street. We sat through most of a horrible sci-fi flick, with the intrepid spacefarers accompanied by gorgeous women scientists, discovering an ancient alien race, and bringing back an alien virus that devastated Earth. We left before the cannibal zombies got their first meal. When we got home, we drank Clar's awful herbal tea, talked for a while, then went to bed.

On Sunday we rehearsed the attack over and over, taking a break every two hours to clear our heads and give us a chance to make sure we weren't forgetting anything. By Sunday night we had covered every detail thoroughly, set a timetable for each particular action, and felt confident that we were ready. We decided to stop for the night and do one more review on Monday, to be sure we weren't overlooking anything.

TJ officially ended the session by cautioning us, "We seem to have prepared thoroughly, but remember, things can go wrong. If something doesn't work the first time, give it a moment, then try again. If it still doesn't work, tell me and I'll see if I can help. Questions? Comments?"

"The Cayman bank charges one percent for each transaction," I complained. "That's highway robbery."

Clar laughed. "That's from the guy who reminded me it's not our money."

"I was just remarking on excessive business fees," I mumbled, with an attempt at dignity, which really cracked them up.

"One thing you're not, Little Brother," Clar replied, "is dignified. Right, TJ?"

"You've got many fine qualities," TJ said, "but dignity isn't one of them."

"So you rats are selling me out," I rasped in a gangster's voice.

"We got a great price," Clar gloated, and before I could respond, she and TJ grabbed me and poked and prodded me.

"Don't worry, Pete," TJ consoled. "We wouldn't sell you cheap."

Monday morning, we ran, then went to the dōjō and had a vigorous workout. Sensei Omura told us the next testing would be Saturday, February 1, and he urged us to test for the next level. We thanked him and bowed, but just before we left him, TJ expressed some doubts about whether he was ready to test for the brown belt.

Sensei Omura was blunt, as usual. "It is good that you don't wish to hurt anyone, TJ san. But the more skillful you become, the easier it will be to avoid violence."

This was very reassuring to TJ and he bowed respectfully. "Thank you, sensei."

Omura smiled mischievously. "Run away fast when trouble comes, TJ san. Unless you cannot run."

On the way home, Clar and I teased TJ, describing when he should run away and when he should stay and fight. We almost fell down laughing when Clar said, "You should always fight if someone tries to steal your *flan*."

He sniffed disdainfully.

"I don't fight for pudding."

She scampered up his body like a monkey, wrapped her arms around him, and whispered, "Apologize for insulting my Hispanic heritage, or you'll have to carry me home."

"Hang on tight, Old Lady," he retorted. "I wouldn't want you to fall on your *flan*."

She glared at me when I roared with laughter and mock beat him with her fists. People were staring at us, but we ignored them, enjoying ourselves in a lighthearted break from the serious mood of the last few days.

When we got home we had turkey sandwiches for lunch, then we reviewed the attack plan one last time, which TJ pronounced ready. He said he was going to make a special Christmas Eve dinner for us tomorrow and went shopping. Clar went to her room and phoned her family. I settled down on my bed and started to read *Crime and Punishment*, by Dostoyevsky. I had started it in college and had trouble with the Russian names, except for Sonia, because there was a girl named Sonia in my fifth grade English class, whose budding breasts I checked regularly. Somehow it seemed appropriate, now that we were setting out on a life of crime.

Chapter Twenty-Two

Something had been nagging at me ever since Clar pointed out the many flaws in our attack plan. I put down the book just as Raskolnikov was planning the murder of his landlady. The irony of people thinking they are superior to others didn't escape me. I poked and prodded at my elusive thought and suddenly it popped into mind. Just as we couldn't do all the delightful things to the skags at Parsec, we couldn't destroy the company, or steal their money. That too might be traceable to disgruntled ex-employees. I considered it for a few minutes, then went and knocked on the partition next to Clar's curtain door.

"Come in," she welcomed.

"We need to talk with TJ about the plan. Let's go to the kitchen."

"Sure. What's up?"

"I'll tell you when we're with TJ."

She sprang off the bed like a puma and followed me. TJ was busily stirring pots and pans, referring to cookbooks and mumbling in English, French, and some alien language. I started to speak, but he cut me off and insisted we taste the work in progress. He shoved spoons, forks, and some kind of flat thing in our mouths, which produced an array of delicious sensations that whetted our appetites. When I suggested we eat that wonderful meal tonight, he looked at me disdainfully.

"It won't be ready until tomorrow. Tonight you can pick up some take-out, or we'll order in. Now what's on your mind?"

"We can't destroy Parsec," I announced

"Why not?" he demanded.

"For the same reasons that Clar gave us for not doing the IRS or mortgages. We could be possible suspects."

"So what's left?" he asked in exasperation.

"We'll have Lou steal $13,000 with a fake bill of sale and we empty Phil's offshore account."

"That's all?" he grumbled. "After all they did to us?"

"Pete's right," Clar declared. "I'm very proud of you, Little Brother. I know how angry you are at them."

"When I finally accepted what you told us, it became obvious that total revenge would have to wait."

"Then this is only step one?" TJ chortled.

"Absolutely," I replied. "But what comes next will have to be thought out very carefully."

"So our Christmas presents are very simple now," Clar said. "I place the fake sales bill in Parsec's file. TJ moves the money to Lou's account and you transfer Phil's offshore money to another account."

"That's it," I confirmed. "How long will that take, TJ?"

"With everything loaded beforehand, about two minutes, most of that spent powering up and shutting down."

"How much time do you need to prepare us now, TJ?" Clar asked.

"About ten or fifteen minutes. I think we're pretty organized on what we have to do."

"We should do our attack one at a time, so we can keep an eye on what's going on around us," Clar suggested, then added, "We should get rid of the money right away. Do you still want to give to those charities, Pete?"

"Sure. TJ can get their account info tonight and I'll work it out with the bank to send the money to them as soon as it clears. I think we're finally ready."

TJ nodded. "You transfer Phil's money, Clar places the receipt, and I'll transfer Lou's money. We should have wine with dinner tonight and toast to our successful attack," TJ stated. "I don't think we should drink tomorrow night."

"We should drink champagne if all goes well," I said.

"I'll get a bottle tomorrow," TJ offered.

We ordered Japanese food for dinner and drank a bottle of very pleasant Rhine wine, selected by TJ. When we finished, I disposed of the food containers, TJ went back to cooking, the tantalizing aromas almost an intoxicating perfume, and Clar returned to her budget chores. I got the charities information, interrupted TJ so he could get their bank accounts, then continued reading *Crime and Punishment*. Raskolnikov was convincing himself that his superiority justified his murder of the landlady when I fell asleep, book in my hands. I instantly went into a deep rem sleep. When I awoke in the morning, a piece of a strange dream lingered in which Raskolnikov, as I pictured him, was approaching Phil's office at Parsec with a big knife in his hand. That's all I could remember.

We went for our morning run, then to the dōjō, frequently looking at each other and smiling, the secret knowledge of what we were finally going to do building a glowing feeling of satisfaction. We didn't talk much during the day, but felt closer than ever, sharing the anticipation of revenge to come. We skipped lunch and sat down to a glorious meal at 5:00 p.m., just after dark. TJ proclaimed it a traditional English holiday feast, the highlight of which was a roast goose, stuffed with all sorts of tasty morsels. We laughed when TJ called the Brussel sprouts "Irish golf balls". By the time we got to the plum pudding I was so stuffed I could hardly move. It was the most delicious meal I ever ate and I recalled reading about a Christmas feast in one of Charles Dickens' books. TJ's had to be better.

We lolled around like farm animals, occasionally mooing to each other, but we were too full to even laugh.

At 7:00 p.m., Clar took a deep breath, sighed, then said, "Alright, boys. It's time to get moving."

"TJ has to carry me," I pleaded.

"Fat chance," he replied. "I cooked. You carry me."

It took a while, but we finally got moving. We took the 3rd Avenue bus downtown, got off, and walked the few blocks to Water Street. It was a clear, crisp night and I could see thirty or forty stars, as much as you ever see in the blinding light of cities. I had never paid much attention to the thousands of stars I could see in Binghamton, but now I sort of missed them. We found a comfortable spot in a doorway, pulled out our computers one at a time, while the others kept watch and in a few minutes the attack was done. We walked home, exchanging greetings with passersby, who said, "Merry Christmas." We stopped regularly to discard pieces of our computers in trash cans, after wiping off fingerprints. We broke the hard drives into small pieces and dumped them in sewers.

A strange apathy possessed us that night, and we tried to absorb the letdown after so much preparation, realizing we might never find out what happened to Phil and Lou. We idly discussed some possibilities, but they were a bit silly since they hadn't been thought out, and our hearts weren't in it. Clar suggested we follow the local news carefully for the next few weeks and TJ and I nodded agreement. Then TJ asked if we should delete Cybersnarer from Phil's computer, but Clar instantly vetoed that idea.

"They'll know right away who did it and they'll automatically suspect us of taking Phil's money. I don't know how long it'll take them to discover Lou's theft, but we don't want them suspecting us."

We knew she was absolutely right, so we dropped the idea. But a part of me was still burning with rage at them, and I fantasized about breaking into Parsec, stealing all their discs and deleting all the data from their hard drives. I made a mental note to talk to TJ and Clar about a B&E in a few weeks, once enough time passed from our attack. We were in a peculiar mood, an odd combination of mild satisfaction after accomplishing the attack, and frustration that we couldn't do more, or even find out how they'd respond.

Clar went back to work on the budget, TJ got involved in a violent video game and I cleaned the kitchen. It felt like TJ imported an array of dishes, pots, and silverware, but I finally finished, went to bed and continued reading Crime and Punishment, just as the Police Inspector got his first suspicions of Raskolnikov. I hoped this wasn't an omen. My last thought as I fell asleep was this was the weirdest Christmas Eve ever.

Chapter Twenty-Three

I don't know if it was aftershock, mental fatigue, or laziness, but we slept late Christmas morning, didn't go for a run and skipped the dōjō. If the three of us weren't bonded so closely together we might have felt completely detached from the rest of the human race. Instead, we seemed to sense each other's mood, didn't talk much and lolled around all day. TJ served leftovers from the great feast for dinner. It may not have been as elaborate as the night before, but it was just as delicious. Once again we stuffed ourselves on roast goose and plum pudding.

"There's no more, is there?" Clar moaned, but TJ just burped at her. "Because I'm getting fatter and fatter. I eat one more meal like that, you'll have to trundle me around in a wheelbarrow."

I just grunted, then asked idly, "Do you know what a wheelbarrow is?"

"Sure. It's those chairs with wheels they use in hospitals."

"No, silly. It's a one-wheeled cart they use on farms and in construction sites."

"Whatever. As long as I don't have to walk."

"Do you feel like doing anything tonight?" TJ asked.

"I'm going to hibernate until morning," Clar declared. "Then, if we're up to it, we can start to talk about what we do next."

We tottered off our separate ways, too full to do more than mumble goodnight. I read a few pages of *Crime and Punishment*, but was too sated with good food to feel much sympathy for the sufferings of Raskolnikov.

We felt slightly more human in the morning, went for our run, then to the dōjō. Sensei Omura reminded us testing was two weeks away and after looking us over carefully, wondered if we'd be ready. We made reassuring noises that didn't sound very convincing to us, but seemed to satisfy him. We bowed and scurried to the locker room, a little self-conscious about not being entirely candid to the one person in New York City who cared about us. On the way home we talked about him and realized we knew nothing about him, except he was Japanese, a highly skilled teacher, and had a strong moral code. Clar suggested we ask him about himself, but I suspected he wouldn't be very forthcoming.

"I bet someone else doing the dishes he won't say much."

"Tired of cleaning up, Little Brother?" Clar asked.

"I do it cheerfully. As soon as we can afford a maid, I'll let her do it."

When we got home we discussed what we'd do for the rest of the week and through New Year's Eve. Clar said she'd continue working on the budget and outline a corporate model. She said we'd get salaries of $300,000 a year for the two-year investment period of 20 million dollars, and 17% each of the stock, giving us 51%. This was very satisfying to us, but she added it all had to be negotiated. We decided that I would work on Cybersnarer and TJ would work on Castle Keep. We briefly chatted about what we wanted to do for New Year's Eve and agreed we wouldn't go to Times Square. We admitted one at a time that it might be fun, and I fantasized about the hot girls I could meet. The thought of standing around for hours in a closed-in cattle pen was just not appealing enough to make me change my mind.

The next few days passed quietly as we slowly got used to a routine again. Saturday morning, right after we came back from our run, Clar used the bathroom first. Suddenly we heard a scream and heard her yelling for us and we rushed in. She held up her hand for silence and we heard the radio newscaster.

"Philip Hapgood, age 33, CEO of Parsec, Inc, a well-known software development company, was found dead last night in his Tribecca condo, allegedly of a self-inflicted gun-shot wound. His wife, Rebecca Hapgood, 31, a fashion designer, had been out with clients and found him on the living room floor, a pistol in his hand. She insisted he didn't own a gun. Next, the four-day weather report."

Clar slowly reached out and shut off the radio. We stared at each other, trying to digest the news, and I quickly realized that I didn't feel anything about him. This alarmed me a little and I hoped I wasn't reading too much Dostoevsky.

"Did we do that?" TJ asked wonderingly.

"I didn't do a B&E and shoot him," I replied.

"Maybe someone else did," Clar offered.

"Can you picture him committing suicide?" I asked.

"No," Clar answered. "He was too full of himself."

"We don't know how he'd react if he lost his money," TJ stated.

"True," I said, "but he had a good job and would have made a lot more money when he sold Cybersnarer."

"Let's keep it simple," Clar declared. "It's either suicide or murder, right?" She didn't wait for an answer. "If it's suicide, we'll never know if we caused it or not. If it's murder . . ."

"Yes?" I encouraged.

"Then I don't see that it has anything to do with us."

"We don't know enough to conclude that," I retorted.

"You think what we did got him killed?" TJ murmured.

"I don't know. If it was suicide, Clar's right. We won't know if what we did caused it. But if it's murder, and we caused it, we may have a problem."

"Why?" TJ asked.

"Because they didn't kill him for his money. We already took it."

"Why would someone kill him?" Clar asked.

"I don't know. But let's hope it doesn't involve us," I replied.

"Should we talk to the police?" TJ asked.

"And tell them we stole his money and got him killed," Clar snapped. "No way."

We were quiet for a while, then TJ asked, "How do you feel about his death, Clar?"

"I don't know. A little numb maybe, but he's not someone I cared about."

"What about you, Pete?"

"I don't feel anything for him," I answered coldly and they stared at me. "I hope we didn't cause it, but I don't feel guilty. We wouldn't have done anything if they hadn't stolen our life's work." They slowly nodded agreement. "We have to think about this and try to figure out what happened. If the police come around, we were very happy with their generosity when they ended our project."

"Do you think the police will come?" TJ quavered.

"Maybe. We need to do some brainstorming and see if we can come up with some possibilities about why he was killed," I proposed. "Let's talk about it as soon as we get used to the idea he may have been murdered."

Chapter Twenty-Four

We ran in the morning, went to the dōjō, and our bodies may have been there, but our minds kept coming back to the initial news report. Phil was dead of an allegedly self-inflicted gunshot wound. After non-stop discussion of the situation, we had two big questions: If he wasn't a suicide, why was he killed, and who killed him. It was obvious that he wasn't killed for money, even though the loss of his money may have provoked the murder. So why was he killed? It was either business or personal and we didn't know enough to even speculate about his private life. If it was business, it had to go beyond Parsec. He couldn't have embezzled more than a million bucks without being discovered long ago. Parsec wasn't in the big leagues.

By common consent we concentrated on trying to figure out why someone might have killed him. The best answer we came up with sounded more like cheap crime fiction, than a reasonable explanation.

The only thing that made sense was that he was selling Parsec's software secrets to someone and they killed him when he demanded too much money. Clar punched holes in that theory by reminding us it didn't account for his reaction to the loss of his off-shore money. TJ suggested he might have been demanding too much money for Cybersnarer, but that didn't make sense. If he was pirating software, he couldn't peddle it on the street. He had to have a customer. Would he be killed for wanting more? That wasn't logical. It was business. He wasn't stupid. He'd negotiate and get the most he could. I couldn't see him blackmailing his customer. Neither could TJ or Clar.

It was a virus infecting our cognition. Why? Why? We had a lot of detective story speculations, but no conclusions. And there was no one to ask. We kept thinking about it and talking about it, but made no progress. TJ went uptown and got the local West Side papers, bought the Times, Post, and Daily News, but there was no mention of Phil. Just a few days later he was another obscure death with a minimal impact in a city fighting crime, poverty, obesity, joblessness, and a new mayor who was soft on stop and frisk, one of the few initiatives to combat the proliferation of handguns on the streets.

When we came back from the dōjō on Monday, two men waiting outside our building approached us. They were neatly dressed in suits, ties, and dark-blue wool overcoats. Clar turned and went to a defensive stance and TJ and I, responding to her reaction, prepared to defend ourselves. Before we could do anything the men took out ID folders and the big black man, though small compared to TJ, said, "I'm Special Agent Jamison of the FBI. This is Special Agent Bellini. We'd like to talk to you."

"About what?" Clar demanded.

"Can we discuss it inside?" Jamison asked. "Some of what we have to say is confidential."

Clar looked at me questioningly, and I thought of suggesting we go to Starbucks, but one glance at their severe expressions convinced me it was a silly idea. I put on my eager to please, not too bright, puppy face and said, "That okay with you, TJ?" who put on his dumb mask and nodded. "Sure, guys. C'mon in."

Although we had folding chairs in the closet, Clar and the two agents sat, while TJ and I stood nearby. It was obvious that they weren't comfortable with us hulking over them, but if *we* sat it would have seemed more like an interrogation, rather than what I hoped was a simple inquiry. I reminded myself not to think about Raskolnikov and waited silently, along with TJ and Clar. Apparently our visitors expected nervous questions and tense behavior, but when we didn't react, Bellini asked, "You worked at Parsec, didn't you?"

"You already know that," Clar said condescendingly. "How else would you know about us?"

"No need to take an attitude, little lady."

"Excuse me? What did you call me?"

"I was just being polite."

"I'm Ms. Rodriguez or Dr. Rodriguez. Now why are you here?"

Bellini looked at TJ and me, hoping we'd be more responsive, but we just looked back at him blankly.

"Does she speak for you guys?"

"Dr. Rogriguez speaks for us and we're not 'you guys'," TJ corrected. "I assume you want to be called Special Agent . . . sorry, what's your name?"

"Bellini."

"Well, Special Agent Bellini, I assume you earned that title . . ." Bellini managed a surly nod. "Then please extend the same courtesy to us."

Bellini turned to me. "Is he serious?"

"My brother is always serious."

"Your brother? But he's—"

"Yes. Now why are you here?"

Before Bellini could reply, Jamison said smoothly, "We're investigating the death of Phillip Hapgood. You knew him, didn't you?"

"You know we did," Clar snapped. "Why are federal agents investigating a suicide?"

Jamison looked questioningly at Bellini, who nodded.

"There are some doubts that it was suicide." He paused a moment to assess our reaction.

"Are you suggesting he was murdered?" Clar asked in a shocked voice, and TJ and I looked startled.

"That is to be determined. Do you know if he had any enemies?"

"We worked for Parsec for a few months. We barely knew Phil," Clar answered. "But you still didn't tell us why the feds are involved."

"Parsec has several government contracts for developing national security software. We understand that you're working on a security software project."

"Where did you get that idea?" Clar demanded, "We never discussed our personal projects with anyone at Parsec. How do you know about it? Have you been spying on us?" she yelled angrily.

He held up his hands placatingly. "Some people at Parsec suggested the possibility."

"Well it's none of their business, or yours," she retorted.

"You're not being very cooperative," Bellini said.

"About what?" Clar challenged.

"Well you don't seem very disturbed by Mr. Hapgood's death."

"Of course we're sorry about it. But as I said earlier, we barely knew him."

"Were you angry at Parsec for firing you?"

"They didn't fire us," I replied. "They ended the project we were working on."

"Did you want to get back at them for that?"

"No. They gave us a very generous separation package. Will Phil's death affect that?"

"You'll have to ask them."

"You still haven't told us why you're here," TJ said.

"We're just making certain there were no security leaks. Did you discuss your work there with anyone?"

"Just among ourselves," I replied. "Do you suspect some kind of corporate espionage?"

"Why do you ask that?" Bellini said.

"It goes on all the time in this business."

"Do you think it was a foreign government?" TJ asked.

"Look. We're just making sure there are no problems." Bellini said abruptly. "Here are our cards. If you have any information, please call us," and they got up and headed for the door.

"Goodbye, Officer Bellini," Clar said.

"It's Special Agent," and he slammed the door closed behind him.

We heard the front door slam and I went to the window and saw them walking down the street.

"They're gone."

We looked at each other and burst into laughter. Just as it was dying down, TJ said, "Did you kill Phil, little lady?" which really cracked us up.

When our laughter subsided, I said, "You handled them well, Clar."

"Thanks, Pete."

"Could you picture Phil killing himself?"

"That *puta*? No way."

I looked at TJ and he shook his head no.

"It's obvious someone killed him," I stated, "otherwise why would the FBI come here. We have to consider how this involves us."

"Why should it involve us?" TJ asked. "They didn't seem to think we're involved."

"They know about Cybersnarer," Clar said.

"That means they had to be monitoring Parsec, or us," I explained. "TJ found Cybersnarer on Phil's desktop, so they were probably monitoring Parsec."

"Would they monitor Parsec if it was corporate espionage?" TJ asked.

"Probably not," Clar replied. "I doubt that some businessman would kill him over unfinished software."

"So it was a foreign government. Who could it be?" TJ wondered.

She shrugged. "Russia, China, Iran, other countries. They all steal information."

"Do you think our taking his money had anything to do with it?"

TJ's question got me thinking. "If a foreign government was paying Phil for information, that might explain his offshore account. What if he thought his paymaster stole his money? Maybe he threatened them and they sanctioned him."

"Sanctioned?" TJ queried.

"Whacked. Offed. Hit. That's what they say in the movies."

"This isn't the movies," Clar muttered. "Do we have to worry about this?"

"Absolutely," I answered. "If they'd kill Phil in a money dispute over software, they might be interested in us, now that he's gone."

"Is it too late to get those FBI guys back?" TJ quipped, which made us smile.

"What do we do?" Clar asked in a serious voice.

"Do you want to tell them we took Phil's money?" I replied.

"No."

"Then we're on our own."

"To repeat Clar's question," TJ said. "What do we do?"

"For starters, we don't go anywhere alone. We work on the new computers with no link to the internet, and we check regularly to see if we're being bugged."

"We can always go back to Branville U." TJ murmured.

"What makes you think they couldn't find us there?" Clar said.

"Oh."

Chapter Twenty-Five

We were still uneasy by New Year's Eve. We tried to reassure ourselves that all was well, though I don't think we believed it. TJ made an exotic fondue with different kinds of cheeses that we dipped into with a crusty French bread. I didn't dare tell him that a grilled cheese sandwich would have been okay. Just before midnight, we opened the bottle of champagne meant to celebrate our attack, and listened to the old year counted out on the radio. When the announcer shouted, "Happy New Year," we hugged each other and Clar whispered, "To a good year." We touched glasses and toasted the new year. TJ told us it was a fairly good vintage, but I didn't like it. I guess I'm not the champagne type.

We ran in the morning. A cold, chilling wind may have left the usual runners at home, or perhaps they were recuperating from booze and drugs from the night before. We kept looking around nervously as we ran, until Clar stopped. "We can't see everything, no matter how much we try, so there's no use acting like paranoid freaks. We should just try to be extra aware of what's going on around us."

"We could plan ahead and pick places to duck into, if we see some kind of threat," I suggested.

She nodded. "Good idea. I think for a while we should go shopping with TJ." I groaned and she glared at me. "Maybe we can eat a bit simpler for a while."

"Sure," he replied. "What do we do when the girls get back?"

She looked around and noted how deserted the East River Park was.

"Let's talk about it when we get home."

We did talk about it later, but couldn't find any practical solutions. If we were at risk, the girls might be also, just by being with us. It came down to not seeing them for a while, or taking a chance that nothing would happen.

"It's not fair to the girls to put them at risk," TJ said softly.

Even though I yearned for Janet's supple body, I was forced to agree.

"We could discuss it with them," TJ offered.

"And tell them what we did? No way," Clar stated.

"We can tell them a disgruntled employee is making threats, so we can't see them until it's resolved," I proposed, and when they looked at me in surprise, I told them, "We've got to tell them something, if we're not going to see them. Do you have a better idea?" They both shook their heads. "Is it possible that whoever killed Phil knows about them?"

My question really shook up TJ. "Why should they?" he quavered. "We haven't seen them since . . ." and he trailed off. "So whoever was monitoring us may know about them."

"We've got to be sure no one knows we're still involved with them," I said.

"We have to contact them without anyone finding out," Clar advised.

"We can call their cell phones from a pay phone in Grand Central Terminal," TJ proposed.

"Let's do it now," I responded.

"Sure. And after we'll go to the Oyster Bar for a treat."

"I'm not eating those slimy things," Clar yelled.

"We'll get you a shrimp cocktail," TJ soothed.

By the time we reached Grand Central, I had seen menacing foreign agents from Iran, Pakistan, China, North Korea, Russia, and Lichtenstein. I was definitely getting paranoid. It was even worse inside the station. Hundreds of agents seemed to be watching us, until I noticed them, when they quickly moved on. I turned to Clar.

"Am I crazy, or are there spies everywhere?"

She smiled sweetly. "You are crazy, but I see them. I bet TJ does, too."

"What do I see?"

"Spies watching us," she replied.

"Do you see them?"

"Yes. So does Pete."

"I didn't want you to think I was crazy, so I didn't say anything, but it was really getting to me."

"We're all crazy," she said, "but we're all seeing threats everywhere. Make your calls, then we'll go to the Oyster Bar, and I'll watch you slurp mucus."

TJ was preparing an indignant reply, but I took him by the arm and led him to a bank of phones. Clar stood near us watching alertly while we dialed. Her fierce awareness was reassuring. Janet answered on the first ring and we chatted about what we had been doing since we last saw each other, my info severely edited.

"You sound strange," she said. "Aren't you glad to talk to me? I'll be back Monday and we can see each other Monday night."

"There's a problem with that."

"I don't care if we're not alone, as long as I'm with you."

"It's not that."

"Then what? ... Are you breaking up with me?" she asked in alarm.

"No. No. Definitely not. I miss you all the time. We have a situation. Somebody we used to work with made some threats to us, accusing us of stealing his work."

"Did you?"

"Absolutely not. He's a nut job. But until this is resolved, TJ and I want to be sure he doesn't know about you and Lakeisha, just in case he's really dangerous."

"Did you go to the police?"

"No."

"Why not?"

"Because we have no proof. We're going to call him and assure him we didn't take his work, and try to convince him it must have been someone else."

"Do you think he'll believe you?"

"I don't know. But it's worth trying. Clar will talk to him and she can be very persuasive."

"When will I see you?"

"Hopefully in a week or two. I'll call you from a payphone at night, when I can. Don't call me."

"This is really weird."

"I know."

"But you really want to see me?"

"Oh, yes. You're the girl for me. I'll call you in a few days and I'll work something out so we can see each other."

I didn't know how convincing I was. After I hung up the phone, I wondered if she believed me.

TJ's conversation with Lakeisha was similar to mine with Janet and she was as disappointed as Janet. When he told us he felt his excuse was lame and I nodded agreement, Clar said, "That's because it is lame. We'll have to think of something better."

But we couldn't. At least not without making up an entirely new story, which would have strained our credibility. So our only choice, except revealing our criminal activities, was to stick to a dubious story and hope the girls would accept it. Clar was very sympathetic and said she'd help us find a way for us to see them safely. TJ was really moved by this, since he was completely besotted with Lakeisha and he thanked her profusely. I also thanked her, though my feelings were more carnal then his infatuation.

Then something else occurred to me. "I don't think we should go on job interviews alone."

"That's easy," Clar said. "We'll go together and wait for whoever has the meeting."

"Speaking of meetings," TJ added. "I don't think we want anyone to know about our investor meetings."

"Then let's go back to Grand Central and I'll call Bonnie," I said. "I'll tell her there are some complications because of Phil's death and we want to make sure it doesn't affect her, or our potential investors."

"That should reassure her," Clar said. "One thing though."

"What?" I asked.

"Do I have to watch you two eat oysters every time we go to Grand Central?"

"What do you have against oysters?" TJ asked in a hurt voice.

"Nothing. As long as the squishy things stay in the ocean, where they belong."

Chapter Twenty-Six

Clar finished the budget and corporate plan on Sunday. We reviewed it and it seemed functional. All we needed was $20,000,000 to find out if it worked. On Monday morning we went to Grand Central Terminal and I phoned Bonnie, who asked us to come right over. After several starts and stops in the terminal, and circling back, we were fairly certain we weren't being followed. We walked uptown, cut through a lobby in a building off Park Avenue on 52nd Street that went through to 53rd Street. We hung out for a few minutes studying the faces of whoever entered and when none of them looked familiar we went to the Seagram Building.

Bonnie was glad to see us, but expressed concern about what we may have gotten ourselves into, particularly with the FBI.

"Don't worry," TJ said expansively. "We can deal with the situation. It really doesn't involve us."

He was getting off on our counter spy precautions. Clar nodded agreement, so I guess I was the only one who was still paranoid. I knew if I alarmed Bonnie it might jeopardize relations with our investors, so I nodded also. Bonnie looked over the budget and said she'd forward it to both investor groups. We arranged to have her email me, as if responding to a Google job application from us, to confirm they received our resumes, which would inform us an investor meeting was arranged for the next day. Whatever time she wrote, the meeting time would be two hours later. On the way home, TJ bubbled about getting disguises, until Clar bopped him on the head.

"How are we going to disguise you?"

"You mean because I'm black?"

"No, silly. Because you're so big."

"I could dress as an Arab sheik."

"I'll get you a white stallion," I offered.

"Who do you think you'll fool?" Clar asked.

"I'm just trying to be helpful," he muttered.

"I know, Baby Brother," she said soothingly, "but we've got to be practical."

He moped for a minute, then his usual cheerful disposition reasserted itself. "I guess that wasn't a good idea."

"It's a good thing I know how brilliant you are," I remarked, "otherwise I'd wonder about you."

Despite twinges of anxiety and several irrational alarms at loud noises when we were outdoors, we managed to get back into our usual routine; morning run, dōjō, work on Cybersnarer and Castle Keep. TJ confessed that he had been thinking about all the accidents he had seen in the movies that spies arranged to murder their targets. He laughed self-consciously, then admitted that he worried about bus accidents. We laughed with him and admitted our imaginations had been working overtime.

I cautioned, "Let's all look both ways before we cross the street."

Except for occasional apprehensions, things seemed to be normal. Our biggest excitement was preparing for testing at the dōjō on Saturday. We made another trip to Grand Central so I could phone Bonnie. She told me she sent the budget and business plan to the investors and she expected to hear from them in a week or two. She asked if there were any developments regarding Parsec and I told her there was nothing new, which reassured her. TJ and I phoned the girls and chatted briefly. When we hung up he asked me if Janet sounded a bit distant. Apparently Lakeisha had been cool with him and he was worried about losing her.

Clar said firmly, "This'll be over soon and you can see her again and make up for lost time." He gave her such a sweet smile, that she added, "Let's go to the Oyster Bar."

We tested on Saturday and Clar advanced a degree in black belt. I got my black belt and TJ got his brown belt. A new assertiveness had come over him, and Sensei Omura told him he was ready for black belt testing, which pleased all of us. TJ hadn't cooked elaborately since Christmas, so he decided to make a special dinner. We watched him shop at Todaro's, his favorite food store, where they loved him for his enthusiasm and being a gourmet cook, which he discussed as he shopped. We walked home laden with bags of food, making one more stop at a wine shop, where he bought a good burgundy.

We unloaded the bags in the kitchen and helped TJ sort out the purchases. He just started explaining what he was going to make, when our apartment doorbell rang. We looked at each other with the same question, *who was in the building?*

I went to the door and said, "Who is it?"

"Police. We'd like to talk to you."

I looked through the peephole and saw two men, one black, one white. They definitely weren't the android FBI. The black man was wearing a dark-green down jacket and the white man had on an ancient tweed coat that looked like a thrift shop special.

"What is this about?"

The black man answered, "We'd like to talk to you inside."

"Show me your badge."

He took out a gold shield, which looked real enough.

"Show me your ID."

He took out a folder that identified him as Detective Jason Chestnut. His partner showed his ID, Detective Arnold Gluckman. I opened the door.

"What can I do for you gentlemen?"

"We'd like to talk to you and your friends about Parsec," Chestnut said.

"We already talked to the FBI."

They looked at each other in surprise.

"When did you talk to them?" Gluckman asked.

"Last week."

"What did they question you about?"

"Phil Hapgood's suicide."

"Why were they interested in you?" Gluckman said.

"They said Parsec had government security contracts and they were checking anyone who worked there."

"Did they suggest that he was murdered?"

"You'll have to ask them. I'll give you their cards."

"That's not why we're here," Chestnut said. "May we come in?"

"Sure."

I let them in and introduced them to TJ and Clar. Unlike the FBI, they didn't sit. They both looked stressed, tired, and cynical, but definitely human, a distinct change from the FBI

"Do you know Lou Perkins?" Chestnut asked.

"You mean from Parsec?" Clar replied.

"Yes."

"I didn't remember his last name, but we know him."

"He was your supervisor?"

"Yes."

"Did you like him?"

"Not particularly. He was a jerk."

"What do you mean?"

"He wasn't very bright and was always questioning the accuracy of our work, even though he didn't understand it."

"Did you hate him?"

"I didn't like him, but hate him, no."

"Is he dead?" I asked.

"No," Gluckman said. "He's been accused of stealing money from Parsec by making phony equipment purchases. He claims he's innocent and someone is setting him up. Do you have any reason to do that?"

"No," I answered. "Parsec gave us a very generous separation package when we left. We don't have anything against anyone there."

"Any idea who might?"

"Not really. We weren't there that long and didn't get to know anyone well."

"Has Lou been arrested?" Clar asked.

"No. He's under investigation. He said you three might have done it."

"I don't know why he would say that." Clar replied. "We have nothing against Lou."

"Would you mind if we looked at your computers?" Chestnut asked.

"No way," Clar said. "We have confidential material on our computers."

"I tell you what," I said. "If you find out what day he claims we did it, we'll let you look at our computers for that day."

"What will that prove?" Chestnut asked.

"If we did it, there'd be a date and time on anything sent from our computers."

"We'll have to get back to you on that," Gluckman said, and looked at Chestnut, who shrugged.

"Well if you think of anything, please give us a call," and he handed me his card. So did Chestnut. They started for the door and Chestnut turned to TJ.

"You're a big guy. Play college ball?"

"I played computers."

They left and Clar said, "Good thing you didn't tell him you're a karate killer."

"I could take him with one hand," he boasted.

"He carries a gun," I said.

"I bet I'm faster."

"Let's not find out," Clar retorted. "It looks like they've got Lou, so congratulations. At least one part of our plan worked well."

"Not yet," I cautioned. "They're just investigating. We may never know what happens to him, unless we monitor police reports."

"I can do that," TJ asserted.

"Then keep us posted."

Chapter Twenty-Seven

We were definitely getting tired of running to Grand Central Terminal to make our phone calls, but it seemed too expensive to keep buying throwaway phones. Besides, I liked looking at the women who passed through the terminal. Some of them were hotties. I knew they were way beyond my current economic sphere. Maybe someday. Karen Haskell phoned me several times, but I let it go into voice mail. She repeated how much she wanted to see me. I just got off the phone with Janet and I was feeling real horny, when I got another call from Karen. I let it go into voice mail, but I was tempted to see her. I didn't care about her, I just wanted her body, so I wasn't too concerned that someone might follow me there. I phoned her and she asked me to come right over to her brownstone on East 38th Street, where she lived, as well as had her office. TJ and Clar weren't thrilled when I told them.

"You gotta be kidding," Clar said.

"Don't do that to Janet," TJ added.

"I know you're a dog," Clar said, "but that isn't the issue. If you go alone, you're at risk and maybe we are. If the threat landscape is real, and we've been living as if it were, you can't go off on your own. And we're certainly not going with you."

"What were you thinking?" TJ asked.

I was a bit embarrassed about saying it in front of Clar, but I answered, "I wanted sex. I wouldn't risk Janet, so I figured I would see this woman."

Clar shook her head. "You couldn't wait another week or two?"

"I've been waiting a long time. It's like I was in the desert since I was a teenager and Janet is the oasis. If I had an alternative . . ." and I looked at her for a moment.

She smacked me on the side of the head. "Don't even think about it."

"I can't help it. We're together all the time and you're a beautiful woman."

She looked at me, hands on hips, exasperated. "I don't know whether to punch you out or kiss you."

"Do I have a choice?"

She started to smile, then laugh, then TJ joined in, and a moment later I began to laugh.

"Just keep your thoughts to yourself, okay?"

"Sure."

"Now call that old lady and tell her you won't be coming around."

"Yes, Clar."

Karen responded very maturely when I told her I couldn't see her, curtly saying, "Fuck off, sonny."

We shopped at Todaro's and were just a few blocks from home when Clar got a phone call.

"Dr. Rodriguez?"

"Who is this?"

"My name is Li Po. I got your number from Mr. Rogers, at Parsec."

"What do you want, Mr. Po?"

"Actually my family name is Li. Chinese last names come first."

"I repeat. What do you want, Mr. Li?"

"I'd like to talk to you and your colleagues about a software project."

"One of yours?"

"Actually one that you and your colleagues might make."

"We're not interested in a job."

"I meant a funded project, not a job. Mr. Rogers told me you might be developing a cyber security program. My company is marketing security software all over the world."

"Well thank you for calling, Mr. Li. But I don't think we're interested."

"Don't you even want to discuss it with your colleagues?"

"They trust my judgment."

"At least let me take you to dinner at a restaurant of your choice, so I can tell you a little more about my company."

"Are you from China, Mr. Li?"

"Taiwan."

"Hold on a minute." She covered the phone with her hand and turned to us. "A Mr. Li got my number from Rogers at Parsec. He wants us to do a funded cyber security project. I started to tell him no and he invited us to dinner at a restaurant of our choice, for further discussion. What do you think?"

"It can't hurt to listen," I answered.

"Tell him Michael Jordan's, in Grand Central Terminal," TJ advised. "I know a lot of better restaurants, but this one is in a public space."

She nodded. "Alright, Mr. Li. We'll meet you at Michael Jordan's, in Grand Central Terminal. When would you like . . . tomorrow night at seven?" She looked at us and we nodded yes. "We'll see you tomorrow night then. Goodbye."

We talked about Mr. Li's phone call and invitation to dinner at length that night and the discussion continued the next day. TJ wanted to go, so we could find out more about what Mr. Li knew and wanted from us. Clar was naturally suspicious and commented that Mr. Li might be behind Phil's death. As the biggest paranoid among us, I assumed Mr. Li was probably dangerous and possibly meant us no good. I visualized several different scenarios of assassination attempts in Grand Central Terminal, all ending with a call of, "All aboard". I started imagining all the vantage points where deadly enemies could shoot, stab, poison, or otherwise knock us off, until I had enough of apprehensions.

"If anybody's after us, they were skilled enough to fake Phil's suicide. No matter how many precautions we take, or how careful we try to be, we'll always be vulnerable."

TJ nodded and Clar, albeit reluctantly, agreed.

"I suggest we have dinner with him, find out what he has to say and unless it's too crazy, tell him we'll consider it."

"As long as he's clear we're not making any kind of commitment and we don't tell him what we're working on," Clar said.

"If he's behind Phil's death," TJ explained, "he probably knows what we're working on."

"But he won't reveal that," I replied. "So are we going?"

"Yes," Clar said. "I could enjoy a good steak dinner."

"With a good Bordeaux," TJ added.

I had been getting fond of Grand Central Terminal during our recent visits, admiring the architecture, appreciating the enormous transportation center with the subway system and trains going to so many different places. Except for seeing spies everywhere, I particularly enjoyed the people hurrying somewhere, thousands in transit, some pausing to dine or shop in the huge terminal. Only the homeless had no purpose, other than staying warm and using the bathroom. Unlike many city public spaces, the terminal police encouraged the homeless to move on without abusing them.

Mr. Li was waiting for us at a table on the rail overlooking the main concourse. He stood to greet us and shake hands. He was about 5'6", taller than Clar, but TJ and I towered over him. He had dark hair, a smooth complexion, and almost delicate features, except for a scar at the corner of his mouth that gave him a sardonic look. He was wearing a well-tailored, obviously expensive, blue pin-stripe suit, with a muted red tie. I couldn't help wondering if that was homage to China. He held Clar's chair for her and we sat down.

"A pleasure to meet you," he said smoothly. "I took the liberty of ordering shrimp, crab meat, and oysters for the table, along with a nice California white wine. I thought we could chat after we order our main course."

TJ and Mr. Li got into a discussion about California wines, Clar surreptitiously studied Li, and I looked around for potential assassins. The busboy brought water and bread. A moment later our waiter brought large platters of shrimp, crab, and oysters and we helped ourselves. I offered oysters to Clar and she gave me a scathing look that Li noticed.

"You don't care for oysters, Dr. Rodriguez?"

"No. But my friends do. Please call me Clara."

"Thank you. Please call me Po."

"That's TJ and Pete."

"My pleasure."

The waiter brought the wine and Li signaled that he should let TJ taste it, which he did and approved. We ate for a while, sipped wine, and tried to appear civilized to our host. The food was good and if I could stop thinking about poisoned oysters, or snipers, it would have been enjoyable. The waiter appeared when we finished the appetizers and took our orders, filet mignon for us, salmon for Li.

"I know you must be curious about me and why I wanted to meet you. We can start by my telling you what my company wants, or you can ask questions."

"Please tell us," Clar said.

"We are a cutting edge, Taiwan based company with government contracts, as well as international contracts with other governments and corporations. We specialize in cyber security and we're always looking for new talent to create viable software."

Clar nodded. "Do you deal with China?"

"We only offer commercial, off the shelf software."

"Why are you interested in us?" she asked.

"Mr. Rogers spoke highly of you and sent me your resumes. Very impressive. You're the kind of talent we look for."

"What exactly did he tell you about us?" she persisted.

"That you were doing exemplary work on a firewall project that was cancelled and he assumed you were working on projects of your own."

"Why did he assume that?" she asked.

"You'll have to ask him. Now I'd like to make you an offer, unless you have any questions?" and he looked at TJ and me. We shook our heads no. "We'd like you to do either a firewall project, or develop an invasive program. You can work at our New York City office in the Citi Corp Building, we can help you find a workplace of your choice, or you can work at home. We would hire you as consultants, so there is no benefit package, but we'll give you a twenty-week contract at $5,000.00 a week each. An extension to be discussed in the tenth week, depending on your progress."

Gary Beck

Before we could respond, the main course
arrived, along with two bottles of a very good
Bordeaux. We ate and drank, with each of us
digesting the highly lucrative offer. After we
finished large portions of meat and ordered
dessert, Clar said, "That's a very appealing offer,
Mr. Li. We'll certainly give it a lot of thought and
then get back to you."

"One more item. If, as many young entrepreneurs,
you are seeking capital investment for a project, we
would consider funding your venture."

We declined an after dinner brandy, thanked
him for his hospitality, and got up to leave. He
gave Clar his card, nodded politely to us, and
said, "I look forward to hearing from you."

As we left the terminal, I kept looking
peripherally for lurking spies, but I saw so many I
gave up, disgusted with what I hoped was an
over-active imagination.

Chapter Twenty-Eight

For some reason we didn't discuss Li's offer that night. The next day, when we came home from the dōjō, TJ finally brought it up.

"What can we do about Mr. Li?"

Clar looked at me and I gestured for her to talk.

"It's a lot of money. $50,000 each for ten weeks. Maybe another $50,000 for the next ten. After that, who knows? We won't get a better salary offer."

"That's for sure," TJ said. "We'd have to pay for our health care and taxes. What do you think that would cost?"

"We have about four months left on the Parsec healthcare package, unless they rescind it, so we wouldn't have to pay that for at least the first part of the ten-week contract. As for taxes, we'll have to get an accountant. But we'd have to do that anyway, if our investors come through. We'd probably have to pay between 20 to 25%."

"That much?" TJ wondered.

"Maybe more. Only the one percent get away with lower taxes."

"We'll have to join the one percent," TJ declared.

"You haven't said anything, Pete," Clar prompted. "What do you think?"

"I don't like Li. I think he's probably behind Phil's death. He might have arranged the break-in and bugging of our place. I suspect he's from China and they want our software to use against us."

"I guess you have some reservations about him," TJ quipped, and we laughed.

"You asked. I suggest we put him off very tactfully, until we find out if the investors come through. We can reconsider his offer if they don't fund us."

"That sounds good to me," TJ said.

Clar considered for a moment, then nodded.

"You'll have to call him," I told her.

"Why me?"

"You've been our spokesperson so far. Just tell him his offer was so unexpected that we have to reconsider our plans and decide if that's what we want to do."

"Why don't you talk to him?"

"Because you can do it much nicer that I would. My dislike of him would probably show."

"Alright. I'll call him tomorrow," she agreed begrudgingly.

"Good girl," I said as if to a child, which got me a dirty look.

"You're messing with the wrong girl," she growled and stomped off to her room.

Clar phoned Mr. Li the next morning, told him how pleased and impressed we were with his offer, but we needed some time to reconsider our plans. He was very suave in his response and told her he was very impressed with us. He assured her he'd like our participation with his company and looked forward to a creative, profitable association. She told us he seemed very polite and reasonable and was quite willing to wait to hear from us. TJ suggested she do a follow up call to him in a week or so, to let him know we were actively considering his offer. We were certainly tempted by $100,000 each for twenty weeks, but I guess my misgivings affected my friends.

Later that day, TJ announced loudly, "I've been hacked."

Clar and I immediately checked our old laptops that were connected to the internet and they were running slower, a probable indication that we were being hacked also.

"What do you think, TJ?" Clar asked.

"I'll have to check it out, but it seems to be the same pattern as last time."

"What do you think, Pete?" Clar asked.

"If TJ says it's the same, I go along with him. One thing for sure . . ." my voice trailed off.

Clar asked impatiently, "What?"

"It isn't Phil."

They looked at me for a moment as if I had two heads, then burst into infectious laughter. When the laughs subsided to chuckles, TJ murmured, "He's with the boss hacker now," which triggered more laughter.

I replied, "Down below somewhere," which started us laughing again.

"Seriously guys. What do you think?"

"My money is on Mr. Li," I replied. "I guess he's too impatient to wait for our reply."

"If this is a pattern," TJ said, "the next step will be a B&E, to copy our hard drives."

"Weren't you clever in having us work without an internet connection," I complimented him.

"Thanks, Pete. Obviously from now on we have to take our working laptops with us when we go out."

Clar nodded. "All they can get off the old ones is the material they already have."

"I'll put a telltale on the door again. The real question is what happens if they break in and learn they got nothing new?"

"They'll have to make some kind of deal with us," TJ said.

"Unless they threaten us, or do something more drastic," Clar responded.

"Why would they do that?" TJ asked.

"Clar has a point. Look what they did to Phil," and this time there was no laughter.

"You really think they killed Phil?" TJ whispered.

"Yes," and before I could say anything else, Clar said, "I do too."

"Alright," TJ replied. "Say they did it and they might be a threat to us. What do we do?"

We looked at each other for a moment.

I said, "We'll need protection. Police or FBI."

"What a choice," Clar quipped. Our responding laughs were weak. "I guess the FBI. They're better equipped to deal with this kind of thing."

TJ and I nodded agreement, and she declared, "We call if they break in."

"If this is what I think it is," I said slowly, "then it's not just simple hacking. My guess is Mr. Li has an organization, and if he's from China, as I suspect, this is a lot bigger than we can handle."

"So, as TJ asked, what do we do?"

"We have to go to the FBI."

"Why not the police?" TJ asked.

"Because this isn't just murder, it's espionage. If I'm right, we're going to need protection. I don't think the police can do that."

"I agree," Clar said. "What do we tell them?"

I thought about it for a minute, while the implications of our situation began to sink in and my two best friends looked more and more concerned by the moment.

"We were hacked a month or so ago and someone stole some of our cyber security program. They didn't get all of it and we started using new laptops, unconnected to the internet. After talking to the FBI and the police, we began to be suspicious about Phil's death. Then a few days ago, Mr. Li approached us, and was interested in our cyber security program. He told us Mr. Rogers at Parsec gave him our resumes. He made a very substantial offer to work for his company, and we told him we'd consider it. Then we were hacked again, but they didn't get anything new. The more we thought about it, the more frightened we became and we decided to call the FBI."

"You didn't mention the break-in," Clar pointed out.

"That might raise suspicions about why we didn't report it to the police."

"Good thought," TJ said. "What about the electronic bugs?"

"Same thing. Why didn't we report it?"

They both nodded and Clar said, "Let's go over our story once more, then we'll each say it our own way, so it doesn't sound rehearsed."

"When should we call?" TJ asked.

"Tomorrow afternoon," Clar decided. "After we get back from the dōjō."

Chapter Twenty-Nine

We left the dōjō early and didn't stop to shop, anxious to get home and call the FBI. It started to snow, so we hurried the rest of the way. When we got to our building I noticed a black SUV with tinted windows parked out front. I saw fumes coming from the tail pipe, so I knew the motor was running. I was tempted for a moment to go knock on the window to find out who it was, but I realized it could have been anyone, so I turned to unlock the outside door.

Suddenly, two men in ski-masks and dark clothing burst through the door, knocking me backwards. TJ grabbed one of them, but the other one pulled an automatic pistol, fired a shot in the air, then pointed it at us. TJ released the man he was holding. They jumped into the SUV and sped away. Clar got the first few numbers of their license plate, but they were gone too fast for her to get the rest.

We stood there for a minute, waiting for the surge of adrenalin to subside. I looked around and saw no one showing the least bit of interest in us. Either no one heard the shot, or like contemporary American city dwellers, they scurried off at the sound of gunfire. I complimented TJ on his quick reaction in grabbing the guy, and his smart, quicker response in letting him go when the gun was pointing at us. Then I complimented Clar on trying to get the license number.

"I didn't react fast enough," she mumbled.

"On the contrary," I chided. "If you went into the street they may have come back and shot us."

"It's a good thing we didn't catch them in the apartment," TJ remarked, "or they might have shot us."

I realized how calm we were, despite a dangerous confrontation in which we might have been killed. My admiration for my friends' quick reactions felt good, but I knew the situation was moving past our control.

It was clear what we had to do, when Clar said, "This has gone past hacking."

"I think it's time to call our friendly, local, FBI agents," I announced.

"Let's go in and see what they did," Clar suggested.

"Sure," I replied. "But you're calling right away."

Nothing was missing and, except for my laptop that was turned around, there was no evidence of a break-in. Obviously these guys were pros, and if we hadn't come back early they would have been gone without a trace. Clar called Agent Jamison, who seemed very happy that we needed him. He told her that he and Agent Bellini would be there in thirty minutes. We went over our story one more time and appointed Clar our spokesperson. We sat, reluctant to touch anything on the faint chance that they had left fingerprints. A few minutes later we heard a siren that got louder and louder, then stopped in front of our building a moment later, followed by our outside door bell ringing.

Clar answered sweetly, "Who is it?"

"You know damn well who it is," Agent Bellini growled and Clar buzzed them in.

"I'll bet that's the first time they ever drove fast and used their siren," TJ remarked.

"They should thank us for that," I replied.

"Now boys, behave," Clar said with a twinkle in her eye as she went to answer the door.

Bellini and Jamison stormed in with their pistols drawn, as if the perpetrators were still here, ready to resist arrest.

"Put your toys away, boys," Clar said. "The bad guys are long gone."

Bellini flushed and gave us an angry look. Jamison merely shrugged as they put their guns away.

"Now tell us what happened," Bellini ordered, "and spare us your sass."

We laughed and TJ said, "Don't worry. She's got plenty of sass to spare."

Jamison held up his hand for quiet.

"You called us. If you want to play games, we're leaving."

He turned and went towards the door and TJ started to call him back, but I signaled him to wait. It was obvious these guys were desperate for an important case and weren't going anywhere. When Jamison reached the door, he turned.

"Well?"

I smiled pleasantly. "Sorry. We only have tap water."

TJ and Clar laughed. Bellini turned even redder in the face and looked like he would have a coronary. I hoped we wouldn't have to call EMS. Before he could erupt, Jamison said in a conciliating tone, "Alright. You've had your fun at our expense. Now do you want our help or not?"

"Tell them what happened, Clar," I said softly.

Clar told the story we rehearsed and the not so dazzling duo listened intently, Jamison recording on a hand-held device, Bellini writing in a notebook. When she finished, they looked at each other triumphantly, as if they'd discovered electricity. I couldn't help but compare these two to my former image of bright, fearless, FBI agents dedicated to serving the public.

Bellini asked Jamison, "What do you think, Jamie?"

"I'm considering the implications. What do you think, Bell?"

Bellini took a deep breath and said reverently, "We've got a national security case."

"I agree. What's the next step?"

Bellini looked at Clar.

"What do you think is going on?"

"I think you should lend us your badges and guns and we'll deal with the problem." Before he could respond, she said, "I told you what was going on. It's up to you to investigate Mr. Li and find out if it's a Chinese cyber-attack that's getting violent."

Bellini looked like he would explode. He glared at Clar and I tensed, ready to defend her if he went for her. Jamison put his hand on Bellini's arm, and said placatingly, "We're just trying to get all the information so we can formulate a plan of action. We'd appreciate it if your attitude was more appropriate to this serious situation."

I suppressed a laugh, thinking we might have been better off with the police. In the most reasonable voice I could manage, I said, "We're aware of how serious this is. That's why we called you, instead of Homeland Security. If you'd rather not help us, I'll call them," and I reached for my cellphone.

"Your safety and wellbeing is our primary concern. Then we'll deal with the cyberattack and the criminal incident," Jamison said, oozing sincerity, and Bellini nodded affirmation.

They were so urgent to get the case that I felt I could manipulate them at will. Shades of

Raskolnikov. TJ and Clar, aware of what I was doing, watched me without revealing their amusement.

"The reason we called you," I explained, "is that we think you can see the big picture. We suspect that China is trying to steal our cyber security system and they may be willing to commit murder to get it. Are you prepared to give us protection 24/7?"

Jamison started to speak, but Bellini cut him off.

"We'll have to review this case with the Special Agent in Charge and get approval in order to allocate the necessary resources."

"And how long will that take?" Clar demanded.

"Just a couple of days."

"And what do we do if they come back tomorrow, Agent Bellini?" TJ challenged.

Before he could respond, I said, "We better call Homeland Security. They'll protect us right away."

"No need for that," Bellini said. "I'll leave Agent Jamison here, while I confer with the Agent in Charge."

"Not in the house. He waits in your car, down the street," Clar stated.

"But . . ."

"No buts, Agent Bellini," she said. "Get us coverage by tonight, or we call Homeland Security."

"I'll call you later," and he rushed out the door, followed by Jamison.

Clar went to the window and when she saw them reach their car, she burst out laughing.

"Pete. You are too much. I love the way you threatened them with Homeland Security."

TJ and I laughed, and I replied, "Had to get the boys moving," which made us laugh a little longer.

"Joking aside," Clar said. "That guy might have shot us if TJ didn't let his guy go. We may be in some deep doo-doo."

"Is that Spanish?" I asked with a straight face.

She slapped me playfully. "This is serious. They might come back to kill us."

"They wouldn't do that until they got the rest of our program," TJ reasoned.

"What if you're wrong," she retorted.

"Maybe we should get guns," I suggested.

"Not yet," Clar replied. "Let's consider our options after we hear from Bellini."

We were much too tense to relax and every effort to do some work ended up with us drifting aimlessly around the apartment. When I collided with Clar for the second time, she said, "We've got to settle down and take it easy."

"How about some lunch?" TJ offered.

"I'm not hungry," she replied.

"Neither am I."

"We've got to eat. I'll make a mushroom omelet."

"Put some cheese in it," Clar requested.

"You changed your mind pretty quickly," I remarked.

"TJ tempted me."

That gave us a little bit of a laugh that went a long way to clearing the atmosphere, which was becoming gloomy.

TJ went to the kitchen and began preparations. Clar went to her room and I was just about to try to do some work when I heard what sounded like gunshots. I rushed to the window and saw what looked like the same black SUV in front of our building, with two men wearing ski masks crouched behind it and firing down the street. I looked in the direction they were shooting and saw Jamison firing back. Suddenly he was hit and fell. The men jumped into the SUV and roared off. I called TJ and Clar, then rushed outside.

Jamison got up and was standing in the street, blood dripping down his left arm, pistol still aiming at the disappearing SUV. I dialed 911 and requested an ambulance, gave them the address and my name, then disconnected.

"Are you alright Jamie?"

He gave me a big grin.

"I've been shot in the line of duty."

Clar and TJ came up to us right then, and Clar said, "Don't look too pleased. You might have been killed."

"You don't understand," he said, grinning non-stop. "It's just a flesh wound. It won't keep me off duty. It's the first time I discharged my weapon in the field. Now our superiors will give us whatever we ask for. Thank you. Thank you so much."

"You are one peculiar dude," TJ muttered.

"I can shoot you in the other arm, if it means a commendation," I offered.

His grin was threatening to split his face.

"Do you have any idea how many agents get to discharge their weapons on duty, let alone get shot? ... I've got to call Bell."

The sound of a siren approaching made him end his call.

"Agent Bellini will be here soon with a protection detail that will cover you 24/7."

The ambulance arrived, the EMS guys jumped out, quickly putting Jamison in the back. Just before they closed the doors, he yelled, "See you tomorrow."

Before we could go inside, a siren announced the arrival of a police car. The officer got out and approached us cautiously. I raised my hands slowly and told them the ambulance just left with the wounded agent. They started questioning us, but were interrupted by the arrival of detectives Chestnut and Gluckman, who immediately took charge of the crime scene. They told the uniformed officers to canvas the street and try to locate witnesses.

Chestnut turned to us. "I knew you guys were trouble. Now tell us in your words what happened."

"I don't use anybody else's words," I stated.

Gluckman started to say something nasty, but looked around when a convoy of SUV's, sirens blaring, turned the corner and pulled up in front of us. Bellini jumped out, rushed over, and asked worriedly, "How's Jamie?"

"It's just a flesh wound," I answered. "The ambulance probably took him to Bellevue Hospital."

"Thank god," he murmured. "And you guys are alright?"

"We're fine, thanks to Jamie," Clar said. "He engaged the attackers in the street, before they could get in our building."

"I should have been here with him."

Chestnut and Gluckman had been standing there impatiently and Chestnut demanded, "Just who are you?"

"Special Agent Bellini. FBI," and he flashed his credentials.

"And exactly what are you doing here, Special Agent Bellini?" Chestnut asked sarcastically. "And why are you responding to a police matter?"

Bellini, secure in being involved in a big case, said calmly, "We are here to protect these people and investigate the shooting of an FBI agent."

"This is a New York City Police Department jurisdiction," Gluckman challenged.

"Not any more. This is a national security case," then he said expansively, "Let's discuss this away from the civilians."

The two detectives looked at each other for a moment, then followed Bellini to his SUV.

Chapter Thirty

Instead of watching the official dispute, we went inside, joking inanely to relieve the tension.

"Every Bellini will have his day," TJ murmured.

"Don't be a meanie to old Bellini," Clar chanted, which made us laugh.

I tried to think of something witty, but drew a blank, so as soon as we got into the apartment, I said, "Now that we know they're coming for us, what do we want from the FBI?"

"Who are *they*?" TJ asked.

"It doesn't matter," Clar replied. "It's obvious we need protection. The real question is how will this affect our lives. Can we stay here and work, go to the dōjō, run?"

"What if they want to take us into protective custody?" TJ whispered.

That was something we hadn't considered, but I instinctively knew we wouldn't be happy in confinement somewhere. I thought quickly. "Let's discuss our staying here with Bellini," I suggested, "and find out what he can offer."

"We could have bodyguards," TJ said, "like the Secret Service protects important people."

"We're not important," Clar said.

"Maybe we are to Bellini," I reminded them.

"What if the police take over the case?" TJ asked.

I laughed. "Fat chance. This is national security."

About ten minutes later the outside bell rang, and Clar murmered sweetly, "Who is it?"

"Don't start that again," Bellini growled.

"Come in, Special Agent Bellini," Clar crooned warmly.

Bellini came in, smiled expansively, sat down at the table and we hovered around him. He explained that the police would be assisting the federal investigation in the spirit of cooperation between government agencies. He looked at us as if expecting applause for his diplomatic skills, but went on when we didn't respond. He informed us that Phil's death was now under investigation as a possible homicide. The break in to our apartment was to be considered a possible act of espionage, and the attack on us, thwarted by the bravery of Special Agent Jamison, would be considered a possible assassination attempt. Again he paused and looked at us significantly, but this time we applauded, and Clar asked, "Can we visit him at the hospital?"

Bellini positively beamed at her.

"That's very thoughtful of you, but you can thank him in person tomorrow. His wound was superficial and they're releasing him tonight."

Then he described the plan for the next few days. The FBI would station a car in front of the house in three shifts from 8:00 a.m. to 8:00 p.m. in the daytime and the police would cover 8:00 p.m. to 8:00 a.m. during the night and early morning. He grinned smugly when he mentioned how the police objected to the night shift, but that was the only choice he gave them if they wanted to participate. He informed us that this would only be for three or four days, until they determined the threat index.

"What about our morning run and workouts at the dōjō?" TJ asked.

"You'll have to postpone them for a while."

"We need our exercise, or we'll go mad," Clar declared. "Can't you cover us?"

"I'll see what I can do. When do you run and where's the dōjō?"

He noted the information, then asked, "Anything else?"

"What about Mr. Li?" I said. "He's expecting to hear from us."

"We're going to check him out thoroughly."

"I'm glad," I said patiently, "but we don't want to make a public announcement that we suspect him yet, do we?"

He glared at me, then muttered, "What do you have in mind?"

"Can you cover us if we have dinner with him again?"

"Depending on where, sure."

"Then TJ'll pick a few restaurants and Clar'll call him and arrange a meeting."

"Who's Clar?" he asked.

"Me," Clar said. "Why do I have to call him?"

"Because you're Ms. Nice Guy," I answered.

"Alright," Bellini conceded "You let me know what restaurant you pick. Is there anything else?"

"Yes." I replied. "You should have our apartment checked for listening devices or cameras. They may have done that at the break in."

"Good idea. I'll have a crew here tomorrow morning."

"In the afternoon, after our run and workout," TJ said.

"Sure." he growled.

"One more thing," I added.

"What?" he said in growing exasperation.

"Can I borrow your cell phone for a minute. I need to make a call and my cell might be compromised."

He handed me his phone and I stepped into the bathroom. I called Janet and left a message on her voice mail. "This is Pete. Our situation has changed. There was a break in to our apartment and an attack on us that was prevented by the police. We won't be able to see you and Lakeisha for a while. TJ and I don't want you girls exposed to any danger. I'll call you when things are resolved. If you don't want to see me, I'll understand."

I returned Bellini's phone and he instructed us to stay indoors for the rest of the day, then he left. I told TJ about my call to Janet and he reluctantly approved. I couldn't risk calling Bonnie on Bellini's phone and told them I'd call her from the pay phone at the dōjō.

We talked for several hours about what happened and agreed that Li was most probably behind the break in and attack. We discussed his possible connection with Parsec and decided to save that piece of information if we needed leverage with the FBI. TJ was brooding about Lakeisha and I told him to call her from the dōjō tomorrow, which perked him up a little. By the time I asked him to select a restaurant, he cheerfully suggested a seafood place on Park Avenue South and 17th Street. He explained his choice by describing an upper level that looked down on the main floor, from where it was an ideal place to monitor what was going on below.

"Thank you, TJ," I said. "You've become a first rate secret agent." Then I turned to Clar. "It's time to call Mr. Li."

She dialed his number and made faces at me while she waited.

"Hello, Mr. Li. It's Clara Rodriguez. How are you?"

We huddled next to her so we could hear the conversation.

"I'm well, Dr. Rodriguez. How are you?"

"Fine, thank you. And please call me Clara."

"What can I do for you, Clara?"

"We've been thinking about your generous offer and we'd like to discuss it further with you."

"I'm glad to hear that. May I take you to dinner again?"

"That would be very nice. There's a seafood restaurant on Park Avenue South and 17th Street, if that's acceptable to you."

"Certainly. Are you free tomorrow evening?"

She looked at me and I nodded yes.

"That would be fine."

"Seven o'clock?"

"Yes, Mr. Li."

"Call me Po. I'll see you then," and he disconnected.

"He's a smoothie," I remarked. "You did really well, Clar."

"Thank you, kind sir. I'm working on my secret agent skills."

"It looks like we're going to need them," I whispered.

Clar smiled sweetly. "We seem to have gotten ourselves into a mess."

"We'll figure a way out," TJ said.

"I hope you're right," Clar responded.

I went into the hallway, phoned Bellini and gave him the dinner information for tomorrow night. I mentioned the upper level as an observation point, which he thought was clever. He seemed to be less hostile now that his big case was unfolding, so I reminded him that we wanted coverage for our run and workout in the morning. He begrudgingly agreed to send agents with us, then confirmed that a tech team would come by in the early afternoon and check the apartment for electronic bugging, as well as fitting Dr. Rodriques with a recording device.

"You want to wire her?"

"Of course. We might gain vital information at your meeting."

"What if Mr. Li wants to check her?"

"It's just a tiny device that he'd never find and he didn't check you last time." When I didn't object, he said, "Agents will follow you there and back, and there'll be a presence in the restaurant." He paused for a moment. "Are you guys good at martial arts?"

"We're progressing," I replied cautiously.

"Well just remember that you can't stop bullets with kung fu."

"We do Tae Kwan Do, but I get your point."

"I hope so, Dr. Larkspur. This is becoming a dangerous situation and I don't want you to get hurt."

"Thanks, Agent Bellini. Call me Pete."

"Alright, Pete. Call me Bell."

TJ and Clar were pleased with Bellini's improved attitude towards us and relieved that we'd be able to run and work out. We got out our laptops and started to work on Cybersnarer, feeling a little more comfortable about our circumstances, now that Bellini was on our side.

Chapter Thirty-One

It started to snow and by the time we took a break from working on Cybersnarer it was coming down heavily. The huge flakes danced a swirling vision, obscuring the rest of the world. We stood at the window for a while, watching the wondrous display, reminiscing about the snowfalls upstate at Branville U. We hadn't been in New York City long enough to see the pristine white snow turn dirty, then black, or yellow with urine stains from canine donations.

When the outside bell rang, we could see three figures, but not clearly enough to identify them. One of them was holding some kind of large bag or package. TJ and Clar looked at me questioningly and I shrugged, and buzzed them in. Just as they entered and moved out of our sight from the window, two figures moved in behind them. I rushed to the door, opened it and saw two men with guns behind the three people, who turned, saw them and started screaming. One of the two men was oriental. I started to yank the three in and slam the door, when the men pulled out identification and yelled, "FBI."

The three people turned towards me and it was the girls, Janet, Lakeisha, and Brinn.

I stood there trembling with relief, anger, and surprise and said suavely, "Come in, girls," then I turned to the two agents.

"I guess no one told you that we were threatened by Chinese men." They looked at me blankly. "It would have been considerate to tell us there was an agent of Asian extraction, when we're worried about attackers of Asian extraction."

"What do you have against Asians?" The Asian mumbled resentfully.

"Nothing. As long as they're not shooting at us."

Before it could go further, the other agent, a corn-fed, Midwestern looking product said, "Glad to be of service," and he led the Asian out.

I bit back a nasty comment, closed the door and faced the girls, who were slowly getting over their fright. Lakeisha went to TJ and hugged him. Brinn took the shopping bag from Janet that turned out to be Japanese takeout, and put it on the table. Janet confronted me, then said, "Do you intend to explain what's going on?"

I looked at TJ and Clar for back-up, but TJ was nuzzling Lakeisha, and Clar elaborately turned away and helped Brinn lay out the food. So it was up to me. I quickly reviewed what I could and could not say, and stalled for time by asking, "What are you doing here?"

"We missed you and wanted to see you. Brinn didn't think it was a good idea, but Lakeisha insisted. Now will you tell us why the FBI pulled guns on us?"

"Why don't we eat first," Clar suggested. "then Pete'll tell you everything."

"Alright," Janet said begrudgingly. "But then I want to hear it all."

She took her coat off and I gaped at her delicious body, then put my arms around her, but she pushed me away.

"Don't touch me until you explain,"

She went to the table, which was set up like a buffet. Everyone else was happily eating California rolls, miso soup, sushi, dumplings, and rice. Janet quickly dove in, so I followed suit.

I mentally thanked smart, thoughtful Clar, for giving me time to prepare the story with a tasty diversion.

After we finished eating, TJ made tea and Janet turned to me expectantly.

"Well?"

I told the basic story we told the FBI, filling in some details about the hacking, break-in, and shoot out on the street. When I finished, Janet asked, "Why did you tell me it was someone at work who accused you of stealing his work?"

I gave her my most innocent, sincere look.

"When it started, we didn't think it would go much further, so we made up a story that we told everyone that was supposed to be temporary. Then things got out of hand."

"So you're saying you didn't trust us," Lakeisha accused.

"We didn't know you very well," TJ replied. "But we liked you a lot and we didn't want to expose you to danger."

"That was very sweet of you," she murmured and got up and kissed him.

Janet stood up, hands on hips and looked at me, frowning.

"If you're going to be my boyfriend, you have to be honest with me."

"I'll try. But it's not that simple."

"Why not?"

"Because by coming here you came to the attention of the FBI and possibly the Chinese. This is a national security problem now."

"Why is it about national security?" Brinn interrupted.

"Because we're building a cyber program that identifies cyber attackers," Clar explained. "Apparently the Chinese want it."

"So where does that leave us?" Lakeisha asked.

"We can't see you until this is resolved," TJ said softly.

"I just hope the Chinese aren't watching our building yet," I said. "When you leave, just to be sure you're not followed, take the 3rd Avenue bus to 34th Street, get off and walk to Lexington Avenue, then take the bus to 23rd Street. When you get off, cross 23rd Street, then 3rd Avenue, then come back to the dorm."

"Do you think that's necessary?" Janet asked.

"I hope not, but we want you to be safe."

Janet finally came into my arms, looked intently into my eyes and whispered, "Why do I suspect you're a lying dog? If TJ and Clar didn't love and respect you, I probably wouldn't trust you."

I gave her a wounded look, which she just laughed at, and I said virtuously, "If I were the dog you accuse me of being, I would have rushed to see you, without worrying if you were in danger. I think about you all the time. I want to kiss you, pet you, tell you about Raskolnikov . . ."

"Who?"

"A Russian colleague of mine." She wasn't looking at me with the same antagonism, so I kissed her, and said, "I lust for your body . . . And you call me a dog, when I'm trying to protect you."

"Alright."

"Alright what?"

"You got me. When can we be together?"

"I don't know. We should know more in a week or so. I'll phone you as soon as I can. One more thing."

"What?"

"If anything unusual happens, if you think you're being followed, if older men suddenly approach you, or if Chinese men approach you, go to your dorm immediately and phone me and I'll arrange for your protection."

"Do you think that will happen?"

"No. But I want to be sure. Now it's time for this dog to throw you out."

"How long will you keep throwing that back at me?"

"Until you make up for it with your sweet body."

"Then here's an installment," and she rubbed against me, instantly giving me an erection, which she patted. "See you sometime, little doggie."

She put on her coat and headed for the door followed by a reluctant Lakeisha, who was prodded along by an amused Brinn. Just as the girls were leaving, Clar said, "Wait a minute. Get your coat, TJ. We'll walk out with them and go to the corner, then go the other way. Pete. You watch from the window and see if we're followed."

"Sure, Clar."

I watched them walk towards 3rd Avenue, followed a minute later by the two F.B.I agents. I didn't see anyone else following them, but couldn't help thinking about how many ways there were to surveil someone. TJ and Clar returned about ten minutes later and Clar said they watched until the girls got on the bus and she didn't notice anyone who seemed interested in them. I thanked Clar for her thoughtfulness and she grinned mischievously.

"You're welcome, you dog."

"Not you too," I protested.

"Why not? I knew it years before you preyed on that innocent child."

Before I could respond, TJ said, "I think we should get guns."

The idea appealed to me and I nodded eagerly.

"Have you ever fired a gun?" Clar demanded.

TJ shook his head no, then I did.

"Did you?" TJ asked.

"Once, with my older brother, after I was raped. He wanted me to carry a pistol to protect myself. The more I thought about it, I realized if I had a gun I'd go looking for the animals who raped me. Even if I killed some of them, I could get killed, or I'd end up in jail. It takes a lot of practice to shoot well and you might not be able to pull the trigger when you had to, TJ. Pete might be too quick on the trigger."

"What are you saying?" I protested.

"You know what I mean. You have a volatile temper and might overreact."

"I'm learning to control myself," I muttered.

She smiled her inimitable smile, put her arms around me and kissed me. Then smacked me on the back of the head.

"We're not ready for guns yet."

So it was decided, despite any feeble objections TJ and I might come up with. Then she suggested we go to bed, because tomorrow would be a long day.

Chapter Thirty-Two

Our run in the morning, despite a near freezing temperature and not having run for several days, was exhilarating. Two agents accompanied us, one on foot in front of us. The other one paced us in a car and monitored us with binoculars while we were running. I felt a little better restricting my worrying to sniper attack, or helicopter assault. We may have been happy outdoors, but judging from the agent's sullen face, he would rather not be exerting himself on a cold January morning, and would rather be seated in a heated car, comfortably watching our building. When we got near the house, the agent preceding us, Fred something, asked Clar, "Why do you guys wear those packs when you run?"

"We carry our laptops, so no one can get at them."

"You can leave them in our car when you go out," he offered.

"No thanks. We don't trust anybody."

"But we're the FBI," he protested.

"You least of all, agent boy," which so shocked him that he didn't have time to get angry at her insult before we went into the house.

The agents were far more comfortable accompanying us as we walked to the dōjō on 23rd Street. Fred-something preceded us on foot, his partner again pacing us in the car, while two agents stayed in their car and monitored our building. When we arrived, Fred-something went upstairs with us. His partner stayed in the car parked out front, so he could observe whoever went in or out.

Sensei Omura was teaching a white belt class and glanced at us as we bowed to him. He turned the class over to an assistant, Jin Takahashi, an advanced black belt with incredible skills and the mildest, most polite manner imaginable. We could tell sensei Omura was pleased to see us, and he queried Clar with his eyes about the stranger seated near the door.

"He's an FBI agent, sensei. We are having some security problems with our work and he is guarding us."

"Perhaps you should guard him," he replied with a twinkle in his eye.

"If his being here is a problem, sensei, we won't come back until it's over."

"You, Pete san, and TJ san are always welcome here."

Clar said, "Thank you, sensei," and we bowed respectfully to him.

He cracked a smile. "Try not to have gun battle here. I do not dodge bullets as fast as I used to."

He giggled and walked away, as we stared at him, surprised at his frivolous remark and behavior. We changed, warmed up, went through our different forms, sparred lightly with different partners, then showered and dressed.

I phoned Bonnie and brought her up to date on our progress on Cybersnarer. I told her we were still having some security complications, but they were under control. Then I told her about Mr. Li's offer. She eagerly told me that both groups of investors were seriously interested in funding us and we might have to choose between them. She laughed when I asked if we could have a bidding war. Then she said she might have solid offers as soon as next week. This was exciting

news. I said I'd call her in a few days, signaled TJ
and Clar, and we left.

I told them about the investors interest as we
walked, which really excited them. We stopped on
the way back for TJ to food shop. While we
waited, Fred-something sidled up to Clar and
said, "I watched your karate. Not bad. I trained in
self-defense at the FBI academy."

"What belt do you have?"

"We don't get belts. They teach us to subdue
criminals."

"You better rely on your gun," she teased.

"I can take care of myself," he protested.

"I'm sure you can," she said sweetly.

Before he could reply, TJ came out of the
store and we headed home. When we got there
Bellini and Jamison were waiting for us outside.
We rushed to Jamison, said, "Hi, Jamie," and
hugged him, careful to avoid his injured arm.

"I thought you didn't like the FBI," he said.

"The enemy of my enemy is my friend," TJ
quipped.

"Anybody who gets shot defending us is okay
with me," I replied.

We chatted casually, even including Bellini
without teasing him, now that he was
accomplishing things for us. Fred stared at us a bit
resentfully, wondering why we were so nice to
Jamison and Bellini, while not appreciating him,
but we ignored him. Bellini reminded us that the
tech crew would arrive at 1:00 p.m., sweep for
bugs, wire Clar, and set up cameras to monitor the
hallway and the front of the building. Then he
assured us we would be thoroughly covered for the
dinner with Mr. Li, informing us that he had ten
agents assigned to investigate Mr. Li, and he hoped
to get some information from the tech crew. We
reviewed final details, then he and Jamie went to

their command van parked down the street, from where they'd monitor the meeting at dinner.

The tech crew arrived, two men and a woman, loaded with equipment and immediately went to work. The men swept for bugs, searched for cameras, checked our old laptops, and sulked when we wouldn't let them touch our new laptops. One of them started to insist, but TJ straightened up and looked mean, book subsided. I had to grin at sweet TJ playing tough guy, and he gave me a quick smile when the man turned away.

The woman tech took Clar into the bathroom to fit the device in her bra. I went to the door, knocked politely, and offered Clar my assistance, just in case the woman was a lesbian and made sexual advances. There was a yell of indignation, followed by whispering, then the woman said, "Thanks for volunteering, Dr. Larkspur. I'll fit you for a penis transmitter when I'm finished here."

"I'll look forward to it," I replied.

She laughed wickedly. "I hope you'll appreciate how we lesbians handle men."

"On second thought, I decline," I turned and went back to watch the much safer men techs.

The crew finished an hour or so later and informed us we were bug free, but reminded us the apartment should be swept regularly, as long as there was a possibility of illegal electronic surveillance. They installed a camera in the hallway above our apartment door so we could see anyone there, and a camera outside the building, so we could see anyone approaching. We thanked them for their efforts, and the woman tech winked at me and said, "Next time," and made a violent twisting gesture with her hands. I involuntarily covered my crotch, which made her and Clar laugh.

We tried to work for a while, but had the same problem as earlier, poor concentration due to thinking about the meeting tonight. So we talked about Mr. Li, speculating about how dangerous he really might be. We concluded that if he was from the People's Republic of China, he was very dangerous indeed. We assumed he would be completely ruthless, with enormous resources at his disposal. We reviewed our story for the evening, stressing that we were definitely interested, but required more information before making a commitment, and especially needing to know what was expected of us. Then we tried to relax until it was time to go.

Chapter Thirty-Three

When we left to meet Mr. Li it was freezing cold, overcast, and damp, with sleet expected. The restaurant was warm and inviting after the short but uncomfortable walk. Mr. Li was already there and we were led to his table. Fred-something went to the bar and perched himself so he could watch us. If our circumstances weren't so serious, it would have been comical how obvious he was. Mr. Li greeted us courteously and we bowed back, then sat. The waiter immediately brought large platters of oysters and a shrimp cocktail for Clar.

Mr. Li grinned cheerfully and gestured to the oysters.

"Unless you've changed your mind, Dr. Rodriguez."

"Definitely not. Those things are nasty. And please, call me Clara."

"Thank you, Clara. I've taken the liberty of ordering lobster and swordfish steaks for everyone. If you prefer something else, we can order anything you like."

"Lobster and swordfish are fine," TJ said. "What about the wine?"

"I ordered a California chardonnay for the appetizers," Mr. Li replied. "Please order whatever wine you want for the main course."

"Whatever you pick is fine," TJ responded.

We ate oysters, to Clar's disapproving looks, and when we finished, Mr. Li said, "Perhaps we can begin to discuss your concerns about working for me. By the way, you might tell your FBI friends that they should learn to be more subtle."

I thought quickly. "They were investigating Phil's death, because Parsec had government contracts, and they questioned us."

"Were they suspicious of you?" Li asked.

"I don't think so, but we had a break-in and two men pulled guns. The next day some men shot an FBI agent who was watching our building. I think they're afraid we may be involved somehow."

"Did they discuss it with you?"

"An agent questioned us again. He didn't think we were very cooperative."

"Why not?"

"Because we told him we didn't know anything that might involve us and we wouldn't let him search our laptops."

"I see. Who do they suppose is behind this?"

"They didn't say, but they've been following us everywhere."

"Should we invite the man at the bar to join us?"

"No," Clar said. "He's obnoxious."

"He's just doing his job," Li said pleasantly.

"Then let him follow someone else," she replied.

"Then to business," Li said. "Tell me about your concerns."

"First of all, Mr. Li," Clar began.

"Please call me Po."

"Alright, Po. We went to work for Parsec after carefully checking them out. I searched the internet for your company and there was no information, just a basic website, with a contact email. We don't know what you do and without knowing who we'd be working for, we're reluctant to make a commitment."

"I see . . ... How do you feel about my offer?"

"It was very generous and that's why we're still talking."

"Do you have any other concerns?"

"Yes," I replied. "What do we have to do to earn that money?"

"Simply finish the program you're developing and sell or license it to my company."

"How will you use it?" I asked.

"We'll sell it or license it to corporations and governments."

"What governments?" TJ demanded. "We're Americans and we don't want our software going to anyone who might be hostile to our country."

"I understand, TJ. I'm certain we can work out sales restrictions that you will find satisfactory," Li answered smoothly.

"I hope we're not offending you by voicing our concerns," Clar said.

"Not at all, Clara. I respect your forthrightness. I admire integrity, especially in young people."

Before we could respond, the main course arrived. The waiter and bus boy served large platters of broiled lobster and swordfish, as well as various side dishes. Then another waiter brought two bottles of German Rhine wine, with an unpronounceable name of at least six syllables. We didn't talk much while we ate, and Mr. Li watched in amusement as we devoured the unexpected treat, eating two lobsters each, then a swordfish steak. If food was any indicator of Mr. Li's character, he had one redeeming virtue.

We declined dessert and accepted tea. It was a delicious meal and we were reluctant to rush out in what had become a winter sleet storm, so we asked Mr. Li about his company. He wasn't evasive, but told us nothing that gave us a clear picture of their activity. He said they were a marketing company that identified cutting edge technology, frequently investing in development, then selling on the world market. He avoided any specifics and painted a picture of a benevolent company making money serving its clients. He reminded us that he was very interested in our project and hinted of more money down the road.

Mr. Li didn't press us for a commitment, but asked if we were seriously considering his offer. We assured him that we thought it was very interesting and were definitely giving it major consideration. He suggested that we make a decision within two weeks, if that gave us sufficient time. We assured him that it was ample time, then stood and thanked him for dinner and said goodnight. He offered to drive us home and Clar accepted without consulting TJ or me. Naturally, I immediately visualized a one-way ride to a Chinese freighter that would put out to sea and dump us in the ocean, after we finished our software program.

Fred-something's eyes bulged out of his head as he watched us go out and get in a large Mercedes limousine and drive off in the night. Mr. Li asked us to tell his driver our address, which I thought was a clever ploy to assure us he didn't know where we lived. He made casual conversation during the short ride and warmly said goodnight. We had to smile when he mentioned that our FBI minder might have an uncomfortable walk. I had to admit to myself that Li made a very good impression for someone I assumed was a monster.

About ten minutes later the outside buzzer went off and kept buzzing. We went to the video monitor and saw Fred, soaked and bedraggled, looking upset.

"Who is it?" Clar crooned sweetly."

"You know who it is. Open up."

"Not by the hair of your chinny-chin-chin," I answered, which made us laugh.

"What's that? C'mon. Open up."

"Sorry, Fred. We're going to bed," TJ replied.

"But I need to know what happened in the car."

"Come back in the morning," Clar said.

"I can't. My shift doesn't start until four o'clock tomorrow afternoon."

"Then if we're available we'll talk to you then. Now goodnight. And don't keep buzzing us," Clar ordered.

We watched him walk to the car, disconsolate, without our feeling the least bit of sympathy. TJ made tea, then we talked about Mr. Li for a while. We agreed that he made his offer seem very desirable, but we didn't really learn anything new about his company, or its business activity. We had a Park Avenue address from his business card, but that didn't mean much. Clar suggested that since he gave us two weeks to make a decision, we probably had a week or so without being attacked. TJ said that sounded reasonable, but we had no way of knowing if it was true. So we decided to discuss our situation tomorrow and come up with a plan that would hopefully resolve the situation favorably.

Just before we said goodnight, I said musingly, "In all the spy movies, the villain is always sophisticated and ruthless, but he doesn't take his victims to nice restaurants."

On that amusing thought we went to bed.

Chapter Thirty-Four

A different agent replaced Fred-something in the morning. He kept in front of us during our run to prove how fit he was, but towards the end of the second mile he was faltering and struggling for breath. When we turned back he could barely keep up, and he wasn't happy that we didn't wait for him. By this time, we didn't have much tolerance for the FBI, except Jamison and Bellini, who had shown their concern. Newbie agent sneered at us at the dōjō as we went through our forms, to the displeasure of sensei Omura. Clar noticed his growing annoyance at the rude visitor, went to the agent, stooped in front of him, then did a 360° side kick that ended up an inch in front of his nose, held it for a few moments, then recovered and walked away. He looked after her wide-eyed and observed the rest of the workout politely.

After lunch we talked about Mr. Li, his offer and the danger he represented. I mentioned that we might find out in a week or so if we had investors. So aside from our safety, the investors and the girls were our biggest concerns. When I declared that we had to resolve the situation before we went ahead with the investors, they agreed.

"So the only question," TJ said softly, "is how do we do it? How do we deal with the threat?"

Neither Clar nor I had an answer and I summarized the problem.

"If we want a start-up, we can't leave. If we want to see the girls, they're at risk. If we work for Mr. Li that might buy us some time. One way or another we have to deal with Mr. Li."

"What if we kill him?" Clar murmured.

My eyes lit up at the thought of removing Mr. Li forcibly, but reason prevailed.

"We don't know if he's the only one who knows about our work. It would be fun to off him, but that may not solve the problem."

"Then what do we do?" TJ demanded.

"Let's discuss it again tonight," Clar suggested, "and for the next few days until we find an answer. Now let's work on Cybersnarer for a while."

We discussed Mr. Li that night and for the next two days, without finding a practical solution. We clarified the situation to the point where there weren't many options. If we didn't work for Mr. Li, the start-up and the girls were at high risk. We knew that the shield of protection by the FBI would certainly prevent a mugging, but it would not stop a sophisticated attack. If we went to work for Mr. Li, we might buy some time, but we'd basically be in the same situation and our usefulness would end as soon as we finished Cybersnarer. It was getting frustrating as we realized there was no simple solution to our problem.

For the next two days we kept up our routine of run, dōjō, and work on Cybersnarer. We didn't go out at night and either TJ cooked, or we ordered in. That evening Clar suggested a possibility.

"What if we sell Cybersnarer to Mr. Li, you two leave the girls, and we go back to Branville?"

"And give up our start-up and the plan to become millionaires?" TJ said.

"Do you have a better idea?" Clar asked.

TJ shook his head no, then replied, "I don't like giving up what we've worked so hard for."

"Do you mean Cybersnarer or Lakeisha?" Clar teased.

"We put years into this," he insisted. "Everything we dreamed about is within reach."

"But it could cost us our lives," she said. "What about you, Pete? You're being remarkably quiet."

"I've been thinking about how we could leave New York City and set up the start-up somewhere else, like San Francisco or Miami." They looked at me in surprise, and I continued. "Even if it might work that still leaves certain problems. Would the investors accept our situation? Would we have to tell them why we were relocating? Unless we had a good reason, they wouldn't want to risk potential threats. And the biggest question of all; would Mr. Li be able to find us if we moved?"

"So where does that leave us?" Clar asked.

"We need more time to consider our options," I answered.

"How do we do that?" TJ said.

"Clar calls Mr. Li and tells him we're still interested in his offer, but we haven't discussed our share of the earnings of the program. You explain that we planned to either market it ourselves, or find investors to back us. The only reason we're considering his offer is that we lost our jobs at Parsec and we'll need money soon."

"And?" she prodded.

"You suggest we meet again next week and discuss money. Meanwhile, we'll do a review of Cybersnarer and assess what has to be done to finish it."

"That sounds reasonable," TJ said.

"Let's hope he thinks so," Clar offered.

"Call him," I told her.

Clar stuck out her tongue and I couldn't help thinking how appealing she was. She took out her cell phone and called Mr. Li. TJ and I moved closer to her to listen to the conversation.

"Hello, Mr. Li. This is Clara."

"Always a pleasure to talk to you. And please call me Po."

"Thank you, Po. We've been giving your offer a great deal of thought and it's very interesting. The only thing we haven't discussed is our share or percentage of the sales, or an outright purchase of the program."

"I see. What did you have in mind?"

"We're still talking about that. We'd like to meet with you again and discuss some specifics."

"Are you sure you don't just want to have dinner at my expense?"

"We'll meet at your office, if you like. We can afford our own dinner."

"I was teasing, Clara. Please don't take offense. It's just taking a long time for you and your colleagues to decide about a job offer."

"That's the problem. We're not just looking to be employees. Governments and corporations will pay millions for this program. We created it, so we want to profit from it."

"Then let us have dinner again. When do you suggest?"

She quickly looked at TJ, who mouthed, *The Oyster Bar*, which she told him.

"For someone who detests oysters, you seem to pick places that specialize in them."

"What can I say. I've fallen into bad company."

Li laughed. "I enjoy humor. Shall we say this Saturday, at 7:00 p.m.?"

"Yes. We'll prepare a summary of where the program is at and what remains to be done."

"Good. Until then," and he disconnected.

Clar turned to us. "How did I do, boys?"

"You did great," I enthused. "He's one smooth operator."

"Too smooth for us?" TJ worried.

"He better not be," Clar said fiercely.

"In any event we bought three days," I stated. "That'll give us a little more time to consider our options. Can you prepare the summary, Clar?"

"Maybe TJ should do it and make it as technical as possible."

"Good idea," I said. Then I had a thought. I got up went to the closet and pulled out the RF detector.

"What are you doing?" TJ asked.

"Making sure no one is listening, including the FBI."

While I was sweeping the apartment, Clar asked, "Speaking of the FBI, do we tell them about dinner with Mr. Li?"

"We better tell Bell," TJ replied.

"You call him, TJ," Clar said. "and mention that they shouldn't be so obvious."

I finished checking for bugs and announced we were clean.

"Good," Clar declared. "Then nobody'll know what we're planning to do."

"That includes us at the moment," I added.

"We'll think of something," TJ responded.

Chapter Thirty-Five

Thursday morning it started snowing early, and by the time we left for our run at 8:00 a.m. the snow was sticking to the ground. When we got to the East River Park the snow was coming down so heavily that we could see only fifteen to twenty feet ahead of us. The few runners who were daring enough to run in this weather suddenly popped out of the white screen, startling us, keeping Fred-something on high alert. The snowfall kept getting heavier and we had to move carefully on the way home. When we left for the dōjō, there were at least two inches on the ground and the sky was a dark contrast to the swirling flakes. Fred-something muttered resentfully about going out again in this weather, but we ignored him.

We had an excellent workout, which we appreciated even more because of Fred's sulking by the time we finished and left for home. It was almost a blizzard outside. It was very dark for daytime and visibility was limited to ten or fifteen feet. Traffic had mostly disappeared, and the few delivery trucks that went by drove slowly. We were really enjoying the walk and stopped to throw snowballs at each other. Clar hit Fred with one and he loudly protested. We reached our corner, laughing at Fred, when we heard a car engine roar, followed by gunfire, then screaming.

We rushed to our house, ignoring Fred's orders to wait, and saw three people sprawled on our steps. We ran to them and it was the girls, Janet, Lakeisha and Brinn, slowly sitting up.

"Are you hurt," I yelled, and quickly inspected Janet for injuries.

She had what looked like a flesh wound on her upper arm and I immediately called 911 for an ambulance. I ignored the operators request for my name and said, "Officer down. Send an ambulance," gave her the address and disconnected.

I barely noticed the FBI car roar off in pursuit of another vehicle. TJ was checking Lakeisha's leg, which had a flesh wound that looked like no more than a scratch. Clar was checking Brinn's arm, which she twisted when she fell. The girls were in a state of shock and kept babbling that they didn't really know what happened. Janet said she heard loud noises, suddenly felt something hit her, then pain. She saw Lakeisha fall into Brinn and knock her down. They didn't even know they had been shot, until we got there.

As soon as I realized that the wounds weren't serious, I couldn't help thinking that the three people who were shot going into our building could have been us. I led Janet inside, followed by TJ carrying Lakeisha, and Clar helping Brinn. I quickly cleaned the wound on Janet's arm with peroxide, which made her wince. TJ and Clar helped the other girls. Sirens were getting louder and louder outside, then we heard police, FBI, and EMTs pounding at the door. I told the police and FBI to wait until the EMTs went in, which provoked an outraged howl from the police. The local precinct was only a block away and officers had responded on foot when they heard the call, "officer down."

The EMTs took the girls into Clar's bedroom and I tried to answer the angry questions from the police, particularly why I reported an officer down. My explanation, that we had a shooting incident a few days ago and my first thought was that the bodies in front of the building were FBI agents, was not appreciated. One furious cop yelled, "They're not officers," and the clamor for my blood grew louder. There seemed to be a police debate whether to beat me or arrest me. Fred-something and the other agents were standing around, possibly enjoying my discomfort.

Then I heard a familiar voice shout, "Alright. Let's make some room here. Agents, if you're not doing anything, step into the hall. Officers, please step into the hall."

Some of the cops objected, but Bellini was firm and ushered them out. He turned to me.

"What happened?"

"We were coming back from the dōjō. We heard a loud car, then gunshots. We rushed to the building and found our girlfriends had been shot. I called 911, we brought the girls inside, and a few minutes later this mob arrived."

Bellini held up his hand and took a call, muttering, "Yeah. Yeah. Yeah," then disconnected.

"Our agents pursued a vehicle, but lost it in the snow. Anything else?"

"Could you have Fred pick up the food bags that the girls dropped?" Clar asked.

Bellini grinned, called Fred, and told him to get the food. Clar smiled as he walked out stiff-backed. Just then Detectives Gluckman and Chestnut arrived and got into a jurisdictional debate with Bellini and Jamison, which they took into the hall.

The EMTs came out, assured us there was no need for the hospital, and left. Clar led us into her bedroom, while I tried to figure out whether this was a warning attack or a serious attempt on our lives. I swore to myself that Mr. Li would pay for this.

The girls were starting to get over the trauma of being shot and were looking quite young and frightened. Janet looked at me wide-eyed and whispered, "I guess you weren't kidding when you told us we could be in danger."

I felt a genuine affection stirring for her and resisted the temptation to say, "I told you so." I put my arms around her and held her close.

"You were lucky. It's not serious and your arm'll be fine in a few days."

"I guess this is what we get for trying to surprise you," she said with a smile.

"It's not that I don't like surprises," I replied.

Brinn snapped, "I told them it was a bad idea."

I started laughing and Brinn glared at me.

"I don't think getting shot is funny."

"It's not that," I protested. "It's just that I resisted saying 'I told you so'," which gave everyone a laugh.

Clar had been comforting Brinn, but now she stood up and announced, "I hope you're beginning to understand that this situation is serious. We'll work out a way to get you back to the dorm, but after this, don't surprise us. Don't visit us. Don't phone us. I think even TJ will agree that it's best if you forget us, at least for a while."

He looked at Lakeisha longingly, then reluctantly nodded.

"What if we can't forget you?" Janet asked.

"Then you'll have to wait until this situation is resolved," Clar replied.

"How long do you think that'll be?" Lakeisha quavered.

Clar shrugged. "A week. A month. I wish I knew. What I do know is you could have been killed today. And we're not taking any more chances."

We talked with the girls for a while, avoiding the real issues that concerned us. Then Bellini and Jamison came in. Bellini told us the police were gone, a bit frustrated that they couldn't arrest us, but finally accepting that the event was under federal jurisdiction. I asked Bellini to have the girls taken to their dorm and he ordered Fred to do it. Fred wasn't happy when I told him to make sure they weren't followed. He started to say something, but Bellini cut him off.

"Get going. And make sure you're not followed."

"Yes, sir," he muttered, then stalked out, glaring balefully at me.

Bellini's concern for us and the girls was genuine. When Clar told him about our Saturday dinner date with Mr. Li, he promised thorough and discreet coverage. He added that an additional ten agents would be assigned to the investigation, with particular interest in a People's Republic of China connection. We thanked him and he left, saying he'd stop by tomorrow to discuss the situation and help us prepare for Mr. Li. It was finally quiet and Clar started for her room, then turned back to face us.

"We really have to do something about Mr. Li," she said before pulling the curtain across her door.

Without revealing how he felt, Li Po sat at his desk, simmering with anger at the two men standing before him. He had assigned what he thought was a simple task, fire some warning shots at the three programmers. Instead, these dolts wounded their girlfriends. The spy camera his men had installed in a nearby tree revealed their complete failure to deliver a subtle warning to the right targets. He was tempted to send these two home, but after hard reflection concluded the replacements might not be any better. He wondered why his countrymen made excellent assassins, but lacked the requisite qualities for less violent activities. He sighed, gestured in dismissal, then concluded he'd have to wait until his next meeting with the young Americans to determine his course of action.

Clar was doing whatever Clar did when she was alone in her room. TJ was puttering around in the kitchen preparing dinner. I paced up and down in the tiny living room, too restless to work or sit, occasionally looking out the window as the snow continued to fall. An image of Jack London's "To Build a Fire", flashed through my mind, and I visualized myself huddling in a tiny cave while darkness fell, and the snow built up deeper and deeper in front of the cave, as I desperately tried to light a fire with my last match, the only way to keep from freezing to death.

I shook my head to clear the distracting thoughts and focused on Mr. Li. It didn't matter if *we* were the target or it was the girls. The earlier incidents were belligerent acts, but this was a declaration of war. I thought about the shooting and decided it was probably meant to be a warning and shots went astray because of poor visibility in the snow. Yet I couldn't reject the possibility that it was a murder attempt that didn't succeed because of the snow. I tossed both possibilities back and forth without reaching a conclusion, and decided to discuss it with TJ and Clar later. What had become clear was that one way or another we were at war, and it was time to defend ourselves and punish the enemy.

Chapter Thirty-Six

We didn't go for a run Friday morning, due to the snow accumulation of ten to sixteen inches. It would not have been shoveled yet at the East River Park, where the drifts might be as much as three feet deep. Instead we slept a little later than usual, then went to the dōjō, escorted by sullen Fred and his partner in the car. Sensei Omura noticed Fred's unhappiness and remarked on it to Clar. She told him he was discovering his limitations the hard way, which brought a twinkle to the inscrutable master's eyes.

I phoned Bonnie and told her work was progressing on Cybersnarer, which reassured her that all was well. I didn't tell her about the latest shooting incident with the girls, figuring that might frighten her and possibly lead her to postpone the investors meeting with us. She said both groups were still eagerly interested and she hoped to discuss meeting dates next week. I thanked her for her efforts and disconnected.

TJ phoned Lakeisha and I could tell by watching him that both of them were mooing with happiness. I had the silly thought that if the investors came through we could buy a dairy farm. When he finally finished, the big guy looked ready to bawl and Clar took him aside and consoled him for the enforced separation from his dream girl. I phoned Janet and she insisted her arm was fine, just a scratch that already scabbed over. She added that Brinn was alright, with just a minor sprain, which was a relief. I told her how worried I had been about her, and she said that was sweet of me, then we chatted for a few minutes. I reminded her how serious the situation was and firmly stated no more surprise visits. She assured me that she understood and I told her I'd see her as soon as possible.

On the way home I couldn't help thinking about the peculiar relationships TJ and I had gotten involved in. TJ grew up in foster homes, poor all his life, looked like a monster, but was really a gentle giant, if not riled. Lakeisha was from a well-to-do middle class, urban family and grew up in a nurturing environment. I didn't know if it was puppy love, infatuation, or first love, but they were obviously swept away on an emotional tidal wave.

I came from a broken family that ended up living in a trailer, so I definitely qualified as trailer trash. Janet's parents were doctors, her brothers were all doctors or lawyers, and she was expected to do something meaningful when her dancing days were over. I desired her, more accurately lusted for her body, and certainly cared about her well-being, but I didn't love her.

For the first time I allowed myself to accept that what I felt for Clar was more than brotherly love, which I had always suppressed, since it could be a disruptive problem in our relationship.

Agents Bellini and Jamison were waiting for us at our building and Clar invited them in. On an impulse I invited Fred, but Bellini shook his head no and Fred went to the watch car. Bellini brought us up to date on the investigation of Mr. Li, which was disappointingly brief. The FBI had a file on him, which they had for all prominent foreigners legally residing in the United States. All they knew was that he was an international business man from Taiwan, with offices in New York City, Washington, D.C., San Francisco, London, Berlin,

Moscow, and Dubai. He specialized in computer security software, had extensive government contacts whom he entertained lavishly, and he had enormous resources, including lots of cash.

We considered the information for a moment and I asked with a straight face, "Is he a commie rat?"

Everyone looked at me, then cracked up.

"If you mean, is he an agent of the People's Republic of China?" Jamison said formally, "we don't know."

"But you suspect?" Clar prodded.

Jamison looked at Bellini, who shrugged.

"We have no evidence one way or the other," Jamison replied.

"What do you think, Jamie?" TJ asked.

"It's possible. We're certainly looking into it."

"We'll go into that another time," Bellini answered. "Now let's plan your coverage for the dinner tomorrow night."

The rest of the day passed quietly and we worked until TJ served dinner. Afterwards we talked for a while, then worked on Castle Keep, which we had neglected of late. We ran on Saturday morning, thanks to the Parks Department clearing pathways at the East River Park. We had to be careful because there were slick spots, but we enjoyed it, even if Fred didn't. Only a few of the regular runners had ventured out and I noticed that we checked them out carefully as they approached, with special interest in anyone we hadn't seen before. I remarked to TJ and Clar that Fred didn't seem to be looking around very much.

TJ smiled. "We could try to teach him to point."

Clar made a dismissive gesture. "Let's get him reassigned."

I nodded approvingly. We wouldn't miss Fred.

The workout at the *dōjō* was fun and sensei Omura mentioned that he was pleased we were enjoying ourselves. Then he added casually that we didn't seem to have any problems in the world. I guess we looked at each other ruefully, because he said, "If you ever wish to talk to an old man who cares about you, please let me know."

We were touched by his concern and bowed respectfully. Clar answered for us, "Thank you, sensei. We appreciate your kindness. I hope you know how much we esteem you."

"A nice way to say 'mind your business'." Before we could reply, he added, "You may all test for the next level on Saturday, February 8," and he walked away.

On the way home, Fred kept teasing Clar about why we went to the *dodo*. She suddenly turned, grabbed his arm, and squeezed a pressure point until he yelled, "Stop. I'm sorry." I could tell by the look on her face that she was thinking the same thing I was. If we didn't have bigger things to worry about, we'd kick the annoying jerk's ass.

The same tech crew as the last time was waiting for us, including Ms. Ball-Twister, who seemed surprisingly glad to see me. I didn't know whether or not to worry about her. The crew swept for bugs and pronounced the apartment clean. Miz BT miked Clar and left with the crew without making any threats.

Bellini and Jamison came by an hour before we were to leave and described how we'd be covered on the way to Grand Central Terminal, and once we got there. They apologized for Fred's clumsiness at the last dinner with Mr. Li, and assured us this time there'd be undercover agents who would be difficult for Mr. Li to identify. We appreciated their efforts and didn't mention our lack of confidence in their undercover agents. However, it would be nice if neither we nor Mr. Li could recognize them. Both Bellini and Jamison were much more concerned about us and were aware of our changed attitude towards them.

We left a little early that evening and walked to Grand Central Terminal. The pure white snow had already begun to blacken from urban toxic emissions that also colored the lungs of city dwellers, who mostly didn't seem aware they were being poisoned. It was a cold, clear night and I could see ten or twelve stars. Without pollution or lights, several thousand stars should be visible. I idly wondered when was the last time people saw lots of stars at night in New York City. Probably not much later than the Civil War. The Terminal was still crowded, even though rush hour was over. The people hurrying back and forth reminded me of prairie dogs scurrying through their underground tunnels.

As usual, people were hulking in the arched corners in front of The Oyster Bar, where, in an audio phenomenon, they could whisper in one corner and be heard diagonally across in another corner. I noticed that teens seemed more interested in whispering than their elders. As we turned towards the restaurant, I saw Mr. Li standing there and I nudged TJ and Clar. He bowed to us in greeting and we bowed back.

"The Oyster Bar is closed for renovation," Mr. Li announced. "I took the liberty of reserving a table at Michael Jordan's. I felt it was courteous to tell you in person. If that is not acceptable, we can go somewhere else, or meet another time."

"Michael Jordan's is fine," TJ said.

"Then let us go," Mr. Li said.

We didn't talk on the way there and were seated a few minutes later at a table overlooking the main concourse.

"I took the liberty of ordering appetizers. I'm afraid their choice of oysters is limited, which will disappoint Clara."

The busboy brought water and bread, followed by the waiter with a large platter of oysters, shrimp, and scallops, which we heartily enjoyed. The busboy removed the platters when we finished and the waiter gave us menus. It only took a moment for us to order filet mignon, while Mr. Li ordered fish.

I casually looked around, trying to identify FBI agents. I suspected a few, but wasn't sure. Mr. Li had noticed my survey and remarked quietly, "They are a bit more subtle tonight", and nodded at a touristy looking couple who seemed a little more alert than other diners.

I nodded back and found myself staring at him in a different way. He was still smooth, polished, urbane, but a contained power emanated from him that was definitely not the jovial persona of a genial host. This time he had ordered servings of lobster to accompany our entrees and we ate heartily. I couldn't help thinking that if he was fattening us up for the kill, this was a very nice last meal. After we finished and ordered dessert, Clar told him about our concern of wanting a big payoff for our work. I could swear that nothing changed in his expression, but the atmosphere was less cordial.

"How much did you have in mind?"

Before Clar could reply, I said, "Don't misunderstand, Mr. Li. We're not trying to get you to raise your offer. We've worked on Cybersnarer and Castle Keep for years, with the goal of a start-up making us rich. If there's some way we can do that together, we'll be glad to work with you."

"I see. What amount are you thinking about?"

"We have a preliminary operating budget of twenty million dollars, with the three of us retaining fifty-one percent of the stock."

"This puts a different light on things. Send me your budget and we'll meet again, once I've had a chance to consider it. I must go now. I'll take care of the bill. Enjoy your desserts."

We started to get up, but he gestured us to remain seated and we watched him leave. I was afraid that we had provoked a fire-breathing dragon.

Chapter Thirty-Seven

TJ and Clar had the same misgivings about Mr. Li that I did and we looked at each other for a moment, a glance that was almost a farewell to innocence. The two people I loved most in the world had experienced difficult childhoods, as did I, yet our spirits hadn't been crushed, as happens so often to disadvantaged youths, whose wrecked lives litter our streets, prisons, and asylums. We had escaped that tragic trap, and a chance meeting brought us together in the most improbable way. The protective environment of Branville U. let us discover our abilities and leave behind the horrors of our past. Now we were faced with a frightening adversary and our protectors were questionable. I stared at the undercover couple and saw the woman talking into her lapel, obviously a concealed mike. I mimicked talking into my lapel, and she glared at me. I could only hope that Mr. Li's agents were as clumsy as the FBI.

Dessert had lost its appeal so we left the restaurant, and we didn't feel like phoning the girls. TJ shopped at the food market on the upper level of the Terminal and bought all kinds of goodies. I hoped he wasn't preparing for the last supper. Clar and I scanned the area, looking for assassins and FBI agents. I paid particular attention to the few oriental shoppers, then realized they looked much too middle-class to be assassins. I laughed to myself at what might be a fatal assumption, realizing that Mr. Li wouldn't be restricted to low-life, or oriental agents. He had money and money could buy anything. I leaned over to Clar and whispered, "I've been looking for Chinese guys, but he could use anyone."

She looked startled. "You're right. I was doing the same thing. How do we identify threats that could be from anyone?"

"Let's get home safely and we'll talk about it."

She grinned. "That's assuming we get home safely."

I grinned back, delighted as usual with her indomitable spirit.

"You mean you don't trust the abilities of the FBI? Let's collect the giant gourmet and get out of here."

"What are you two giggling about?" TJ demanded.

"We don't giggle," Clar said with dignity. "We were laughing at how silly you look inspecting each spear of asparagus for imperfections."

"That's gratitude for the delicious meal I'm planning for tomorrow night."

"Let's hope we're still here to enjoy it," she responded.

He got a very solemn expression and said, "I'm as aware as you are of the dangers we face. That doesn't mean I'm not going to enjoy myself as much as I can."

Clar hugged him and sent some of the food packages flying.

"Well said, Baby Brother." She laughed as she helped pick up the bags. "Finish up and we'll go home and discuss your future as the happy chef."

For whatever reason, my recent paranoia subsided as we walked home down Lexington Avenue. I did look around on the way, but not more than before the threat to our lives became real. It was cold enough that most of the people on the street moved along briskly, eager to get to a warm indoors. There had been more homeless in the Terminal than usual, and they would no doubt be evicted and have to survive the cold elsewhere. Some of them wouldn't make it alive until morning. I found it very strange that in the richest city in the world, there was no emergency plan to help the homeless when the temperatures fell below freezing. Perhaps the authorities preferred that the homeless would freeze to death, thus obviating the need to deal with them. I forgot my bleak thoughts when I saw a car go by with the FBI *tourists*. I mimicked talking into my lapel again, but I didn't know if she saw me.

Bellini and Jamison were waiting for us when we got home and we invited them in. They questioned us about the meeting, even though they heard every word live and probably listened to it several times. Jamie asked for our impressions of Mr. Li.

When it was my turn, I said, "At first I thought he was sophisticated and experienced. Tonight he scared me. I saw the real Mr. Li and he wasn't a kindly businessman looking to purchase our talents. I have no doubt that he had Phil killed."

"You may be right," Bellini murmured, "but we have no evidence that would stand up in court."

"Just remember," Clar said sharply, "if you find us dead it may not have been suicide."

"No need to be sarcastic," Jamison said. "We're trying to help you. We're not the secret police. We can't do anything without probable cause or evidence. So far, Mr. Li just comes across as an international business man."

"You didn't see his face when we told him we wanted to make a lot of money," Clar insisted. "I don't scare easily, but that man has me worried."

"Alright," Bellini said heartily. "You'll be safe tonight. I'll advise the police to be extra alert. We'll talk more about this tomorrow. Maybe it's time to consider the witness protection program."

"I hope you can come up with something better than that," Clar replied, as she walked them to the door.

"We're doing our best," Bellini muttered. "Goodnight."

Clar stood by the door and didn't say anything for a moment after they left, then turned to us.

"Any bright ideas, boys?"

"I'm thinking about it," TJ responded.

She looked at me. "Pete?"

"We have to kill Mr. Li."

Clar went to TJ and sat on his lap.

"Little Brother is bloodthirsty," she whispered.

"Yes. He is," TJ agreed. "But I think he's right."

She stared at him. "Baby Brother is bloodthirsty."

"What about you?" I asked.

She grinned wickedly. "I'm not going to let you boys drink alone. How do we do it?"

"That's going to take some thinking," I replied. "We're escorted by the FBI whenever we go out, and the police watch our building at night. The only info we have on Mr. Li is that he has an office in the Citi-Corp building. We don't know if he uses it. We don't know where he lives."

"What else do we know?" TJ asked.

"He has plenty of money and he travels in a Mercedes limousine," Clar answered.

"He may have at least two assassins working for him," I added. "Probably a lot more than that."

"We have to find out everything we can about him, then make a plan," Clar offered.

"I'll do a thorough search," TJ said.

"Good," I stated. "What if that isn't his real name?"

"Let me see what I can come up with."

"How much time do you think we have?" Clar asked.

"That depends on several things," I replied. "How much does he want us, did our demand for big bucks piss him off, and does he have an alternative."

"So what's our next step?" Clar asked.

"You send him the project budget tomorrow, with a nice note. TJ gets us info and I'll figure out how we can come and go without alerting our babysitters."

"What are our chances?" There was a note of apprehension in her voice.

"Us against China? I'm betting on us," I replied confidently.

Chapter Thirty-Eight

We were extra alert during our Sunday morning run, also going to and from the dōjō, without letting our FBI minders sense anything different. Bellini and Jamison stopped by to continue to discuss our meeting with Mr. Li the previous night. They had listened to the recording of the meeting several more times and felt that Mr. Li was not delighted with our request for a lot of money. I idly wondered if one of the requirements to be an FBI agent was to identify the obvious.

We listened politely to their opinions of the situation, then Clar asked, "What did you learn about Mr. Li?"

Jamison shrugged self-consciously. "Not very much yet. We're assembling a list of his business contacts, a team is looking into his background, and we're trying to examine his bank records."

"You do understand," I said without sarcasm, "that he might be planning to eliminate us, and we may have escalated the situation a notch by asking for a lot of money."

"We do understand, Pete," Jamison said reassuringly. "We're working on it. It's not as if we're investigating a petty criminal. This man is a major player. It takes time."

"We know that, Jamie," Clar said. "We're relying on you and Bell to protect us. We'd just like to know more about Mr. Li. It would make it easier to deal with him the next time we meet. If he's who you suspect him to be, there's no way of knowing how patient he'll be with us, if he doesn't get what he wants."

"We know you guys are afraid," Bellini said sympathetically. "I don't blame you. He's a dangerous guy. I'll push everybody to work harder and as soon as we learn anything, we'll pass it on to you. Meanwhile, we'll increase your protective detail."

"Thanks, Bell," Clar responded. "We appreciate your efforts."

The agents left happily, their big case expanding daily. The only possible disruption to their moment in the spotlight would be if we got killed. Then they might be held accountable for the murders of three government witnesses by foreign agents. I wasn't comforted by the assignment of more feds to protect us. Maybe they were great at catching bank robbers, but I suspected it was because most robbers were stupid, not like the real robbers in our society who stole billions, and were never caught and punished. It didn't make me feel any better thinking about the inequalities in America. I didn't know enough about economics to understand why there wasn't enough to go around for everyone, but I grew up poor and I didn't want to live that way. Unlike most people, I actually had a real chance for the good life, if the Chinese Menace didn't prevent it.

I hadn't really thought through the idea of killing Mr. Li. Obviously, if he was out of the picture, we'd be poised to achieve our goal of getting rich. So there was no doubt he had to go. But I had to wonder if we were actually capable of murder. That would require a very serious discussion with TJ and Clar. If we decided we could do it, the real problem was how. We couldn't walk up to him in the Oyster Bar and shoot or stab him. Even if we could kill him that way, we'd be apprehended, tried, convicted, and spend the remainder of lives in the penal system, courtesy of an ungrateful government that didn't appreciate our removal of an enemy of the nation. Just then Clar touched me on the shoulder, startling me.

"What's up, Pete? You were a million miles away."

"I was thinking about Mr. Li."

TJ ambled over. "And what were you thinking?"

"That we have to get him, before he gets us."

Clar smiled grimly. "That sounds like a line from a western movie."

I had to laugh. "We either get out of town by sundown, or we have to fight."

"I've been thinking about it too," TJ said. "Are we capable of murder?"

"If it's him or us? Definitely." I answered. TJ and Clar nodded and I continued. "The real problem, if we decide yes, is how to do it. I can't think of any way to get up close to him with a hand-held weapon."

"That means some sort of remote method," TJ said.

"Without collateral damage," Clar added.

"That sounds like a line from a movie," I quipped.

"Well, we don't want to kill innocent bystanders. This isn't Iraq or Afghanistan."

"It almost seems like that sometimes, with the daily shooting rampages in schools and shopping malls," TJ offered.

"We can't let that happen," she insisted.

"First things first," I said. "Do we kill him?"

"Do we have any other options?" TJ asked.

"I don't think so," Clar declared. "Even if we give him what he wants, he's not going to keep us around to interfere with his plans."

"I agree," TJ said.

"Then are we capable of murder?" I asked.

"When it comes to our preservation," Clar stated, "absolutely."

"Then if you agree, TJ," I said, "you better get started on research for how to commit remote killing."

Clar shook her head with a wry smile. "Did you ever imagine when we first met that we'd end up plotting murder?"

"I never imagined I'd love anybody the way I love you two," I whispered. "I'll do whatever is necessary to keep you alive and well."

TJ and Clar hugged me and a feeling of happiness swept over me, knowing that after an empty childhood I had a family.

I took a deep breath that helped me control the surge of emotion possessing me, then managed in a steady voice, "We have to consider how to commit murder from far away. That means a bomb, fire, some kind of gas, or a deliberate accident."

"You've been thinking about this," Clar stated.

I nodded and turned to TJ. "Can you access the web for your research, then remove every trace of your search? We don't know who may be monitoring our on-line computers, Mr. Li, the FBI, and we don't want to alert everyone, or leave any evidence of what we're planning."

"I'll take care of it," TJ answered confidently. "Do you have any starting point to consider how we'll do it?"

"Not really. If we're going to avoid collateral damage, whatever we do will have to be completely controlled. You'll have to find something that can be contained."

"I'll see what I can find."

"I can always disguise myself as a messenger or UPS person," Clar murmured, "and take him out up close."

"That's the dumbest thing you ever said," I snapped.

"I was only trying to be helpful," she mumbled.

"That's not the way," I retorted harshly. "If you want to help, use your brains, not your macho impulses."

She stared at me, then burst out laughing.

"Is that what you think of me?"

"I've always thought of you as a warrior without a war."

She absolutely glowed. "That's the nicest thing anyone ever said to me."

"I don't know how you got from dumbest to nicest," TJ offered, "but it's time for me to get to work."

"Should TJ be using his own computer here to go on-line?" Clar asked.

"It's not practical to go anywhere else right now to do research," I replied. "If TJ says he can erase all traces of his search, then we should be alright."

"I don't doubt you, TJ," she said. "I just don't want us to end up in prison."

"Don't worry, *chica*," I teased. "We'll all join separate gangs and pretend to hate each other, until we can make peace between the warring factions."

"On that encouraging note I'm going to work. You and Clar can discuss prison life as much as you like."

"That's alright, Baby Brother," she said sweetly. "You'll be sorry when Pete and I are prepared and you become someone's bitch."

He huffed and went to his computer. She winked at me, then went to her room.

Chapter Thirty-Nine

Several hours later TJ was not very encouraging when he reported preliminary results. "The need for contained attack is going to be a big problem. I can't see any way to use fire. Gas is out of the question, unless there's some way to deliver it in a personal size capsule that he'll activate. I haven't the faintest idea how to do that. Even if we could figure out a way, we aren't chemists or biologists, so we couldn't prepare it. Also, we'd leave a trail by acquiring the ingredients. As for a bomb, that could be more controlled as a method, but how and where to use it, and how to only target Mr. Li is beyond me."

"You've just started," Clar said encouragingly. "I'm sure you'll find something practical."

"I'll keep trying, but don't get your hopes up."

"Maybe there's something we should do first," I offered.

"What?" Clar asked.

"Let's consider every way to commit murder. That might suggest how we could do it."

"There are lots of ways to commit murder," TJ said.

"Sure," Clar replied. "But we can eliminate almost all of them immediately."

"We can send him a letter with anthrax," TJ suggested.

"How do you know he opens his own mail?" Clar replied.

"I see what you mean."

"We can get out of here through the basement door without being seen, if we're lucky," I proposed. "That means we can do things outside. It's easier to get out at night, and we can probably do it two or three times before someone notices us. If we can figure out what to do, we'll have the chance to try it. So let's wrack our brains and see what we can come up with."

Before we started a discussion, I suddenly remembered the apartment had been checked the other day for listening devices, but my paranoid mind couldn't reject the possibility that the FBI bugged us. I went to the closet, took out the RF detector that was hidden under a pile of shoes and sneakers, and began to sweep the apartment. TJ and Clar watched me without saying a word, making me conclude that perhaps I wasn't as paranoid as I suspected, or they were getting paranoid. They waited patiently until I finished and pronounced the apartment clean. We recited the many ways to commit murder that we could think of without going to Wikipedia, which we planned to do later.

The methods that we advocated, albeit humorously, may have revealed something about our characters, though I couldn't figure out what. TJ liked a bow and arrow, Clar favored a gun, and I preferred a poison dagger. Clars' choice seemed normal to me, but I couldn't decide whether TJ's choice or mine was stranger. We bantered back and forth until TJ said, "We could use a gun to shoot a poisoned dart."

Which diverted us for a moment from the morbid conversation. The complications of committing a perfect murder, at least perfect enough so we didn't get caught, were becoming more obvious. We decided to resume our search tomorrow and work on our projects, alternating between Cybersnarer and Castle Keep.

Monday morning, I phoned Bonnie from the dōjō, and she told me she arranged meetings with both investor groups for the following Wednesday, at 1:00 p.m. and 3:00 p.m. This was exciting news and she advised me that both groups were ready to go, and we would have to pick one of them, probably within a week after the meeting. TJ and Clar were delighted that our long term dream was about to come true. The only problem was Mr. Li. Even if we had only ten days to paradise, Mr. Li was the serpent, threatening everything. Fred was trying to eavesdrop on our conversation, but Clar glared at him and he turned away.

We went home, had lunch, and just had started to look up murder on Wikipedia, when Clar got a hysterical phone call from Brinn, who told her Janet and Lakeisha were in the emergency room at Beth Israel Hospital after a hit and run accident. Brinn was so agitated that it took a minute for Clar to find out that the girls were alive and the injuries weren't life threatening. TJ and I realized something bad happened, so when Clar told us, we grabbed our coats and rushed to the hospital.

Fred ran after us, but we easily outdistanced him in the short run of only five or six blocks. We hurried to the reception desk for the emergency room, alarming the startled nurse by demanding to know where the girls were. The security guard approached us, just as Fred arrived. Clar quickly explained what happened. Fred showed his credentials and the nurse led us inside. Brinn was sitting nervously in a chair and jumped up when she saw us, hugged us one at a time, crying, babbling almost incoherently, until Clar calmed her. I went to Janet's cubicle and TJ went to Lakeisha's. Janet looked ashen and was obviously in pain. I started to get upset and was about to call for a doctor, when she motioned me closer.

"I saw the doctor. He thinks I may have a broken hip bone and I'm waiting to go to x-ray. He checked me for concussion and thinks there's no problem and he's pretty sure there are no internal injuries. It hurts, but I can deal with it."

"How did it happen?"

"You'll have to ask Brinn. All I know is we were crossing 23rd Street when something hit me and I went flying. I could see what was going on around me, but it didn't seem to register . . . Am I making any sense?"

"Yes. Especially considering what happened."

I leaned over and gently kissed her on the forehead.

"That was sweet," she murmured. "Maybe you're not the dog I thought you were."

Before I could respond, an orderly pushed the curtain open and announced he was taking her to x-ray. He looked more suitable to be a grave robber bringing bodies to a mad scientist. I could only hope x-ray was their actual destination. A nurse came in and they carefully moved Janet onto a gurney. She moaned a little as they put her down, then bravely winked as the grave robber rolled her away, I know not where. I went to Lakeisha's cubicle, where TJ was crooning in her ear and she had one arm holding him tightly.

"She just has some bumps and bruises," TJ explained, "and she didn't see anything. Find out what you can from Brinn."

"Sure." I leaned over and kissed her on the forehead. "Take it easy, Keish."

I went to a waiting area where Clar was talking to Brinn, while pushing Fred away if he got too close.

"You've got to hear this, Pete," Clar said. "Tell him, Brinn."

She managed to stop crying. "We were crossing 23rd Street and this big, black SUV came out of nowhere and swerved towards us. I was the only one who saw it and I shoved the girls out of the way, but it hit Janet and knocked her into Keish. I tried. I did."

I reached out and hugged her, which surprised Clar.

"You did good, girl. If you didn't react they might have been killed. Well done."

She held me like a little girl. "You think so?"

"Definitely. What else did you see?"

"The car turned on 3rd Avenue and went downtown. The windows were tinted, so I couldn't see anyone inside. It happened so fast I didn't get the license plate."

"You saved the girls. That's the important thing."

"I guess someone called 911, because an ambulance came. They brought us here and I called Clar."

Clar hugged her and told her she did well. Fred had been trying to get close and Clar turned to him. "You heard what happened. Start playing boy agent and see if you can find that car."

He flushed at the insult, but pulled out his phone and headed for the outside waiting room, where he could talk freely.

Clar took me aside. "What do you think?"

"That was no accident."

Playing defense attorney, she said, "There are hundreds of SUV's in New York City with tinted windows. There is no evidence to indicate this vehicle was sent by Mr. Li."

I could tell she was as angry as I was and trying to provoke me, so we could both vent. I controlled myself and just said, "I don't believe in coincidence, and *you* mentioned Mr. Li."

She put her arms around me and looked up at me solemnly.

"It really is war."

I held her close sensing her fear, but knowing she'd never give in to it.

"Yes. Whether we like it or not."

"What do we do now?"

"You take Brinn to her dorm, then go home. Be careful, and I don't just mean of the icy streets. I'll stay until Janet comes back from x-ray. Once I know what's happening with her, I'll get TJ, if I can pry him away from Lakeisha, and we'll come home."

"This was more than a warning. They could have been killed."

"I know. We'll have to figure out if there's anyone else they can threaten. Maybe it's time to talk to your brothers."

"I don't want to involve them in this."

"I think it's a good idea to warn them to keep an eye on your parents, just in case."

"Do you really think Li would go after my family?"

"We don't want to find out the hard way."

"They're going to want to help me."

"Tell them the FBI is protecting us and you'll let them know if they can do anything. For the time being tell them to escort your parents everywhere and be alert."

"They're going to want to know who's threatening us."

"Say we don't know, but it's probably some big corporation that wants our software, and the FBI thinks they can find them"

"They're going to give me a hard time."

"You're tougher than they are. Tell them what to do."

"You really think I'm tougher than they are?"

231

"Absolutely. You're the bravest woman I've ever met."

"I know how you feel about me . . ."

I didn't know how to respond and just stared at her.

"I've known for a long time. At first it was the way you looked at me when you thought I wasn't looking. Then I could sense your feelings . . ."

"This isn't the time or place to talk about this."

"I just wanted you to know. I'll get Brinn now and see you later."

I watched her say goodbye to Lakeisha and TJ, then help Brinn on with her coat and lead her out. I felt a little foolish thinking about how hard I tried to conceal my true feelings for her from myself, and she saw right through me. It didn't seem to bother her. That was a relief. I could only hope her knowing wouldn't affect us in a bad way. I sat down, prepared for what would probably be a long wait for Janet, if they brought her back. I idly wondered if life was this complex for Raskolnikov.

Chapter Forty

After several hours I dozed off and TJ woke me when they brought Janet back to her cubicle. The Emergency Room was remarkably quiet, except for a Hispanic woman sobbing over someone I assumed was her daughter. I had never been in an E.R. before and I guess I expected organized chaos, with blood, screams, and personnel rushing like wild to save lives. This was better. I went into Janet's cubicle and she looked tense with pain. I didn't know what to do, unaccustomed to being a consoler, and took her hand.

"How do you feel?"

"Everything hurts. I waited on the gurney for two hours until the x-ray technician showed up. They weren't the greatest body movers. The hospital gown is so short that they kept looking at my legs."

"I don't blame them. They're pretty good legs."

"Don't make me laugh. It hurts."

Just then the doctor came in, a young, tired-looking Indian man, carrying x-rays. He put them in a viewer, studied them, nodded approvingly, then shooed me out and pulled the curtain closed. I stood right outside and listened as he examined her.

"You are a very lucky girl. There are no bones broken. You have extensive bruising and your gluteus maximus is going to be sore for a week or more. We'll keep you here overnight, just to be sure there are no complications, but you'll probably need a wheelchair for a while. I'll stop by later and see how you are feeling."

He opened the curtain, ignored me, and went to the still sobbing Hispanic woman. I went in, sat down next to the bed, and took her hand.

"I heard what the doctor said. You are lucky."

"I don't feel lucky."

"You could have been killed, paralyzed, or injured so badly you'd be in bed for months."

"I guess you're right."

I concealed my relief at learning she had no serious injuries. "May I see your gluteus maximus? For purely scientific purposes, of course."

"It's a good thing I know you care." Her smiled faded as she looked at me. "I guess you were right about us being in danger. That wasn't an accident, was it?"

"No. I'm sorry I got you into this."

"It's my fault for coming to see you so they . . . Who are they?"

I leaned close and whispered, "We think they're Chinese agents. Don't tell Lakeisha or Brinn. They're not as mature as you and might tell others."

"Why shouldn't they?"

"Because we have no proof and it might provoke a drastic response."

"Oh. I see."

"I want you to go home and stay with your family for a while. I'll ask Lakeisha and Brinn to do that also."

"Why can't we stay in the dorm?"

"Security is poor and you wouldn't stay in your room."

"I don't want to put my family at risk."

"I know. We'll resolve this before it can involve your family."

"How?"

"I can't go into that, but believe me, you'll be safer with them."

"Alright. I'll call them and have one of my brothers take me home in the morning."

"Good."

She phoned her family and told her mother what happened and her father got on the phone and said they'd pick her up in the morning. She reassured them that it wasn't serious, she was just sore all over and she'd see them in the morning. She fell asleep with the phone in her hand and I gently took it and placed it on the nightstand.

I went to Lakeisha's cubicle, took TJ aside, and told him to convince Lakeisha to go home for a week or so. Then I phoned Clar and asked her to do the same with Brinn. I went back and sat next to Janet. Watching her battered body fueled the anger that had been building since I learned her injuries weren't serious, but could have been fatal. As the realization grew that we would have to deal with Mr. Li very soon, I repeated to myself, over and over, *Calm, Calm,* until I dozed off.

The doctor woke me when he came in a few hours later to check Janet. She was groggy from the pain pills they gave her earlier. A nurse came in and took her blood pressure and pulse, while the doctor studied her chart. When the nurse finished she entered the data and left. The doctor checked her vision, palpated her stomach area testing for organ tenderness, then said she could go home in the morning. She mumbled something, blew a kiss at me, and instantly fell asleep. I stood up, stretched, walked back and forth around the cubicle to awaken my body, which had become stiff sleeping in the chair. I was just starting to sort through my feelings for Janet, when the nurse told me two policemen were waiting for me in the outer waiting room. I asked TJ to keep an eye on her, in case some pervert, hospital worker wanted to fondle her body parts, and went to see what they wanted. It turned out to be my not desirable acquaintances, Detectives Chestnut and Gluckman.

"What can I do for you, gentlemen?"

"Why didn't you report the accident, or call us?" Gluckman demanded.

"I didn't know I was supposed to."

"Every accident has to be reported," he said aggressively. "Haven't you ever had one before?"

"No. My girlfriend and her friends were involved in a hit and run. One of them called me and I rushed to the hospital. It didn't occur to me to report it."

"It's funny how things keep happening to your friends," Gluckman smirked.

"It's not funny at all. And I don't like your attitude."

I felt the anger boiling up inside of me, but before it could erupt, Chestnut said soothingly, "Detective Gluckman is just concerned you may be into something over your head."

"He has a funny way of showing it."

"Why don't you tell us what happened."

"Brinn phoned me—"

"Who's Brinn?"

"Janet and Lakeisha's roommate."

"What's her last name?"

"I don't know. Shall I continue?" Chestnut nodded yes. "She told me a black SUV hit them while they were crossing 23rd Street at 3rd Avenue. The SUV turned downtown on 3rd Avenue and kept going. The windows were tinted so she couldn't see anyone and she didn't get a license plate number. That's all I know."

"Are they the same girls who were shot at from a black SUV with tinted windows in front of your building?"

"Yes."

"Do you think it's a coincidence?"

"How would I know?"

"You're not being very cooperative," Gluckman growled.

"I can't tell you what I don't know."

"We'll want to question the girls," Gluckman declared.

"You'll have to wait until they wake up and the doctor clears them to talk."

"We'll come back in the morning," Chestnut said.

"You better make it early afternoon. That'll give them time to recover."

They left without saying goodbye, as I wondered if I just committed a crime by misleading the police. I grinned when I realized I couldn't care less. I went back to Janet's cubicle and sat holding her hand. A few minutes later the nurse told me two FBI agents were waiting to talk to me in the outside waiting room.

"You seem to be real popular with law enforcement. What did you do?"

I leaned forward confidentially and whispered, "I'm a suspect in a series of brutal murders of nurses."

Her eyes grew wide for a moment and she moved back a few feet as I got up, gave her the serial killer's arctic smile and went out to see what my F.B.I pals wanted.

I wasn't surprised at how sympathetic Bellini and Jameson were. Our relationship had become personal since Jamison got shot and we had shown our genuine concern.

"How are the girls?" Jamison asked.

"Battered, bruised, scared. Except for that, not too bad."

They both grinned wryly, knowing how TJ and I felt about them.

"Tell us what happened." Bellini said.

"The girls were crossing 23rd Street, at 3rd Avenue, when a black SUV with tinted windows, going east on 23rd Street, swerved at them. Brinn pushed Janet and Lakeisha out of the way, but the SUV grazed Janet, knocking her into Lakeisha. The SUV turned south on 3rd Avenue and sped away."

"Did they get a license plate number?" Jamison asked.

"No. It happened too fast. They were lucky they didn't get seriously hurt. Our friend Mr. Li has struck again."

"We have no evidence of that," Jamison stated.

I shook my head pityingly. "The FBI should be smart enough not to believe in coincidence."

They didn't get angry, an indication of how far we had come together.

"We started a search for black SUV's," Bellini admitted, "but there are thousands of them in the Greater New York area. We'll have to provide protection for the girls."

"I explained the situation to them and they know they're in danger, so they're going home to stay with their families for a while. Hopefully you can resolve this before Mr. Li makes house calls."

"We'll do our best, Pete," Bellini assured me. "Is there anything else you can tell us?"

"Detectives Chestnut and Gluckman were here a while ago. I didn't tell them anything."

"Good." Bellini said, "They're even clumsier than Fred," and we laughed.

"I'll post an agent in the waiting room until the girls leave. Jamie and I will stop by your apartment later to discuss the situation."

"Thanks, Bell. Jamie."

I watched them walk out and couldn't help shaking my head at the present turn of events. They were a lot more involved than I thought possible, but I wondered if they were a match for Mr. Li. I went back to Janet's cubicle to sit with her until morning when her parents would take her home, wherever that was.

Chapter Forty-One

Janet's parents weren't very pleased to meet me, as if I was responsible for what happened to their daughter. They had no idea how right they were. I knew Janet hadn't told them anything about the terrible situation that we had involved her in. But parent love is fierce and I was the only one they could blame their distress on. I was shunted aside as the worried parents took her away in a wheelchair. She waved goodbye and I wondered if I'd see her again. Then I went to Lakeisha's cubicle to see how things were progressing there.

Lakeisha's parents were in the process of taking her away from TJ, who stood there helplessly as his beloved was whisked off. I asked how the meeting went.

"They were almost hostile, until Keisha told them I was a doctor. Then they were polite at least. They kept looking at me as if I was Frankenstein's monster."

"I always thought you looked more like Bigfoot."

He stared at me for a moment as if I was an alien, then burst into laughter that was infectious, and I laughed with him. The tensions we were feeling about the girls eased a bit and he hugged me.

"Thanks, Pete."

"Any time, my main man."

Someone tapped me on the shoulder and I turned. It was the nurse I told I was a serial killer.

"Will you and your girlfriend please do your thing outside. This is an emergency room, not a make-out place."

We were relaxed enough that we didn't get annoyed at her.

"You sound jealous, little girl," TJ whispered. "Would you like to join us?" and he held out his very large hands invitingly.

She grinned. "I don't know which one of you is worse. Get out of here."

We went to the waiting room where an FBI agent was still waiting.

"The girls are gone," I told him. "You don't have to wait here anymore."

"Agent Bellini ordered me to stay with you and escort you wherever you went."

I looked at TJ, who shrugged.

"Alright," I said. "Just don't stick too close. We don't want to make it obvious that you're protecting us. Come along."

We went outside and I phoned Clar. She told me Brinn would be going home with Lakeisha and she'd stay with her until they left, then meet us at home. I told TJ and he seemed relieved that they'd be out of immediate danger soon. I didn't distress him by speculating why Brinn was going home with Lakeisha and her succulent body. Maybe they were just friends. TJ wanted to go to their dorm, but I persuaded him that he already said goodbye and he wouldn't have a moment alone with her. He really had a severe case of love-itis. The agent kept trying to hear what we were saying, so we moved faster. He sped up and we went even faster, until we were speed walking. I was tempted to run, but relented when I remembered he was there to protect us. If our recent experiences were any indication, he was definitely at risk being near us.

When we got home we just hulked around, with no inclination to do any work. I didn't know what TJ was thinking, but I was trying to make sense of what happened to the girls. Clar was a bit annoyed with us when she came home and found us sitting idly.

"Why are you two moping around like a pair of wusses? We have things to do."

"I wasn't moping," I protested. "I've been thinking about the hit and run. TJ's moping."

TJ stood up to his full imposing height and said with wounded dignity, "I'm feeling the pangs of separation from my love. Something you hard-asses aren't familiar with."

Clar glanced at me for a moment and I saw a glimpse of her feelings for me for the first time. A thrill of elation coursed through me, but I forced myself to remain calm and said, "Mr. Li knows who the girls are, where they go to school, and how we feel about them. This is a blunt message. He targeted them to get at us. They could have been killed, or at least seriously injured. It's obvious that he's not ready to remove us yet, but he'll ruthlessly pressure us any way he can. TJ and I don't have any family, but your family could be next on the list."

"I love my family and don't want anything bad to happen to them. My brothers are tough, but they're not in Mr. Li's league. What do we do?"

"We'll get Bell and Jamie to assign a protective detail for them," I replied.

"We have to do something about Mr. Li soon," TJ said. "Before he surprises us with something else."

"You're right," I answered. "He might target one of us next."

"Why would he do that?" Clar asked. "He doesn't know what we do individually for our projects."

"Don't be so sure," I rejoined. "We don't know what he's capable of finding out. Maybe he wouldn't kill us, but what if he kidnapped one of us? I'd do anything he demanded to get you back."

I said this looking at Clar and something passed between us, a recognition of how we felt about each other and a feeling of urgency surged through me.

"If we're going to kill Mr. Li, we have to do it soon," I declared, "Are we agreed?"

TJ and Clar nodded yes. I quickly thought about our options.

"We have to find a way to do it in the next few days or so, or seriously consider going into the witness protection program."

"Then I'd never see Keisha again," TJ murmured. "Let's each of us think about how to do it for a while, then sit down and see what we come up with."

"There must be a web site that has all the types of murders that people have committed, or thought of," Clar said.

"Sure," TJ replied. "You can bet that the FBI and all the other security services know it. If we used something we found there, someone might check it out."

"So you're telling us we not only have to commit the perfect murder," I took a dramatic pose and said in a mock-solemn voice, "but it has to be a new and original method."

They both smiled at my tone and relaxed a little. TJ replied in a playful voice.

"Do you think I'm setting the bar too high for us?"

"Not at all. We've always had lofty expectations," Clar joked. "Who knows. If we pull this off and get away clean, it might open a new career track for us, innovative hits for hire."

"I'm in, as long as I don't have to wear a tuxedo," I quipped.

"I guess I'd have to join my elders, but for now let's start by brainstorming," TJ said.

Clar went to her room, TJ ambled into the kitchen, and I slowly walked up and down our tiny living room area. I hadn't hated anyone since I was young, when my father would come home drunk and beat me. Now a combination of hate and rage was growing in me, not just for what Mr. Li did to the girls, but for the threat to the friends I loved. I found it very hard to think clearly about practical murder methods. Instead, images of my strangling him to death with my bare hands filled my mind so I could almost feel his neck in my grasp, smell his fear . . . I forced myself to stop thinking that way and tried to concentrate on the daunting task that confronted us.

I actually managed to focus on the specific problem of "How to", considering various ways to kill him in his office. After rejecting bombs and poison gas, I succumbed to a fantasy of throwing open his door and shooting everyone with an Uzi. I couldn't seem to come up with anything practical and my last thought was of Clar, wearing a UPS suit, delivering a deadly package. I gave up in disgust and went to my computer to try to do something constructive, before I sat down with TJ and Clar to hopefully find a solution to our troubles.

Chapter Forty-Two

Mr. Li sat back in his comfortable, black leather reclining chair and stared inscrutably at his two agents, who had failed to carry out properly any previous assignments. They tried to stand at attention stoically, but kept shifting nervously under his harsh gaze. He smiled to himself at the thought that if he had a blood pressure monitor, their numbers would be going up like the latest Chinese rocket. He leaned forward before they went into cardiac arrest and said softly, "You did well. It is a difficult task to only slightly injure someone with a high speed automobile. You carried out your instructions perfectly."

They both bowed low and murmured, "Thank you, sir."

"I am pleased with your efforts. Here is a card that will give you admission to a club in Chinatown. They will provide you with whatever you desire."

They bowed even lower and their thank-yous were much more cheerful.

"Do whatever you wish there, except kill anyone. Report back here at 9:00 a.m. Go."

He watched them almost *kowtow*, then scurry out, and made a note in his PDA to have someone pick them up at 7:00 a.m. and get them ready to function.

I wasn't surprised that separately we didn't come up with how to commit the perfect murder. One way or the other we had been thinking about it for weeks. We sat down without the usual joking that preceded a work session and quickly eliminated almost every possibility, except for an odorless, colorless, tasteless gas or poison that could be administered at our next dinner with Mr. Li. I was just starting to describe how TJ would divert his attention for a moment and Clar would deliver the dose, when the doorbell rang.

It was Bellini and Jamison, our favorite FBI agents. I couldn't help saying aloud that their names sounded like a seedy law firm with silly singing commercials on TV, promising to win millions for their injured clients, which made us a laugh. We managed to control ourselves and Clar let them in.

They greeted us warmly and TJ offered tea, juice, or sparkling water. He explained that we didn't drink hard liquor, but said he could open a bottle of wine, which they declined, as well as the other drinks. TJ then suggested he make lunch for them, which they also refused.

"TJ is a gourmet chef," I interjected. "You don't know what you're missing."

"How about he invites us to dinner, once this situation is resolved," Jamison said.

"Gladly," TJ replied. "I'll make something nice. French."

"Let's talk about food another time," Clar said. "Our friends are here in an official capacity."

"We just wanted to tell you how sorry we are for what happened to your friends," Jamison said.

"First they got you," I stated, "then our girlfriends. We've got to do something before they kill us."

"We're working on it," Bellini responded. "You know, when we first met we thought you were smart-ass kids who thought you were better than everyone else. That changed as we got to know you. We were touched by how much you cared when Jamie got shot. We're going to end this threat to you. It'll take a little time, but we want you to trust us. We'll get you out of this."

"Thank you, Bell," Clar said. "That was good to hear. Up to now we've been pretty scared, but it's gotten to the point that we're fearful for our lives. Whatever you're going to do, do it soon."

"If Mr. Li kills us," I said, "we'll tell everyone where we go that it was your fault."

We all laughed, then Bellini said, "We've increased your protective detail and we'll talk to you in a few days. Call us anytime you need us."

We murmured thanks and Clar escorted them to the door. However well they were treating us now, I definitely didn't trust them. The only people in the world that I trusted were right here, TJ and Clar. But I could rely on the FBI, the same way I relied on the tap water to keep flowing and the radiator to keep heating. I guess I should have pushed them to find out what they were planning, but I was too tired to think straight and just told TJ and Clar I was going to bed.

I slept like the comatose, except for a troubling dream. I was running on a beach in the fog, with my friends behind me. The ocean was on one side and a steep cliff on the other. The tide was coming in and the beach narrowed as the fog got thicker. I could hear the water rising behind us and ran faster. Big waves came closer and closer and just as a great breaker crashed over us, I woke up in a cold sweat, shivering. I was breathing hard and my heartbeat was racing. It took a few minutes to calm down to a tense normal.

I went to the bathroom without waking TJ, who was snoring loud enough for a marching band. I showered, dressed, made tea, and by the time Clar joined me I was almost ready for the day.

Clar hadn't slept well. Her eyes were bloodshot and her face was drawn taut. I handed her a cup of tea. She sat down next to me, took my hand, and said, "I don't know which of us looks worse."

A pang of sadness went through me that such a beautiful spirit had been worn down by the terrible events of the last few weeks. A surge of anger possessed me, aimed at Mr. Li for endangering us. But an inner voice told me that we may have started everything ourselves by our attack on Parsec. I felt my stomach heave and for a moment I thought I was going to throw up. I regulated my breathing and slowly my insides came under control. Clar stared at me as if she knew what had been happening to me and she squeezed my hand, reminding me I wasn't alone.

"I'm not up to running this morning," she said. "Unless you need me for something, I'm going back to bed."

I held her hand for a long moment and she stood up, kissed me lovingly on the forehead, then went to her room. I felt some consolation that my feelings for her were out in the open and she felt the same way towards me, so if Mr. Li killed us at least she'd know I loved her. I laughed to myself thinking how I had been identifying with Raskolnikov as I read *Crime and Punishment*. But there was no *gulag* with redemption in my future. I brooded about whether I should discuss with TJ and Clar what I now admitted was our fault for triggering a retaliation against us by attacking Parsec. Then I thought how tired and distressed they were and decided to wait until the situation was resolved. The more I thought about wanting retribution against Mr. Li, I began to accept that it was happening to us.

I worked on Castle Keep until TJ and Clar woke up, then we had a light lunch, followed by an internet search for poison or gas. After a guided tour that would have warmed the cold hearts of the Borgias, it became clear that the only substance that was not only odorless and tasteless, but relatively quick-acting, was botulism. It was painfully obvious that it was beyond our resources to obtain any, so there was no point in further consideration of a delivery method. We had run out of bright ideas for any kind of subtle murder. Since we didn't have a gun, the only remaining method seemed to be stabbing him.

"Maybe he'll drop dead of a heart attack," TJ quipped, "and save us a lot of trouble."

"He could get a blood clot on the brain and go into a coma," Clar offered.

"He could get hit by a car," I said, but this was too close to what happened to be funny.

"Could you stab him?" TJ asked me.

"If I was defending us. If I had to go up to him and do it, I don't know."

He turned to Clar, "What about you?"

"If there was no other way, maybe. But I'm not sure."

"I thought all you Hispanic chicks used a knife," I said with a frown.

"Only the well-bred ones, who use it to cut their food," she retorted.

TJ said, "Let's go over your preparation for the investors meetings tomorrow. We can go back to murder 101 tomorrow night."

"Alright, spoilsport. But I have a question."

"What?" TJ waited for the jest.

"Will we get our money before Mr. Li kills us?"

"Why?"

"Because I want to do something extravagant before I die." We were still able to laugh.

"We forgot something very important," I announced.

"What?" TJ asked.

"To make our wills."

This brought a howl of outrage and they picked up pillows from the couch and threw them at me. I picked up the pillows and put them back, then said in mock indignation, "If you're through with childish games, it's time to go to work."

Chapter Forty-Three

Wednesday morning, we ran, careful not to slip on the black ice that refused to melt and go away, courtesy of two new snow storms per week, and frequent sub-freezing temperatures. We did enjoy Fred's discomfort and I kept hoping he'd fall, but he refused to cooperate. Then we went to the dōjō and had to endure Omura's scrutiny, since we hadn't been there for more than a week.

"You are all scheduled to test this Saturday. If your preparations match way you look, you will get butts kicked. I think that is how you say it."

"We appreciate your good wishes, sensei," Clar responded. "As soon as I have the time I will learn Japanese. I'm sure I'll find some suitable phrases to reply to you."

"I will not wait more than ten or twenty years for you to learn the divine language."

He waited expectantly for Clar to ask why it was called that, but she just bowed politely and said, "We have to get to work now, sensei, so we don't get our butts kicked."

"Perhaps one day you will appreciate the grace of my culture. Perhaps."

We worked out diligently, possibly overdoing it to show Omura that we were really trying. When we finished, we showered, went home and changed into business suits. We went to Bonnie's office in the Seagram building a half hour early so there'd be time to talk to her before the first meeting.

She looked at me closely and remarked how drawn my face was. "You're so tense, Pete. And you've got bags under your eyes. With just a touch of make-up you'd look like a raccoon. Is anything wrong?"

Her antennae were up, so I used my most reassuring voice.

"Nothing's wrong, Bonnie. We've been working long hours on the software, to be certain of its current status for the investors."

"Are you sure that's all? You look so tense."

"I will admit we're a little uptight about being so close to fulfilling our dream. I'm fine. Once this is resolved I'll sleep for a week."

"Are there any problems with the software that can worry the investors?"

"It's fine, Bonnie. No problems. Now who are we going to meet with first?"

"The young group. They're excited and eager to commit."

"Great. Anything you want to tell us about them before they get here?"

"No. Just be yourselves."

The first group, the cool yuppies, arrived a few minutes before 1:00 p.m. They were trying to be professional, as if they had done this many times before, but I could tell they were as nervous as we were. This was very revealing to me and suddenly I felt in complete control of the situation, a refreshing change after the recent period of fear and worry. It became clear, after a few minutes of casual chatting, that they were trying to impress us with invitations to their beach house in West Hampton and a day trip on their yacht. When I asked if they all had yachts, they were taken aback and said they shared the same yacht. I nodded sagely and said knowingly, "I see."

I guess they assumed I meant something critical and redoubled their efforts to win us over. TJ and Clar recognized my attitude of polite interest and mirrored it. I went through a brief recapitulation of the origins of the project, then brought them up to date with a confident description of our progress. When I elaborated on the programs' projected completion and added that they were already performing at least twenty percent above expectations, Jessica started clapping, followed by Elaine and Mort.

Clar smiled sweetly. "Normally we get applause after a particularly good lecture. But we appreciate your response."

TJ nodded benignly and Bonnie, sensing the growing enthusiasm, asked, "Any questions?"

Jessica stared at me, trying to get me to talk, but I remained calm and detached, certain that we were in control.

"How much do you expect the program to earn, Pete?" she asked.

Before I could reply, Clar answered, "We estimate between 50 and 100 million the first year, 200 to 300 million the second year, and 100 to 200 million the third year."

"Why does it go down in the third year?" Mort asked.

"Because the programs will begin to be obsolete late in the second year," TJ replied.

"So that's the end of our business?" Elaine asked.

"Only if that's your preference," I said. "We'll start working on Cybersnarer 2.0 and Castle Keep 2.0, about the middle of year one. They should be ready for preliminary marketing by the end of year two."

By this time Jessica was almost salivating.

"How much do you think they'll earn?"

"This is just an educated guess," Clar said, "but the success of the first versions should create a greater demand for the second versions. I think it's reasonable to expect double the return."

We watched the cool yuppies not too coolly exchange glances, then Jessica said, "If there are no other complications, or liabilities, we are prepared to finance your start-up."

"That's very gratifying," I said. "We have one more meeting with another investor group. We appreciate your interest and will get back to you within a week."

They looked shocked that we weren't falling over with glee and thanking them profusely. Bonnie made some pleasant remarks and they left, slightly deflated that we didn't snap up their offer, but obviously enchanted at the fabulous numbers Clar gave them. Bonnie looked at me strangely, as if discovering a side of me that was new to her.

"I hope you know what you're doing," she said. "You didn't exactly jump for joy at their offer."

"We have another group to see," I said curtly.

"Right. Don't treat them the same way you treated the young group."

"We call them the cool yuppies." At her alarmed look I added, "Don't worry. We'll be completely business like with the morticians."

"That's a relief. I never saw anyone play hard-to-get with 20 million at stake. Do you two agree with him?"

"We go along with Pete," Clar declared.

"All the way," TJ put in.

The next presentation was very formal with no frills. When I concluded with the timetable, Clar stated the earnings estimate. The three grey financiers went into a blue-pin-stripe huddle, then their spokesman said, "We are prepared to go ahead with this venture."

I thanked them and told them we'd get back to them within a week, and they left without comment. We chatted with Bonnie for a few minutes, who needed reassurance that we were still sane, but Clar soothed her.

"Trust Pete, Bonnie. He knows what he's doing."

When we got outside, Clar turned to me.

"Are you out of your mind? They're waiting to throw 20 million dollars at us and—"

"Not *pesos*?" I interrupted. "I wish you'd told me that sooner."

She and TJ burst into laughter and she said, "What are you thinking?"

"I want them to know who's in charge and that they're investing in our product, not buying us."

"I go along with that," TJ responded. "Which group do you prefer?"

"The cool yuppies."

"Why?" Clar demanded.

"Because I think we can dominate them, but not the morticians. But we should discuss it at length."

We revealed nothing to Fred about our business, letting him believe that it was just a visit to our lawyer. We contained our elation on the way home, maintaining self-control until I got out the RF detector, swept the apartment, and pronounced it clean. Then we did a victory dance around the tiny living room, cackling like loons as we bumped into the furniture and each other. Finally, TJ held up his hand and said, "Let's sit down and decide what group we're going with. I can't wait any longer."

"You heard my opinion. Now it's up to you two."

"What if we don't agree with you?" Clar asked.

"Whatever we decide, the three of us have to be in total agreement. If you two prefer the morticians, I'll go along with you."

"I was just wondering," Clar murmured. "I vote for the cool yuppies."

"So do I," TJ said.

"So it's decided." I declared.

"First we need a new-millionaire's hug," TJ said, "then we should have a celebratory dinner. I'll make something special, with an exceptional wine."

We sat there looking at each other in delight, as we reveled in the approaching fulfillment of our dreams. Then Clar's phone rang and we were harshly dashed back to earth. It was Mr. Li, who told Clar that he had reviewed our proposal and would like to discuss it further. He invited us to dinner Saturday night at the seafood restaurant on Park Avenue South and 17th Street. Clar accepted without consulting us and when she disconnected, told us the details.

"I guess it was too soon to be happy." she said. "We still have to deal with Mr. Li."

Chapter Forty-Four

It snowed again during the night, covering the ice that remained with a white coat that hid the filthy surface. The path along the East River was clear and we were extra alert for any possible threat from Mr. Li. There were small chunks of ice in the river quickly flowing to the sea, with the usual city detritus dumped in our waterways; plastic bottles, garbage bags, old tires, anything that could float, thoughtlessly discarded to add to the growing pollution of the ocean. Again I noticed there were no ships or boats on the river, traffic abandoned for air freight.

Fred was whining bitterly about the cold, so we ran an extra half-mile, just to add to his misery. He was still sniveling on the way to the dōjō and I couldn't help hoping that Mr. Li's next attack would miss us and get Fred. I laughed at the thought and when Clar asked what was so funny, I told her and TJ. They laughed, looking at Fred, and he mumbled some complaint, as unhappy with his assignment as we were with him. When we got to the dōjō, sensei Omura noticed that we looked a little better than the day before and remarked that he was glad we were taking better care of ourselves. I didn't tell him that if Mr. Li killed us now we'd at least die knowing we almost got rich. We worked out intensely, but I could tell that TJ and Clar were as distracted as I was, awaiting the next surprise from Mr. Li, so we were not really focused on preparation for our forthcoming tests on Saturday.

We showered, took a walk to Todaros, where TJ shopped for a special dinner that he refused to reveal. On the way home we stopped at a wine shop on 3rd Avenue where TJ bought two very expensive bottles of Burgundy, which he knew we liked. We worked on Cybersnarer and Castle Keep for several hours, then Clar and I kept working and TJ made dinner. After a while the delicious aromas drifting through the apartment were distracting, but when we tried to peek in and see what he was cooking, he shooed us away. Clar finally went to her room to take a nap and for the first time in weeks I went back to reading *Crime and Punishment*. Somehow, after all the turmoil, fear, and attacks of the last few weeks, Raskolnikov's growing fear of being discovered seemed much more poignant.

Dinner was everything TJ promised: crabmeat cocktail, French onion soup, rare roast beef, asparagus hollandaise, and *crème brulée* for dessert, which I, of course, called *flan*, and Clar responded by pelting me with breadsticks. Clar and I did the dishes, as well as an assortment of pots, pans, and utensils. I washed and she dried, while TJ relaxed. I worked as slowly as possible to draw out the pleasure of feeling her next to me in the cramped space. I passed a plate to the dish rack and our hands touched. I gently took her hand, dripping soap on the floor, and kissed it, looking into her beautiful, chestnut-colored eyes. Her hip pressed against me and it was the most sensual feeling I ever experienced. I could have stood there forever, but TJ called out, "Are you loafers through yet?"

We knew we'd have to proceed slowly to prepare TJ for the change in our relationship, but except for someone trying to murder us, I felt I had all the time in the world. We finally sat down together and TJ brought out a bottle of cognac and three snifters, then demonstrated how to properly drink cognac. I wasn't much for hard liquor, and neither was Clar, but TJ was enjoying it so much we sipped politely. I followed each sip with a sip of coffee, which took away the harsh taste. TJ shook his head pityingly at what he considered our barbaric lack of appreciation for the wonderful beverage. I had to smile to myself thinking about how former-foster-care-boy developed such aesthetic tastes.

I had just hoped he wouldn't start liking opera when, as if by ESP, he said, "I was listening to this Puccini opera on my I pad. It's about these starving artists living in a garret in Paris, falling in love, then losing their loved ones; one to illness, the other to a wealthy man."

He looked at us, waiting for a response and I shrugged.

"You want us to listen to some fat ladies squawking?"

"It's not like that," he protested. "It's very melodic and beautiful."

I turned to Clar. "Just before he said that I was hoping he wouldn't discover opera. Talk about weird."

"You're a fine one to talk," she replied. "Reading that Russian novel and mumbling to yourself about the tragic hero."

"I don't mumble," I said with as much dignity as I could muster. "And we were talking about opera."

"Just try it," TJ urged. "If you don't like it I won't ask you again."

"What if I like it?" I asked suspiciously.

"We'll go on from there. It's not a disease."

I mumbled something and Clar said, "If you culture enthusiasts are through, we have to discuss Mr. Li."

We sat there quietly, absorbed in our apprehensive thoughts and I said, "We either find a way to kill him, or we go into the witness protection program, unless either of you have an alternative."

"What if we go to work for him? That might buy us some time," TJ offered.

"I think it's too late for that," Clar answered. "He'd never trust us."

TJ nodded agreement. "You're right. So what do we do?"

"There are two questions," I replied. "First, can we find some way to kill him where we don't get caught, and, second, can we commit murder?"

"I've been thinking about that non-stop," TJ admitted. "I'm not sure I could just go up to him and shoot or stab him."

"I don't know if I can," I said. "But if there's any chance to stab him, it would probably have to be Clar. He watches you and me too closely and has no idea how capable Clar is."

"I've thought about it as much as you two. I don't think I could do it that way," she responded.

"So we're back where we started," I said, "with the additional complication of possibly not being able to do it, even if we find a way. Let's work on Cybersnarer and maybe something will occur to one of us. If we don't get any ideas, we'll start again in the morning."

Chapter Forty-Five

We woke up early Friday morning, went for our run without much enthusiasm, and cut it short, which pleased Fred. I briefly thought of extending it just to torment him, but didn't bother. We weren't very energetic at the dōjō and when we finished a desultory workout, sensei Omura took us aside.

"I know something has been troubling you. I became very fond of you when we first met and that feeling grew as you demonstrated your respect for our ideals. If there is anything I can do to help you, please tell me. If you need money, I will gladly assist you."

We bowed deeply and Clar said, "Thank you, sensei. We respect and admire you and appreciate your offer, but we'd only be endangering you if we involved you in any way."

"I did not think the FBI was here to study your erratic training habits."

We had to smile at his reminder that he knew a lot more than he said. I bowed and said, "We hope to resolve our problem soon and we apologize if we have disappointed you."

"Not so. But we talk of that another time. For now, we postpone your testing until you can approach it properly."

"Thank you, sensei," TJ said and we echoed him.

We hadn't even worked up a sweat, so we didn't bother showering and went home. TJ didn't feel like shopping and cooking, so we decided to order dinner later. Over and over, we discussed the question of whether we could commit murder, with growing despair at our lack of ability to put an end to the threat to our lives. I made sandwiches for lunch and actually managed to place the tuna between the bread, a distinct accomplishment. We really didn't notice what we ate and sat around feeling sorry for ourselves, with no inclination to do anything . . . an unaccustomed feeling. When Bellini and Jameson rang the bell, Clar let them in and barely acknowledged their greeting.

"We know why you look so depressed," Bellini said heartily, "but cheer up. We solved the problem."

We didn't seem very responsive, so Jameson asked, "Didn't you hear Bell?"

"Sure," I replied lethargically. "Tell us."

"We met with the deputy director last night and brought him up to date, then told him the threat to your lives was imminent. He called a good friend, a federal immigration judge, who, once she heard all the possible felonies Mr. Li committed, his men's attack on a federal agent and his cyber-piracy, issued an order to deport Mr. Li on the grounds that he was a danger to American citizens and a threat to national security."

"So what's going to happen?" I asked with growing relief.

"Tomorrow evening, in front of the restaurant, when Mr. Li arrives, Jamie and I, accompanied by an immigration officer, will take Mr. Li into custody and convey him to a detention facility, where he will be held until he can be put on a plane to Taiwan."

"Holy shit," Clar gasped. "I hope you're not kidding?"

"Bell wouldn't kid about that. You'll stay home tomorrow, with an additional protective detail, who will accompany you to the restaurant. They'll be ready to deal with Mr. Li's men if they offer resistance."

"Will it work?" TJ asked.

"Certainly." Jamison said. "It's so simple we don't even need a response team. And if for any reason he doesn't show, we'll pick him up at his apartment."

"You can sleep easy tonight," Bell said. "It'll be over tomorrow night."

"Do we have to worry about retaliation from Mr. Li's men?" I asked.

"I don't think so," Bell replied. "We'll maintain your protective detail until we're certain."

Clar went to them and hugged them, one at a time. TJ and I shook their hands and patted their shoulders.

"I probably won't sleep tonight," I murmured. "But I'll look forward to a sleep without nightmares tomorrow night."

They headed for the door, basking in our heartfelt gratitude, then Bellini turned. "You may not even have to go to the restaurant tomorrow night. It's so close to your house that we may pick up Mr. Li before you have to leave. We'll call you and alert you if you have to come there, and once we apprehend him we'll let you know immediately."

Clar rushed to Bellini and hugged him hard.

"I hope you know that you and Jamie are saving our lives. How can we ever thank you enough?"

"Wait until we get him, then TJ can make us one of his special dinners."

"It's a date," TJ affirmed.

We watched them go with mixed feelings of relief that we would soon be safe and frustration that we couldn't do anything to protect ourselves and the people we cared for.

"Is it too soon to relax?" Clar whispered.

"In the words of my highly educated colleague," I said, "Holy shit," which evoked a real laugh, the first light moment in days. "But we better wait until tomorrow night to celebrate."

"I'll make them the most delicious meal they ever ate in their lives. French . . . maybe Italian . . . I'll have to think about it."

"I hate to be a spoilsport, oh giant gourmet," I said, "but what if they don't get him?"

"What are you talking about?" TJ demanded. "You heard their plan. It's simple. They grab him, lock him up, then put him on a plane to far off Asia and he's gone, and our troubles are over."

"What if he has someone in the FBI on his payroll, and doesn't show and goes into hiding?" Clar asked.

TJ looked genuinely shocked.

"Would an FBI agent sell out his country?"

"Stranger things have happened," she replied.

"It's probably Fred," I asserted.

They gaped at me, then burst into laughter.

"I could give him an accident during our next run," TJ offered.

"Pete's just kidding, Baby Brother . . . aren't you?"

I stared at them coldly for a moment.

"Clar's just telling us to wait until they get him," I replied. "I have no idea who Mr. Li could buy, but I know he's ruthless and capable. I'll wait until Bell calls us and confirms they got him, before I relax."

"So what do we do until then?" Clar asked. "We can't go out and I'm too tense to work."

I smiled expansively. "We let TJ introduce us to opera. I bet he could go on for days."

"I knew you weren't the barbarian you pretend to be, Pete."

"You'll change your mind when I carry off your women and cattle, my Zulu brother."

"Not my cattle," he protested.

"Alright, boys. Enough macho games. How do we learn about opera?"

"We'll start with Carmen," TJ said. "Carmen is a low-class, fiery, Spanish girl who's so alluring that every man falls for her. She makes a young soldier go mad for her, so that he forgets his innocent young sweetheart and his duty. He runs away with her but is caught by the army and put in prison. Carmen makes a famous bullfighter fall for her and he takes her away with him. When the soldier gets out of prison, he follows them and kills Carmen."

"It sounds depressing," I said.

"Give it a chance," TJ urged. "The music is beautiful and you probably know some of it because they use it in the movies."

"Does she carry a knife, like *our* little Carmen?" I joked and Clar mimed waving a knife back and forth at me.

"Just listen to the first ten minutes. If you don't like it after that we'll try something else."

"You could always go back to Raspotatic," Clar teased.

"It's Raskolnikov," I responded huffily. "Alright. Let the opera marathon begin."

Chapter Forty-Six

I wasn't serious when I told TJ to start the opera marathon, but eight hours later we were still listening, although I confess my attention had begun to wander. I was snapped back to full participation when TJ played the Grand March from Aida for the fourth time and urged us to march with him. Clar leaped up immediately, eager to stretch her body that had stiffened from hours of immobilized listening. I followed suit for the same reason, also hopeful this would be the end of opera for the night. I had to admit that Clar would have made an irresistible slave girl and TJ an imposing Pharaoh.

When the final note concluded just before midnight, TJ asked us which one we liked. He, of course, after the grandiosity of the march, picked Aida. Clar selected Madame Butterfly. The passionate tragedy of a woman scorned and abandoned seemed to reveal another side of her character. I preferred Carmen, with its beautiful, stirring music. Then TJ asked if I'd rather be Don José, or Escamillo, the bullfighter, I chose Escamillo. Clar asked why I picked him and I explained that neither of them were too bright, and I had enough anguish in my life, so the simple-minded athlete was preferable.

"You mean you wouldn't kill the woman you loved for deserting you?" she asked.

"I'd kill to protect her and I'd die to defend her, but I wouldn't kill her out of jealousy."

She seemed very pleased with my answer and TJ looked back and forth at us, beginning to sense the change in how we felt for each other. When he asked if we wanted to listen to one more opera, we both shouted, "No!"

"Try to bring culture to the ignorant. I'm going to do my teeth, then go to bed."

As he started for the bathroom I began loudly humming the Grand March. I stopped when he turned and glared at me. When he turned back I hummed again and Clar joined in. As he started to close the bathroom door, he turned and gave us a big smile.

"I see my efforts weren't completely wasted."

"Hurry up and do your teeth, divine one," I said, "so we lesser mortals can get in there."

Clar thought this was hilarious and started laughing. When I extended my arms and bowed low, she really cracked up. Listening to beautiful music had an effect on us that may not have been relaxing, we were still wound much too tight, but it was a temporary escape into magic land, which eased some of the tension eating away at us.

It felt strange in the morning not to go for a run, the first day in weeks that it wasn't freezing cold, but we resisted the temptation, heeding Bellini's warning. It was even stranger not to go to the dōjō, where under other circumstances we would have been testing today. But the thought of Mr. Li's being apprehended tonight convinced us that it was safer to remain indoors and not risk a last minute disaster. I was increasingly restless and kept pacing back and forth. TJ asked if he should put on Aida so I could march to the music, which I declined. It was obvious that TJ and Clar were just as tense.

Clar finally said, "We have a long day ahead of us, and we may still have to go to the restaurant. What do you want to do until then?"

"I'm too keyed up to work," TJ replied.

"So am I," I added, but got a silly idea. "Let's assume Mr. Li goes bye-bye tonight and next week our investors give us 20 million dollars."

"They won't just hand us the cash," Clar reminded.

"I know. Just bear with me. We have the money. What do we do first?"

"Get a nice office," TJ said.

"Take a vacation to someplace warm," Clar said. "What about you?"

"Buy a nice three-bedroom condo, with a swimming pool in the building."

"That's a great idea," TJ enthused. "With a gym."

"I don't think we can afford it," Clar declared.

"How much would it cost?" TJ asked.

"Depending on where, maybe a million, or a million and a half," Clar replied.

"We don't have to pay it all at once," I said. "We can put 20 percent down and get a mortgage."

"That's $200,000 to $250,000," TJ calculated. "Can we afford that?"

"Didn't we allocate a million for us up front in the initial investment?" I asked Clar.

She went to her worktable, pulled out the proposal, scanned the budget, then nodded yes.

"Then I propose we start looking at condos online and show each other what we find if it's anything interesting."

"Sounds a lot better than an office," TJ murmured. "You two start and I'll make something for lunch."

After several hours of condo searching, periodically interrupted when one of us found something of interest, it became clear that the only three-bedroom, hi-end condo we could afford would be in Ramapo, New Jersey.

"It seems to me that a lot of people are making big bucks," TJ remarked. "I've looked at dozens of buildings where one-bedroom apartments start at one million."

"Me too," Clar agreed.

"Then let's look at two-bedrooms," I suggested.

We searched for another hour, pausing occasionally to show the others an apartment of possible interest. At 4:00 p.m. we shut down our computers and discussed the results. TJ, who had been the most efficient of us in the search, summarized our efforts.

"We can probably find an acceptable two-bedroom apartment for one million, but it won't be high end."

"What are our other options?" Clar asked.

"We get a salary or something, don't we?" I asked.

Again Clar referred to the budget.

"We're listed as officers at $150,000 a year", she replied.

"So between us that's $450,000 a year," I said. "If we buy a condo for $1,500,000, we can put $300,000 down and easily manage a mortgage and monthly charges."

"That would be a big chunk of our money," TJ muttered.

"You mean the money we don't have yet?" I retorted, which gave us a laugh. "Let's take another look at three-bedroom apartments and see what we find."

We went back to our computers and by this time I was more interested in keeping us busy the closer it came to dinner with Mr. Li, than finding our dream apartment. I figured that we'd have to get ready to leave around 6:30, and hopefully we'd hear from Bellini by 6:50, at which time we'd have to leave the house. TJ and Clar were as on edge as I was, so I hoped the three-bedroom search would occupy us until 6:00.

We actually found a dozen eligible apartments in our brief search and we discussed the comparative merits with more than casual interest. TJ was already lobbying for one condo that had a chef's kitchen, with granite surfaces on every work space. Clar championed another condo with two luxurious bathrooms, one for the boys, one for the girls. I contributed encouraging remarks, without really caring one way or the other. I was just glad they got involved and for a while forgot the tensions that had been eating away at us. TJ saved the sites so we could go back to them, then suddenly turned to me.

"Thanks, Pete. I was really getting freaked out about tonight."

"So was I," Clar admitted.

"Me too," I confessed. "But it's not over until the skinny man sings."

"Who's that?" TJ asked.

"I don't know. I just didn't want to listen to that fat lady sing anymore."

They managed to smile, which I thought was pretty good, considering the stress we were feeling. We sat quietly for a few minutes, fidgeting, frequently looking at the clock. When we didn't get a call at 6:30 p.m., we slowly, reluctantly, got up and started getting ready to go out. Clar lingered in the bathroom, but I didn't rush her. I was willing to draw out preparations for as long as possible. When we couldn't delay any longer, we put on our coats and headed for the door. Just as we got outside one of our phones rang, and as we reached for our pockets, I reminded myself that it was time to change our identical rings.

We all answered, but it was Bellini calling me, yelling exuberantly, "We got him, Pete. We got him.

And Jamie shot one of his men who pulled a gun on us. This is a terrific bust. We'll get commendations. You should see him, trying to play cool. But we got him. When his man pulled a gun, it scared the shit out of the immigration officer, who'll testify that Li ordered his man to shoot him."

"Hold on a sec, Bell, while I tell TJ and Clar."

Clar signaled they heard and she and TJ started jumping up and down with joy.

Bellini's voice called me back. "Pete. Pete."

"I'm here Bell. Great work. We'll never be able to thank you enough. Congratulate Jamie for us. You guys are super agents."

I could hear his voice bursting with pride as he told Jamie what I said. When Bellini started talking again he was much quieter and TJ and Clar leaned close so they could listen to the conversation.

"We'll be taking him to a secure federal detention center as soon as we settle any questions with the police. Your old friends, Gluckman and Chestnut just arrived, and I'm sure they want to discuss jurisdiction. I'll phone you later, once Li is in a cell."

"Thanks again, Bell. Thanks."

"Later, kid," sounding like a television cop, as he disconnected.

I turned to TJ and Clar, stretched my arms wide and said, "Ho hum. I think I'll go inside and take off my coat."

Clar swatted me playfully. "Don't sound so nonchalant. You were as scared as we were."

"Sure. But I'll sleep well tonight, because I know he can't do anything, at least for tonight."

Chapter Forty-Seven

We calmly hung our coats in the closet and took off our sweaters and shoes. Clar and I sat down, while TJ went to make tea. He asked from the kitchen, "What happens next, Pete?"

"Well I know this will disappoint Clar, but we won't be eating oysters tonight."

Clar threw a pillow at me.

"I don't know how two smart guys can eat those disgusting things," she growled.

"That was a pre-amble to my answering my connoisseur brother."

She giggled. "Give me a break. This isn't a constitutional convention. What do you think will happen?"

"If Li is held incommunicado before being shipped off to Taiwan, and his henchmen don't blame us for his deportation, then we can relax for a while."

"What do you mean 'for a while'?" TJ asked. "Once he's gone aren't our troubles over?"

"Not necessarily, Baby Brother," Clar replied. "There might be someone else he was working with who will take his place."

"I got the impression that he was in charge," I responded. "I don't think someone will take over for him. But how long would it take for him to come back to the country using another passport?"

"He'd have to disguise himself pretty well," TJ offered. "They use sophisticated facial recognition programs at all airports."

"What if he came by sea, on a freighter, or even a cruise ship?" I challenged.

"You've got a good point," he agreed.

"How long would it take him to come back that way?" Clar asked.

I thought about it for a moment.

"He probably has to report to someone, either political or military. That'll take time. They'd have to assess the value of what he got and possibly could still get. Then they'd have to decide the importance of the material and whether or not it was productive to send him back. That could take months."

"So you don't think we have to worry for a while?" Clar asked.

"I didn't say that. I was just speculating out loud. It could be weeks, or not at all. Your guess is as good as mine."

"So we get back to TJ's original question, 'What's next?'"

"We make a final decision between the cool yuppies and the morticians, get the money, buy our condo, then work our asses off and become rich."

"Sounds good to me," TJ said.

"Me too," Clar agreed. "But right now I'm hungry."

"Well I don't feel like cooking," TJ declared, "so we either go out, or order in."

"Let's order in," Clar said. "Anything but seafood. And no smart-ass remarks about mucous on the half shell."

I actually did sleep well that night and for a change didn't have unpleasant dreams. When we went for our run Sunday morning, I felt unburdened for the first time in weeks and really enjoyed being out without looking around for attackers. Then I reminded myself to start looking for threats again tomorrow, but right now I gave myself up to the rapture of the run. By common consent we ran another mile, ignoring Fred's whining complaints, and on the way back, I said, "It looks as if Fred won't get shot in the line of duty."

"We can still hope," Clar replied, which gave us a laugh, that went on a little longer at Fred's suspicious look.

We ate breakfast at a café near our apartment on 3rd Avenue. Then we went home and decadently read the New York Times, instead of going to the dōjō. We decided to just hang out for a while, then decide whether we still wanted to pick the cool yuppies for our investors. I browsed my email, which I had neglected for the last few days and found an invitation from Charles de Croix, our favorite professor at Branville U., and our thesis supervisor in our graduate work. He invited the three of us to do a seminar for his graduate students in the spring, for one or two days, depending on our availability. I sent him an acceptance without checking with TJ and Clar, since I knew they would love to do it. I made a note to recruit Charles for our Board of Directors, once we formed a corporation. Then I found the email from Janet.

"Dear Pete,

I would have preferred to tell you this in person, but that just isn't possible. After talking to my family about getting shot at, then being targeted by a hit and run, we decided that I'm not returning to NYU. We also decided that it's not in my best interests to see you again, so I won't tell you where I'll be going to school. Our relationship may not have gotten very far, but it was full of surprises while it lasted.

Yours,
Janet"

I read it again and for a moment had an image of her desirable body, but then a feeling of relief went through me, since I would be free to explore my changing relationship with Clar. I told TJ and Clar about Charles' invitation, which excited them. Then I mentioned that Janet wasn't coming back. TJ sympathized with me and I didn't say anything. I looked at Clar while he was talking and she saw I didn't care and accepted that I was in love with her. TJ admitted guiltily that Lakeisha told him about Janet.

"You've been phoning her?" Clar asked.

"No. We've been emailing and texting. She misses me and I miss her."

"Then we'll have to get you two together," I said expansively. "But right now let's make our final decision between the 'yups' and the 'morts'."

We took turns presenting what we knew about each group. TJ read Facebook descriptions of the cool yuppies, and background material from his data search of the morticians. Clar reviewed the budget, reminding us that however business-like she made it sound, it was just a working estimate. She pointed out that if we underestimated expenses and operating costs, we'd need more money and we had to consider which group would be more responsive. After TJ and Clar stated their opinions, Clar asked me to finalize our choice.

"Clar was right about the possibility that we might need more money. I vote for the cool yuppies, because I think it would be easier to deal with them, as long as we're producing results, than the morticians."

"Then it's decided," Clar declared. "We go with the cool yuppies."

"I'll phone Bonnie in the morning and tell her our decision," I said. "I'll ask her about how we proceed from here."

"Will she tell the morticians we rejected them?" TJ asked.

"Sure. Unless you want to."

"No, thanks. They give me the creeps. I don't know if the cool yuppies are any better, but at least they don't remind me of the iceberg bureaucrats in the foster care system."

About an hour later my phone rang and it was Bellini. I mouthed to TJ and Clar, "It's Bellini," and they moved next to me and listened. I was particularly aware of Clar's proximity.

"We just put Li on the plane to Taiwan. Jamie and I waited on the tarmac nearby until it took off. He's gone."

"Great!" TJ shouted.

"You're all listening?" Bellini asked.

"Yes," Clar replied. "And we can't thank you enough."

"Well, we have to discuss your future protection, so how about TJ makes that special dinner for us and we'll go over everything then."

"Great," TJ enthused. "How about tomorrow night?"

"Wait'll I check with Jamie." I heard a murmured conversation, then he came back on the phone. "That's good for us. What time?"

"Seven o'clock," TJ answered.

"We'll see you then. By the way, TJ. Tell Clar we like oysters," and he quickly disconnected at her outraged sputtering of what she'd do to him.

I looked at the two people I loved most in the world and said, "We should be dancing with joy, but somehow I'm just not in the mood."

"You'll feel better once the fact that he's gone sinks in," Clar said.

"We just made the decision that'll make us rich and our enemy's gone," TJ looked at Clar and grinned. "The world's our oyster now."

She hugged him fiercely. "I'll punish you for that another time. Right now I feel too good to be provoked."

"As long as Li doesn't come back," I muttered.

"We'll deal with him then," Clar declared. "Right now let's relax and enjoy what we've earned."

About the Author

Gary Beck
www.garycbeck.com

An award winning video documentary and short film director, Gary Beck has spent most of his adult life as a theater director and as an art dealer, when he couldn't make a living in theater.

He has 11 published chapbooks and 3 more accepted for publication.

His poetry collections include: *Days of Destruction* (Skive Press), *Expectations* (Rogue Scholars Press),

Dawn in Cities, Assault on Nature, Songs of a Clerk, Civilized Ways, Displays, Perceptions, Fault Lines & Tremors (Winter Goose Publishing), *Conditioned Response* (Nazar Look*)*, and *Resonance* (Dreaming Big Publications). *Tremors, Perturbations, Rude Awakenings and The Remission of Order* will be published by Winter Goose Publishing. *Virtual Living* will be published by Thurston Howl Publications.

His novels include*:* *Extreme Change* (Cogwheel Press), *Flawed Connections* (Black Rose Writing), *Call to Valor* (Gnome on Pigs Productions), *Sudden Conflicts* (Lillicat Publishers), and *State of Rage* (Rainy Day Reads Publishing).

His short story collections are *A Glimpse of Youth* (Sweatshoppe Publications*)* and *Now I Accuse and Other Stories,* to be published by Winter Goose Publishing.

His original plays and translations of Moliere, Aristophanes, and Sophocles have been produced Off Broadway. His poetry, fiction, and essays have appeared in hundreds of literary magazines.

He currently lives in New York City.

VISIONS VI
GALAXIES

VISIONS V
MILKY WAY

VISIONS V

MILKY WAY

EDITED BY CARROL FIX

VISIONS IV

SPACE BETWEEN STARS

EDITED BY CARROL FIX

VISIONS III
INSIDE THE KUIPER BELT

VISIONS III

INSIDE THE KUIPER BELT

EDITED BY CARROL FIX

VISIONS II
MOONS OF SATURN

VISIONS
LEAVING EARTH

VISIONS
LEAVING EARTH

CARROL FIX

FOREWORD BY
SAM BELLOTTO JR.
EDITOR, PERIHELION SCIENCE FICTION

. . . and coming soon!

VISIONS VII: UNIVERSE